PINOT NOIR

Printed in the United States of America.
For information, address ATS Press: info@PinotNoirBook.com.

www.pinotnoirbook.com

Cover and Interior Design by Lance Buckley:
www.lancebuckley.com

Names: Molnar, Mads, III, author.
Title: Pinot noir : a WWII novel / Mads Molnar III.
Description: Sheridan, WY : ATS Press, 2020.
Identifiers: LCCN 2020907687 (print) | ISBN 978-0-578-66974-8 (paperback) | ISBN 978-0-578-66975-5 (ebook)
Subjects: LCSH: Vintners--Fiction. | Nazis--Fiction. | Poisoning--Fiction. | World War, 1939-1945--France--Fiction. | Detective and mystery stories. | Suspense fiction. | Historical fiction. | BISAC: FICTION / Mystery & Detective / Historical. | FICTION / Thrillers / Suspense. | FICTION / Historical / World War II. | FICTION / Noir. | GSAFD: Mystery fiction. | Suspense fiction. | Noir fiction.
Classification: LCC PS3613.O46 P56 2020 (print) | LCC PS3613.O46 (ebook) | DDC 813/.6--dc23.

ISBN 978-0-578-66974-8 (paperback)

1934

MADS MOLNAR III

PINOT
NOIR

a WWII novel

A NOTE FROM THE AUTHOR

I have the same name as my grandfather, but I'd say he was the greater man. He'd agree. Pictures tell me he was six feet tall and had dark hair and swarthy skin. He tells me his eyes were blue and women liked him. He says the world was more eventful when he was young. It was before wealthy nations realized they couldn't candidly make war. Before the hydrogen bomb, the atom bomb, and the USSR. Men wore hats and women became wives and children were punished … corporally.

My grandfather started his career as a psychologist and performed that role before and during the start of the first war. As he was getting published and gaining notoriety in his field, his first wife died in Budapest. Then he went to the front lines—"searching for Death," as he put it. He found him, and they became pals. After the war, my grandfather said he "couldn't bear fixing broken soldiers." So he became a detective and remained in that role until his death. He told me stories about it; this is one of them. It's based on true events. I pick up where they leave off.

Mads III

PROLOGUE: JUNE 1940

A lesson that you learned in the first war was: don't trust anyone. Now it was the second, and Mads Molnar still hadn't learned that lesson. And he wasn't young.

"*Az anyját!!*" cursed Miles Fekete in the seat beside Molnar. They looked at each other. And then at the group of armed men coming into view behind a heavy-metal crossbar.

"It's a checkpoint!" came a hushed voice from the back of the milk truck. More followed: "What can we do?" and "Quick! Turn around!"

"*Kurvák!* Shut up! Let him think!" yelled Miles into the back of the truck.

Molnar drove on. The desperate whispers turned to silent prayer. He stopped in front of the roadblock that lay across the entrance to a little village. A group of men stood behind it with too-shiny boots and too many guns. They were known in Hungary as the Arrow Cross, and were like little self-imposed brothers to the Nazi party, but with less cash and power.

Things changed for many people when war broke out. For detectives like Molnar, it meant unusual new jobs—such as smuggling people out of places or into places and making more money than normal in doing it. It also meant higher stakes. And now, Molnar found his contact had been wrong about the road being clear.

"Be ready, Miles; you never know how things will land," said Molnar.

Miles, his hired muscle, fondled a big English revolver and nodded.

As Molnar came to a stop, he tapped on the back wall. "Whatever happens, don't make a sound."

One Arrow Cross guard came up to Molnar's window. He had a whistle in his lips. "What's in the back?"

Molnar looked into his eyes. Drawing on his pre-war psychologist career, he dissected him. Most important was the fact that the man's shirt was neatly pressed but had a few pinholes in the left breast. He cared about himself but needed money. That was something. And his eyes said they were used to allowing untruths to pass through his mouth.

Molnar responded, "A bunch of Jews from Hungary, masquerading as milk bottles." As he said it, he reached out a hand and put a heavy piece of gold on the truck door between them, and he watched the man's face. It didn't react so well, so he kept going. "But you'll like them better than milk bottles. They all brought you one of these ... to get you to pretend that they're milk bottles." He lined up more pieces on the door.

"They're paying to leave the country?"

"They're paying so you'll pretend that they're milk bottles," said Molnar. "They're paying me. They're paying you." He shrugged.

One of the other men was coming now. He was swollen up as if he'd been pumped with saline. The curly hairs on his arms were visible to Molnar despite the distance.

The first man turned back to him. Molnar slowly reached for his gun. The first man said, "It's OK! Go back."

The hairy man obeyed, but slowly.

The first man turned back to Molnar. "Let's see them," he said.

Molnar let the gun go, grabbed the gold, jumped out of the car, and walked around the truck to the back door. While he did so, he started thinking about whether they should have just plowed right through the checkpoint. He opened the door and placed the gold in a neat row on the rear bumper of the car. The man kept the whistle in his teeth, but a smile crept across his face as he eyed the gold.

A bunch of people stood there like mice in a spotlight. But they didn't run like mice; they simply stared. Most avoided the man's eyes. Some stared right at him. The man's gaze went from the people to the gold, and back to the people. Molnar's eyes were on the whistle. The swollen, hairy man walked toward them again, moving around the truck.

"You OK?"

"Yes, fine!" The first man grabbed up the gold and pivoted.

Molnar shut the door quickly, but not before the hairy man saw into the back of the truck.

"What are you doing, Gyorgy?" asked the hairy one.

"*Kurva*!" said Gyorgy. "It's just milk bottles." He smiled, slapping the man on the back.

"No! You must—"

Gyorgy cuffed the hairy one in the mouth. Molnar walked as slowly as his nerves would allow, back around the truck. He jumped in and cranked the engine. It roared to life just as a shot rang out behind the truck. Miles jumped high in his seat, and a cry came from the milk bottles. The hairy man ran toward them. Molnar hit the gas. The truck plowed into the metal barricade bar, knocking it down with a loud clang. The Arrow Cross men looked at one another before remembering their guns. Molnar kept the pedal down and plowed over the bar. One man raised his gun, and Miles raised his .455 Webley revolver. It cracked like a bullwhip. The man crumpled without a sound.

"Keep your heads down!" Molnar shouted.

Shots rang out as Molnar careened around a corner and out of view. The truck flew through the little town of Pinkamindszent, Hungary, and toward the Austrian border. The milk bottles in the back tried not to clang together.

Only one car came into view in Molnar's mirrors. The hairy man rode passenger, and long barrels stuck out from all sides like a porcupine. "Miles, we have company."

Miles swung his door open and stepped out onto the truck's railing. He leaned far out, holding the revolver in his left hand and the cab with his right. He took careful aim and fired at the car. His first shot hit the grill.

The barrels pointed forward now, training on him.

His second shot hit the hood.

The barrels started firing. A bullet shattered Miles's window. A bump in the road nearly sent him off the truck rail. He glared at Molnar and took aim again. This time, a red spurt went up from the driver's shirt, the windshield turned into a spider web, and the car drove directly off the road and through the front door of an already-crumbling brick home.

"Least they could have knocked," Miles quipped, swinging back into the cab. He smiled at Molnar, who shook his head.

"If you weren't such a good shot, I'd have fired you long ago for your mouth."

"Better fill it, then," Miles said. He took a small, silver canteen out of his jacket pocket and guzzled the contents.

Molnar pressed the pedal down. And without more warning than a rotting sign with green paint flaking off its face, they were in Austria. Shortly after that, they turned and bumped down a long, dirt driveway leading to the small farm where Molnar was scheduled to hand off his cargo.

Molnar pulled the truck to a halt and opened the back door. Faces stared back at him. He reached up to help a pregnant woman down. Then he watched the other milk bottles follow. None had cracked.

Molnar tipped his hat at the last one and closed the door. He started to climb back into the cab of the truck, but one old man tugged his shirt sleeve. Molnar came back down off the truck rail and stood beside the old man and his wife.

"You didn't have to give away your payment," mumbled the shrunken man to Molnar. He tried to put a gold coin in the detective's hand, but Molnar closed the man's hand back on the coin and pushed it toward him.

"You'll need that more than I will," he said. "It was my decision to do it."

The old man shook his head and turned away. His eyes looked wet, but that could have just been age. Molnar looked over at Miles, who was reloading on the other side of the truck. It was time to go back and find another route.

He'd stepped back up on the railing when the old man's wife looked at him closer. "You're that psychologist, aren't you?"

"One of them."

"I knew your wife," said the old woman. "We both got our hair done at *Evike's*."

"She did have nice hair," said Molnar, trying to smile but failing. "Good luck to you."

Molnar and Miles dropped the truck off at an old farm, where the owner was shocked to learn that the Arrow Cross would shoot them full of holes over delivering milk. Then the men climbed into their own cars and nodded to each other before driving off.

Molnar got into the city and drove through its cobblestone streets toward his office. The walls wore a dark film, infected by the spoiled thoughts in the air, by the government that herded the city toward ruin. Only as he neared his side of town did the old architectural beauty of Budapest manage to shine through the filth.

When Molnar was nearly back to his office, he looked up at a billboard and, for the first time, saw a swastika. He drove on, shaking his head. It was time to get out of town.

Molnar pulled up to his office in the castle district of Buda. The light was off in his single bedroom window. He sat, staring through the windshield as the first drops of rain exploded onto the glass. Soon, the glass was all streaks and rivers. He turned up the collar of his trench coat and exited the car.

Walking into his office, Molnar glanced at his secretary's empty desk. He opened a drawer, where an old bottle of scotch waited. He pulled the bottle out with his hand, the cork out with his teeth, the liquid out with his mouth. Bottle in hand, he stared down into the open drawer. Pulling a pen knife from his pocket and flicking it open, he stabbed lightly into the cheap drawer bottom and pushed it toward the back of the desk. It gave way, revealing a thin hidden compartment and, inside that, a stack of krona and a Swedish passport.

The passport looked lonely. Useless, without an exit visa.

Molnar took another drink at the thought of getting a visa. He hadn't been to Sweden since he'd been a boy. Nothing's the way you remember it from when you were a kid. But in this case, he was willing to be disappointed. Maybe there were fewer swastikas up there.

The golden word SVERIGE on the passport burned into the back of his mind as he closed the compartment and the drawer.

3

BOTTLE I

A thousand kilometers away, in Alsace, France, two men sat alone in a dank wine cellar. The stone walls were sweating. A single ray of dust-filled sunset illuminated a black kiss mark branded into a wooden case of wine. The younger of the men had a black eye, and his face sported new patches of encrusted blood. René Neuf, the older man, wore a clean-shaven face and close-cropped hair. You could tell they were farmers by their weathered faces and hands. You could tell they were vintners by the gleam in their eyes. But that gleam was muted tonight.

Neuf tore the aluminum wrapper from a bottle of cognac and poured, then held the glass out to the younger man.

The two drank. "They'll come here in the morning," said the younger, looking across the sea of wine as if it were in danger. "And they'll break up your cellar like they did mine." His voice quavered. "They'll steal your wine and—" He choked on his words, eyes closing tightly.

Neuf shrugged.

"There's nothing you can do to stop them, René."

The old man shrugged again and finished his glass, staring at the last drops of cognac. "*Qui vivra verra.*" He who lives, shall see. "My father said, 'What we hold is the pruning, the water, the treatments, the picking. The rest of the deck is in His hand.'" René pointed to the ceiling and then turned his palm to the sky. "If it rains before harvest, if the beetle comes, if the sun stays away—who am I to say? This is the same. *Qui vivra verra.*"

"But it's not the same," said the young man, hammering his fist on a wooden case at his side. "He respects *les raisins*, the grapes. But these men…" He raised his hands as if surrendering. "They have no reasoning. They don't respect the *raisins*. They respect only the steel."

Neuf poured another drink in silence.

———

Hours later, in the middle of the night, René Neuf lay in bed, searching the dark for answers. His eyes blinked. Then they stopped and stared. He sat up, glanced at his slumbering wife beside him, and crept from the bed.

He stood erect in his cellar, looking around at his life's work turned physical in the form of hundreds of cases of wine. He walked from case to case, touching the rough wood with his rough hands. He stepped into the middle of the cellar, faced a large, round, basket press in the very center of the room. He stood, wavering. His knees buckled, and he fell to the damp stone floor. Surrounding him, various-sized wooden casks of fermenting wine bubbled away—painting cartoonish noise into the pained silence.

Neuf sobbed. Tears streamed down his face. He folded in half, forearms on the stone ground, face on his arms, shaking.

Slowly, the shaking ebbed. He was nearly limp, as if life had left him. Then, he ground his fist against the stone floor. He stumbled to his feet, face streaming with tears, and grabbed a wooden grape-churning fork off an open barrel of pinot noir. He viciously swung it, smashing everything in reach—cracking cases, siphons, jars. He bellowed and swore. His pitchfork hit a closed bottle of chemical compound that shattered into the barrel of pinot.

"No!" shouted Neuf, flinging the fork and running to the barrel. He clawed out the glass and the chemical with his hands, throwing them onto the ground in waves until the white powder was gone.

Panting and soaking wet, he finally stopped. He kicked at the fork and stared into the vat. Then his eyes turned to his stained hands. Trickles of blood sent darker-red rivulets through the lighter-colored wine.

Neuf's hard face smiled. He chuckled softly. He looked to the ceiling. The smile grew, and he fell back to his knees. His tears continued—but another, new emotion winked in his eyes. The gleam had returned.

———

Noonday sunbeams shone through the rows of pinot noir and gewürztra-miner surrounding Neuf's otherwise humble Alsatian home. A procession of armed men dressed in red and black uniforms moved to the front. A leather fist smashed into the door, rattling the hinges. Neuf stood behind it, in at-ease position.

"Please, come in," he said.

Oberst Karlin Riffel barged through, but, seeing Neuf's gentlemanly air, halted. He adjusted his hair before proceeding—swooping a precariously oiled section up, left, and into a shining wave. "*Bonjour,*" said Colonel Riffel. Though his French accent was perfect, he added a strange twinge to Neuf's name, pulling out the middle.

Neuf responded in German that was equally perfect.

Riffel smashed his hand into his chest and saluted. A younger *Unteroffizier*—sergeant—named Charles apathetically mimicked this be-hind Riffel. "The mother tongue!" said Riffel. "You speak with such beauty."

"My mother is German," said Neuf.

Riffel turned, stunned. He looked at his soldiers and back at Neuf and then back at the soldiers. "I love Alsace! Did you hear that? Neuf's mother is German. Perhaps she's your cousin, Charles."

Charles's face was implacable.

"As a fellow German, would you kindly show us your cellar?" said Riffel.

Neuf nodded, closing his eyes as he did so and holding his arm out in front of him. "After me."

Neuf moved down the hall and through a door to his cellar. The colo-nel followed, soldiers spilling in after him, like a hen leading a dozen armed and sweating chicks.

The room filled with the odor of pork grease from the soldiers' boot polish. Neuf opened his mouth and shut it. Then he said, "This is my pride, gentlemen." He clasped his hands behind his back. Before him lay a dozen wooden wine casks, their carved faces showing varying moments in the winemaking process, from *vendange* to pressing to pruning—like stations of the cross in a sanctuary to the grape. Behind the casks and work-space was storage, where wine racks held bottles of crémant—the Alsatian sparkling wine. Behind the racks, like another army, were hundreds of cases of wine. Neuf's silent, composed demeanor instilled in the troops a kind of awe for the cellar's ambiance. None of them moved past him but followed in line, as if on a guided tour of the Louvre.

"This is lovely, Neuf," said Riffel. Breaking the spell, he grasped a dark-green bottle from one of the open cases.

The vintner nodded, eyeing Riffel's bottle-toting hand.

"Charles!"

The young man was by his side.

"The bottle!"

Charles held a corkscrew in the air and slowly opened the bottle, then poured Riffel a glass. Riffel raised the glass to his mouth—and, with it, an eyebrow.

Neuf tried to picture his friend's cellar, where the same officer only a day before had destroyed some of his stock and confiscated more. He waited in silence for the sentence. Riffel paused, glass in mid-air as if he'd smash it to the ground. The liquid swished a final time in his heavily mustached mouth. And his other brow went up. He lowered the glass, took another drink.

"Oh, my." He drank the entire glass and Charles refilled it. "This is good," he said, pulling more of the bright ruby liquid into his mouth and sucking air over it. "I'd normally say, 'It's a shame I have to take it'"— Neuf's eyes were steady—"but really, I like this wine. I respect it. Oh, oh, which is your best year?"

"1934." There was no hesitation.

"Lead on," said Riffel with a sweeping gesture.

Neuf swallowed and nodded in silence. He led Riffel to a wooden box with a black kiss mark burnt into its side.

"The 1934 pinot noir is the finest year of them all. And it must be drunk now. The '29 was also outstanding, but is now past its prime."

"Charles!" Charles was already beside Riffel, blinking at him. "Open it!"

Charles put a lackadaisical hand on his knee and knelt. He began to pry open the box with the kiss mark. Beads of perspiration broke out on Neuf's bare forehead despite the cool of his cellar.

"No, Charles! Wait. Don't disturb the box with the lovely lady mouth. I'll save that. Open the one beneath it." Charles did so. He retrieved a bottle, opened it, and filled Riffel's glass. Riffel drank. His body quivered, looked as if it were going into convulsions, and then straightened.

His brows did not know how to react, so his mustache moved for them.

In a whisper, regarding the box with the kiss mark, Riffel said, "Charles, take that box to my truck." He covered his eyes with his fingertips and took another drink. Then, still muted, he said, "Men, all of you deserve a drink. Take it now. *Prost!*"

The men descended on the cases of wine. But the case with the kiss was lifted to Charles's shoulders and moved above the crowd, up the stairs, through the house, and down the drive to Riffel's personal carriage. Charles stared at the kiss mark for a moment and touched the rough wood panel with his too-soft fingertips before turning back to the house.

A few hours later, Riffel stood at the front door of Neuf's home as the last of his men filed past him and lined up on the dirt road.

"I appreciate the tour, *Herr* Neuf," said Riffel, pronouncing the name with perfect intonation. "I'm impressed by your skill. I'm in the presence of a genius—but no wonder! You're half German!" Riffel slapped Neuf on the back and laughed. Then he added: "No one shall touch your wine—unless we're buying it from you. Here." He held a leather bag to Neuf, who bowed as he took it and held it at his side.

"Go ahead," said Riffel—as if Neuf were his son and was receiving a piece of longed-for cake.

Neuf untied the bag and saw gold dust glint at him.

Riffel smiled hard and breathed out: "May your success blossom under our improved administration. The coming wine *Gauleiter* will hear of your skill." With that, Colonel Riffel snapped his heels together, saluted, and exited the home.

Neuf gazed at the figures as they drove around his dirt driveway and onto the main street, several dozen of his cases of wine in tow. He looked out at his vines—left perfect, untouched.

"What have I done?" said Neuf aloud. The rigidness in his form departed like a moth from a leaf, and his body fell against the rounded doorjamb.

Wednesday, September 4, 1940

Colonel Riffel, now far from Alsace and dressed in a ruby robe, took a cigar from his mouth to gesticulate. He dictated to Charles, who sat at a mahogany table top, donning bifocals. The case was open, its contents on the table in three neat rows. Bows were tied around the 12 bottles—every one with a red, feminine kiss on a white label. Charles packaged one in a small crate. He put a wooden lid on the box and hammered it shut. The ink on the wood read: *Generalleutnant* Troy Bastick.

———

Only days later, on a large veranda outside a thick-walled German manor, stood the very same Troy Bastick at the head of a long, heavy table crowded with officers and women, all of them staring at his powerful, aging physique. His forearms, neck, and calves bulged against their fabric encasing—all sinew, all muscle. His fully gray hair and mustache were still thick, betraying the fact that his natural force had not abated.

"You're all here because of me?" he said, putting his fingertips to his chest and staring back at the crowd. The first few golden leaves of autumn floated behind him, scared to take any of the attention. "Because I survived another year?" He looked slowly from face to face, comfortable in the spotlight. "I suppose in these times, even that's an accomplishment."

Some in the crowd nodded at this; some, sensing a toast, preemptively drank.

"Blame my wife; she feeds me well," he said, pointing at one of the beautiful, aging women in the crowd. She shook her head and turned a new color. "I'm glad I've survived long enough to see this day in our nation's history. I salute you all!" He lifted a glass high. "I toast our mission and the future. No one can say we didn't shake up the world. *Prost!*"

Everyone lifted a glass to Troy Bastick—including a younger version of the man with a jaw like Mount Rushmore and all the pigment retained by his black hair and mustache. This was Troy's son: Detective Wolfram Bastick. He held up a soda water and lime for the toast.

"Emma! Bring me that bottle, will you? I've something for the wine snobs. A *Spätburgunder* from our regained territory to the west."

She brought him a thin green bottle.

"There's only enough for a few to taste," he said to the crowd as he took the bottle from her and opened it. A few guests' fingers already fondled their glasses, and Troy poured them wine after pouring a large glass for himself.

"You should toast your son," whispered his wife in his ear. "It would mean so much for him to know that you've ... forgiven him."

"If he doesn't come up, what am I to do?" He looked down at the nearly empty bottle, at the dregs floating in the ring at the base. "Wolf! Come drink with me! Hurry, or the dogs will lap up your milk. You'll be left in the cold, Wolfram, your stomach empty, your mouth dry."

"Death!" said Detective Bastick, standing and moving toward his parents. They looked at him quizzically, but patiently, as if this exclamation were not out of the ordinary for their sired giant. "I've promised myself death if I take another drink." He grabbed his father's shoulders and squeezed. "If only I can look like you on my 60th birthday."

"If you want to look like me, keep drinking," said Troy, who poured the remainder of the wine into his own glass. The two men, when near each other, worked like gravity on the party, drawing all eyes. The female attendees rotated their bodies in conversation so as to have the duo in their line of sight. Even the singing nightingales seemed to circle the pair.

Troy's face was red as he poured the wine into his large mouth, pulling air in at the same time. His face changed expression. "It is dry as marrow!" He finished the glass in another gulp, grimaced, and walked toward the house. "I need some real German liquor to wash that down," he said. The bottle remained on the table. Evening sun shone through ancient oak trees in the yard, highlighting the dull purple of the leftover liquid and dregs within.

The guests followed Troy inside. A few stragglers orbited his son, Wolfram, who had a gravity all his own—if darker, if stranger.

Wolfram stared at the bottle on the railing and sniffed it. His nostrils flared as if he didn't recognize the scent.

———

The next morning, Wolfram got an urgent message from his father: Troy was in the hospital and needed his son. Without coffee or hat, Wolfram fled his home and nearly killed a dozen people on the road. He shoved through swinging hospital doors just in time to see a nurse rush from one of the rooms with a gasp.

"Oaf!" she yelled, turning back to the room and filling the doorway, her white bonnet clutched to her head. Wolfram heard his father's unmistakable bellow in response and ran toward it, pausing just short of plowing into the nurse.

It took all of Wolfram's strength to stop behind her, hands clasped behind his back, staring down. Hearing his unconscious snorting, she looked back. She gasped at the sight of the giant and moved out of his way. Wolfram nodded a thank you and ran into the room.

His father was sitting halfway up, his mother at the bedside. Troy looked deflated. But upon seeing his son, his face brightened. He turned to his wife. "I must speak with Wolfie alone, darling."

She kissed him and passed the burden of his hand to her son, who, kneeling, assumed the duty.

After his wife had left, Troy sputtered: "Avenge me, Wolf—" He broke off to cough, covering his mouth with a cloth. The handkerchief came back red. Wolfram stared at it and then at his father, puzzling. But before he could question aloud, Troy continued, trying to whisper and failing. "Don't tell your mother—the doctor suspects foul play. A poison. I won't last, Wolf!" Troy gripped his son's hand and leaned close. His dying breath heated the air between them, and Wolfram smelled the scent of death. "Find out who did this," said Troy, again doubling up in pain. His eyes bulged. He gritted his teeth and fell back into the bed.

Detective Wolfram Bastick leaned over to his father's neck and breathed in his odor. He recognized the scent of death and began to cry, his face trying to fight contortions.

Neither Wolfram nor his father could know that the man's cells were being punctured by a ribosome-inactivating protein poison that Neuf had added to the pinot noir. The poison, *Abrus precatorius,* was more common-ly known as the love pea. Its juice inhibited cell protein synthesis, causing Troy's organs to fail.

"Don't lose a moment," said Troy. He added a wry smile. "Who better to avenge me than the famous Gestapo Detective, Wolfram Bastick?"

Wolfram stood, and the tears continued to pour. His jaw was as tight as a fist, and the tendons of his neck stood at attention. He pulled in air as he sobbed silently. "Nothing—" he whispered, but couldn't get the rest out. His father nodded understandingly, but his son pressed on. "Nothing," Wolfram said through gritted teeth, "will stop me."

His father smiled and watched his son leave. Then his face twisted with pain.

Colonel Riffel sat at his ornate, 16th-century German table. A delicate, steaming tea set held black tea and a few crumbling scones. No one was around at this early-morning hour—aside from the kitchen staff, but they were well hidden. Riffel opened the first page of *Das Reich,* and his eyes moved. He smiled. He reached for a scone and took a bite. One cranberry clung to its host by a crumb. Other stubborn crumb compatriots wedged themselves into the man's thick, black mustache in a final effort to stay free and freshly baked in the outside world. But a roving tongue found them out, sticking to one crumb at a time and pulling them into the salivating chasm of its mouth.

"*Mein Gott!*"

Riffel's mouth dropped open, and one lucky crumb leapt from the deadly lips to the paisley carpet below, wedging itself deep into the wool crevices. Riffel's eyes bulged as he read the headline.

Major General Troy Bastick Dead; Foul Play Suspected

The tea set crashed to the floor as the table tipped over. The scones, with nearly audible praise, joined their brother on the floor. "Who did this?" Riffel was on his feet, his legs tensed, the paper held close to his face.

The very next day, in a massage parlor in Budapest, lay Mads Molnar. His face was planted deeply between two brown leather cushions, and his eyes stared at the floorboards beneath. He wondered if the stress of the cushions would finally cause his wrinkle-resistant olive skin to crack. He wasn't 30 anymore. He wasn't 40 anymore.

"Relax!" said the Swedish masseuse, who could have moonlighted as a pinup girl.

"Hand that bottle back and your job will get easier. I promise." His hand flapped toward a bottle of Bollinger champagne that was sitting nearby, nestled in a silver, ice-packed cradle.

"You're not supposed to drink during the massage. I could get in trouble if they caught me," she said, trying to work through the knots in his powerful back. After a few more moments, she let out a sigh. She crossed the room to get the bottle and placed it beneath him. "I can't bear to watch this," she said, tossing her blonde hair all over one shoulder.

"Come on," he said.

She sighed again, hands on hips.

"You know what to do."

She slapped him on the back and walked to the bar in the corner of the massage parlor. She came back with a long straw and bent down low, looking up at his squeezed face. He nodded at her and she shoved the straw between his teeth and into the champagne bottle.

"That wasn't so hard," he said through the straw.

She continued the massage, pouring on the oil, kneading the muscles, and she huffed.

"So?"

"At least it shuts you up," she said. "But it isn't normal. It isn't normal, and it isn't healthy. If you're not careful, one of these days, this will kill you."

"What, your kneading?"

"No," she began, but was cut off by two blinking red lights on the wall and one loud buzz.

"Mads. Someone must be here for you," she said.

His muscles tightened, and he leapt from the bed. "I prefer not to be found," he said, reaching for the doorknob.

"They're coming up that way," she said, as the sound of heavy boots tramped through the house. She took his bare shoulder with her hand and pivoted him toward the window. "Out you go. You should be limber now, anyway." She smiled at him.

He looked around, desperate for something to cling to, and grabbed the bottle.

"Hey!" she said. He poured her a tumbler full, and the white bubbles spilled over the rim as he jumped out the window. A lump of clothes hit him in the back of the head when he landed; he was still clad in only a small white towel held in place by one clutching hand.

Back in the massage parlor, the door burst open, splinters flying all over the room, and half a dozen men spilled through. They wore the bizarre, Nazi-influenced emblem of Hungary's Arrow Cross party on their sleeves, and held Mausers in their hands. Awaiting them was a tall blonde in a white skirt with a tumbler of champagne, sitting on a massage bench with her legs crossed.

"Didn't your mothers ever teach you to knock?" she said, wagging her finger at them. The men looked at one another and found that behind the guns and suits of men can lie the embarrassment of children. But the leader shoved by, grunting at the woman, and rifled through the closet. Then he turned and shoved the men back out of the room with another grunt.

Back on the ground, bottle in hand, Mads Molnar ran to his parked Packard and threw his clothes through the open window. Then he jumped in, revved the engine, and shot down the cobblestone street.

He kept his foot on the gas, and tore across the *Széchenyi* Chain Bridge and through the Buda Castle Tunnel. As evening approached, the shadows of the bridge elongated on the green Danube, forming dark and fearsome lines.

Meanwhile, Colonel Riffel lowered the most recent morning copy of *Das Reich* to the table. His face was paler than usual. There were more crumbs in his mustache than usual. Both of these effects were the result of another unfavorable headline:

Two German Officers Poisoned in Assassination

Riffel recognized the name of one of the article's victims—*General der Artillerie* Johann Schreider: a WWI hero who'd survived bullets, bombs, and poison gas at Verdun only to have his beaten body consumed by a concentrated dose of abrin from the love pea. Riffel thought about the possibility of a coincidence, but were there any coincidences this grand? Just like Troy Bastick, Schreider was the recipient of one of Riffel's bottles of wine. Now both Bastick and Schreider were dead. That fact interrupted Riffel's digestion. That fact caused him to stammer the name of his compatriot.

"Ch-Charles," he said, not even screaming the name for once, as the weight of the situation bore down on his mind.

The corporal slumped into the room.

"That French *frosch*!" shouted Riffel. "*Der Franzose!*"

Charles stared at his commander and slowly blinked.

Riffel stood, the paper crushed in his hands. He ripped it in half. "What have we done? What have we done?"

Charles stood at aloof attention. But a twitch of the mouth made Riffel wonder if he was inwardly gleeful over his supervisor's distraction.

"Get me a plane to Strasbourg," said Riffel in a whisper.

Charles did a half *heil* and moved toward the door.

"But no ..." The commander sat frozen, finger held in midair, mouth agape. An almost silent squeaking gasp emitted from the crumby chasm and died away. Riffel remained frozen until the corporal again began to move away toward the door and then—"Charles, wait!"

The corporal halted.

"No, no!—You have a more timely task!" cried Riffel, coming to life. He stood and moved quickly toward the young man, who tried not to stare at his crumb-peppered mustache. "Poison!" He grabbed the corporal's lapels. "It's poisoned, Charles!" The man's eyes were panicked. Then plead-ing. Then hard. "You must contact everyone who got our gifts." When the corporal didn't respond, Riffel pushed him onward. "I tell you that the wine is poisoned, Charles! Warn them now!"

Charles stumbled toward the door and barely managed a salute as he was rolled into the hall. His face remained aloof, but a rare smirk crossed his lips as he walked toward his own office.

Back at his desk, Charles shuffled through stacks of paper before pulling a list of names out of one pile. His finger helped his eyes find the first name on the list. He lifted a phone receiver and told the operator a name. Moments later, the operator's voice was replaced with that of a veritable angel.

"*Generalmajor* Heideling's office," said the delicate, lilting voice on the other line.

"Hello, my dear, this is Corporal Charles Herzog. I have an urgent message for Major General Heideling," said Charles, unable to keep his mind from imagining the body belonging to the particularly sensual voice on the other line.

"Oh, I'm sorry; Major General Heideling is out of the office. Would you like to call back in a few hours?"

"It's highly confidential. Are you his personal secretary?"

"Yes," she said, and her voice lowered to a whisper—a tone that sent shivers of glee through Charles. "And I have clearance to handle confiden-tial messages."

"This one could save his life, but don't breathe a word to anyone but Heideling. Did you recently receive a package from a Colonel Karlin Riffel?"

"Let me check." The secretary's voice paused. Charles heard shuffling in the background.

"Why yes, we did just yesterday," she said.

"Please destroy it! It's a poisoned bottle of wine. Colonel Riffel was duped and had no idea. We're just happy no one has yet taken a drink."

There was a pause. "I understand," she said. "Rest assured, your secret and the bottle are safe with me."

"You're a doll. Thank you," said Charles. He tried to think of some-thing that might intrigue the *überfrau* on the other line. But he failed and quickly hung up the phone without saying goodbye. His head fell low between his shoulders, and he got back to work.

Meanwhile, Riffel picked up his own phone and asked the operator for the military airport. Then he slammed it back on its prongs and lifted it again.

"Get me René Neuf, in Alsace."

Riffel stood in silence except for the pounding of his pulse. He began to pace as he waited. After a few moments, he heard a noise on the other end. "Neuf!"

"Yes," said Neuf.

"This is Colonel Riffel."

Neuf's mind tried to panic. His legs went weak, and he fell into a chair beside him. "How may I help *Herr—*"

"Poisoned! I sent your bottles to officers all over the *Deutsches Reich,* and you've murdered them. You've made me a fool! You fraudster!" As he spoke, Riffel's hands uselessly squeezed the phone as if to choke the man on the other end. His mind again slipped into its most-comfortable tongue. "*Du geistig zurückgeblieben bauer! Du Schwein, das auf Trauben saugt!*" This string of profanity was followed by a banging that could only be a receiver reverberating off mahogany. Then the voice was back, if muffled from a damaged microphone. "Try to run. Try to hide. I will find you and I will kill you! Good *Gott* in a vineyard, I will murder your wife and flay your belly and watch you bake in the sun!"

"Yes, kill me. It will, of course, affirm your guilt, but at least you'll have revenge."

"I will!" Riffel slammed the cracked receiver down, ending the call. But then he stared at the phone. What? What had the knave said? Affirm his guilt? Whose guilt?

Spindly fingers of panic spread up from Riffel's navel, embracing his lungs. He yanked the phone off the prongs and ordered the operator to repeat the call. It rang thrice. "What did you say, fool?"

Neuf cleared his throat. "You send poisoned bottles of my wine to German officers, and then you kill me. And you think the French police won't notice that? The—"

"*German* police, you mean. Swine."

"*Oui, oui.* Even worse. How could it help you, Colonel, to draw the attention of the press to my wine? Because behind them will be the police detectives asking: who sent these bottles?"

Riffel looked out the window of his office for a moment. "Hold the line." He dropped the cracked receiver on the desk and stumbled toward his liquor cabinet. He poured himself a full glass of scotch and moved back to his desk as if he were walking across the deck of a vessel at sea.

Attaining his seat, he clung to the receiver. He rubbed his mustache in thought, and found one of the clinging scone crumbs with his thin, tapered fingers. He pulled it loose. Looking closely, he identified it, ensured that Charles wasn't behind him, put it in his mouth, and masticated the crumb in thought.

Riffel was about to drink when Neuf's voice came through. "If I myself am killed, you yourself will be caught. You will be a traitor to the fatherland. And you'll be shot. Tell me that I am mistaken."

"You're mistaken," said Riffel. "I'd be hanged." The words sank in as Riffel stared at his glass. His boiling temper bubbled up, roiling the blood in his forehead until it glowed and perspired. "Oh, when this is over, how I will desecrate your corpse, Neuf."

"I see an alternative."

Riffel suckled his soothing scotch. "Go on."

"We remain unlikely allies. You carry on as if nothing happened. I, of course, tell no one." Neuf's pause allowed the emphasis to fully mature. "Then you secretly track down the bottles before your friends drink them. And you destroy the evidence. A couple poisonings are hard to link, but twelve is a different story."

Neuf took his own seat, his soliloquy complete. Riffel stared out the window, sipped his scotch. "Maybe, you slippery stoat." He took another sip. "Maybe it could work. But who could do such a thing? Who would I hire? All the best talent here is loyal to the fatherland. They would betray me, Neuf!"

"Hire a French detective, of course!"

"No! No, I don't trust you slimy French. Who else?"

Neuf shrugged. Since that wasn't audible, he added, "*Je ne sais pas.* You could just tell the truth. You were hoodwinked by a Frenchman." Neuf smiled as he said it.

"*Gott* no!" said Riffel. He rubbed his mustache. "You know, I've heard legends about a Hungarian detective who used to be a clinical psychologist. He was supposed to be the best."

"A Hungarian? How can you trust a Hungarian more than the French? Come on."

"Neuf, the French got me into this! I'd trust a dog with my duck rillettes more than I'd trust the French. No, it will be this man. And I'll know I can trust him because Hungarians can be bribed. And they're expendable. I can kill him when he's through. Nobody misses a Hungarian."

"*Oui. C'est* true." Neuf yawned. His adrenaline was gone. He relaxed back in his chair, the guillotine avoided for another day.

Suddenly, Riffel's eyebrows shot up to nearly touch his hairline. "Charles!" He slammed the receiver down, tossed the scotch to his tonsils, and ran out the front door. He sprinted his little body through the house, toppling chairs along the way.

Charles had just hung up with Heideling's secretary. His hand was reaching for a pen to cross off the man's name when he heard the commotion.

"Charles! Charles! Charles!" came from outside and increased in pitch and volume as a panting Riffel smashed through the door. "Don't tell anyone!"

Charles looked up at the colonel.

"You didn't tell anyone yet, did you? I must know."

Charles's eyes showed that his mind was churning. Then his voice said coolly, "I was just about to call the first. Why?"

Riffel collapsed in the chair opposite Charles. "Good. Good. Oh, thank *Gott*. For once your dawdling has helped us." He leaned back, deep in the chair. Riffel reached his stubby fingers into his stubby pocket and pulled out stubby cigarettes. One caught fire as Riffel audibly consumed it. He held the tumbler out to Charles, who, recognizing the order, stood and fetched more scotch.

"I'm going to call this Hungarian detective immediately, Charles." Charles poured. "He better be able to work miracles." His eyes went down to the paper on Charles's desk—the list of recipients. Riffel reached for the young man's phone, lifted it, and asked for the office names of detectives in Budapest.

———

In Budapest, a hard plastic hot-pink rotary phone *chingalinged* so loudly it caused the very curvy, very dark, very dry Eva Sandor's hand to slip and her nail polish to touch the cuticle of her big toe, which wasn't all that big. She looked like an office ballerina but with nicer feet. Those toes were perched on her desk, and the rest of her was somewhere between them and her chair. She cursed through her cigarette and screwed the top on the polish. Her tanned fingers fondled the phone and stopped the ringing.

"Yes?" She cradled the receiver on a shoulder that seemed shaped for it. Then she unscrewed the polish and performed gymnastics from her chair to reach her outstretched toes again.

"Is this the office of the famous detective, Mads Molnar?"

"It is," she mumbled, blinking against the smoke.

"May I speak with him, please?" said Riffel, using his "office voice"—the one he switched to when his subconscious mind knew he was talking to something attractive.

"He's not here." Eva finished the final toe as she said this. "I can take a message."

"I'm calling to urgently reach him. It's of the utmost importance to the"—Riffel paused—"stability of the Third *Reich*. I must reach him."

"Pope's bastard!" the girl shouted as her heel slipped from the corner, covering her pinkie toe in ... pink.

"I *beg* your pardon!" Riffel's "office voice" flew out the open window.

"Not you. Something happened on this end," said Eva, reapplying the cap and stubbing her cigarette into the ashtray. "And I assure you, I'm very good at taking a message."

———

Clothes and champagne bottle in hand, Molnar entered his office. His secretary, Miss Sandor, was staring at the light-pink lipstick ring on her cigarette. She looked up at him from under long lashes and blew smoke.

"Nice towel. How's your Swede?" Eva Sandor asked.

"She's only my masseuse. Any messages?"

Eva kept mum and stared at him, then at the bottle. She dumped the remains of her coffee in the trash and held out her cup. He poured some champagne as a toll and frowned at the almost empty bottle.

"One message. You might be intrigued. A Nazi colonel wants you to go to Berlin and help him find some bottles of poisoned wine. He said it's urgent. In fact, he got huffy." She sat up, took a drink, and mimicked the no-longer-office voice of Colonel Riffel: "This is a summons under *Wehrmacht* law and is legally binding in German ally states!" She finished the drink. "I don't think he liked me very much."

"He couldn't see you," said Molnar, finishing the bottle. He closed one eye and looked in the neck to make sure it was bare. "But he can summon away. Berlin is out."

"Well, don't look in your office, then. You might get motivated." She raised her eyebrows and started typing, cigarette firmly fixed betwixt lips.

Molnar cocked his head at her and walked toward his office. Shadowy silhouettes—most certainly not coming from blondes—moved behind the frosted glass. He turned back to Eva with a betrayed look. On cue, his door opened toward him.

"Doctor Molnar," said an officer in an Arrow Cross uniform. It was the same man who had chased after him months earlier at the border. He was just as heavy, hairy, and dark as before. "We meet again." He reached his hand out to Molnar, who took the sweaty palm and shook it out of habit. His other hand kept his towel on. Two men appeared behind the officer. These were leaner, meaner and armed.

"You can call me Horváth," said the hairy man. "We sent some men to your favorite haunts." He nodded at Molnar's towel. "It looks like you ran into one of them."

Molnar nodded. "We brushed elbows," he lied. "I explained my side of the story, and he understood. He says you should lay off me. We're good friends now. He's coming for brunch on Sunday."

Horváth smiled and shook his head. "You will not be available Sunday. You will be of most use to the National Socialist movement and Hungary when you're out of the towel and in a noose. And that"—he gestured at his compatriots with a sausage-y finger—"is where we're taking you."

Molnar backed toward the door and looked at Eva for help. Her fingers kept clacking away as she stared down at her machine. A woman scorned, Molnar thought. The two lean men in uniform grabbed Molnar, knocked the clothes and bottle from his hands, and shackled his wrists behind his back.

"Three months, Molnar," said Horváth. "It's been that long since you escaped me, and now I've got you!"

"I thought you were all chased off at the start of the war," Molnar said.

The man struck Molnar as the others held him. A ribbon of blood ran down his chin, but he kept grinning. "Eva, maybe we have some loose change in the desk. I think it'd be nice of us to buy these guys some new jackboots. Theirs aren't up to code."

She didn't answer, but Horváth did. "It's too late for bribes, Molnar. You flouted the authority of the Arrow Cross and murdered my compatriot. I will watch you hang."

"That was Miles. Let's hang him instead."

"All in due time," said Horváth, shoving Molnar forward to end the conversation.

"I think he likes me," Molnar muttered to Eva as they herded him toward the door.

"Officer Horváth," piped up Eva's voice. Her fingers stopped clacking for the first time, and she drew the paper from the machine. "Would you mind signing this notice to Colonel Karlin Riffel in Berlin? He's just summoned Dr. Molnar to work on a case directly for the Nazi party. He said the lives of a dozen officers—some generals—hang in the balance. This letter states that we're declining service on your account. It says you've more need of Molnar than he. I'll call him now."

Her fingers started spinning the dial. Horváth stared in confusion at the paper. "What?" he said.

Molnar tried not to smile at Eva between the two goons.

"Colonel Riffel, there is a problem," said Eva into the receiver. "An Arrow Cross officer said he needs to hang Molnar and you can't have him. So you'll be getting a letter from us declining the job."

"Wait, wait, wait, wait my girl!" said the hairy man, moving toward her. "Don't be so hasty. Let me speak with him."

She handed over the phone.

Horváth stood with the pink phone pressed to his now-rust-red temple and did little nods and grunts of affirmation as shrill shouts emitted from the receiver. His hand found a home in his pocket. Eva lit a cigarette and watched from under her lashes. Molnar tried to look serious.

The man nodded and grunted and ended with a "*Sieg Heil!*" He handed the phone back to Eva without looking in her lovely, round eyes. He did look into Molnar's.

"Run," he said, nodding to the lean men to uncuff Molnar, which they did. Then he got very close to the detective, his hot breath engulfing the man's dark, handsome face. "Wherever you go in the *Reichsmark*, we will be watching, and when the Nazis are done with you …" He leaned in even closer and slapped Molnar lightly on the face with his sweaty palm. "You will be begging to be hanged."

Now uncuffed, Molnar was pushed to the side. The men exited, the door slammed, and Molnar looked at Eva with relief.

"You are beautiful," he said. "You are genius. You are superb." He moved to the desk with his hands out and grabbed her legs, kissing her ankles. She allowed it at first, but pulled away when it lasted too long and shooed him off.

"Better pack," she said.

BOTTLE III

The somber tones of Handel's *Rinaldo* carried through the air as Detective Wolfram Bastick stood on his white marble balcony facing a wall of rain. A brown pipe smoked in his hand. His eyes were closed, his legs braced as if he'd been riding a horse.

The house that framed the man was impressive: its façade nothing but white stone and black shutters. The balcony overlooked a white Mercedes-Benz SSK whose chromium manifold pipes gleamed in the muted light. But most of the scene was obscured by rain. Bastick's eyes remained closed, and his rubbery nostrils flared and twitched as if he used them to think— like a frog uses its eyes to swallow.

The metallic precision of Bastick's mind replayed the evening of his father's death. He remembered the attendants face by face. He remembered the table of gifts. He remembered his father drinking champagne, an all-vodka Martini, a gin and tonic, straight cognac. He remembered faces. So many smiling faces. And finally, he remembered an emblem and the name of a cocktail company.

His eyes opened. He put the pipe to his lips and breathed in the smoke, letting it seep out of his nostrils in circular swirls.

His body spun round and he rushed into the house and down the stairs. He reached for the phone and gave a number to the operator.

"Otto. Be ready to leave in five minutes."

"*Ja!*" said a high-piping voice on the other line.

Bastick hung up the phone and grabbed his jacket from the wall. A butler opened the door for him on his way out and carried an umbrella over his head all the way to the SSK. His tires spun before getting enough traction to fishtail the car out of the driveway and into the street.

The car careened through the streets of Berlin, jettisoning water on pedestrians and dogs and other cars.

The brown pipe remained firmly planted in Bastick's teeth. His pupils were tiny. They stared through the sheets of rain as his 250-horsepower machine whipped through the streets—the back end nearly sliding out too far on every turn.

When his father had spoken his last request, something inside Bastick had galvanized. For the first time since the last war, he was turning the whole of his uncanny forces on a single task.

One word kept creeping into the front of his mind, blurring out all else: purpose. Purpose. This was a purpose surpassing Germany and the foolish Nazi propaganda, surpassing his love for his fiancée. This was something deeper.

Maybe a way to earn forgiveness from his father's ghost.

Bastick pulled up in front of a vacant barracks building. A thin, albino-pale boy with short-cropped red hair and a floating moon for a face ran down the barracks steps and stared into Bastick's car.

"Get in, little Otto!"

The boy obeyed. The car took off.

Minutes later, the white SSK slid into a parking spot in front of an apartment building. Bastick leapt from the car and moved soundlessly to the front door. Otto followed him like a shrunken shadow the color of moonlight.

The front door was locked. Bastick took a deep breath through his nose and closed his eyes. He slicked his hair back with his fingers. Beads of perspiration stood on his forehead as he pressed the buzzer beside the door with a thick finger.

A young man with an obvious blond comb-over and a less-obvious mustache opened the door.

"I am a Gestapo detective," said Bastick, holding his badge close enough to the doorman's face that he could see fingerprints on the copper. "I must speak with Tomas Schreck, one of your tenants."

"But of course," said the young blond, moving backward and to his bar-height desk. Bastick followed him in, and Otto trotted behind. "Please, come in. He may be asleep, but I'll ring him now." The doorman reached for a phone receiver, but Bastick placed his own hand atop the man's, engulfing it and pinning it down.

"I'm not delivering sauerkraut. I must surprise the man," said Bastick.

"Oh," said the blond doorman, pulling back his hand from the phone. "He's on the fifth floor. Room 508."

"Take me there," said Bastick, eyeing him.

They moved into the elevator. One flickering bulb intermittently sent the cage into total darkness as the aging machine churned up the floors. It clanged to a halt. The doorman opened the cage, and they exited at the fifth floor into near-total darkness. Bastick dismissed the doorman toward the stairs with a snort and a toss of his head.

Bastick and Otto moved in front of door 508. "Draw your weapon, Otto."

The boy complied, slick black Mauser flashing in the low light. Bastick's remained holstered. He hit the door with a heavy fist that rang out like a metal knocker. He repeated this many times until the door opened, revealing a bearded ginger with the look of sleep just lifting from his eyes. Bastick stepped into the doorway. He grabbed the man's beard with one hand and gave him a heavy, open-palmed slap on the eye socket with the other. The man let out a grunt of surprise and almost fell down from the shock. Bastick held him up by the beard, pushing him back into the apartment.

"I need you awake, Tomas," said the enormous Bastick, keeping the beard in hand and slowly pushing the man down his own dark apartment hall and into the open kitchen. He kept pushing until Tomas landed in a chair. Then Bastick crouched over him. "The boy behind me has a gun on you. You were bartender at my father's party. Do you remember me?"

Tomas, in shock, took a moment to gulp air and blink away the sting of Bastick's salutation. When his eyes focused in the dim light on the man before him, he nodded. "Yes—yes. I do. And did. I mean, yes. I bartended his party."

"I know," said Bastick. "Now we both know. How was my father poisoned, Tomas?"

Bastick stood back up to his full height and stared down at the man, who seemed to shrink the higher Bastick rose. As Tomas tried to respond, Otto stepped into view from behind the meaty Bastick, revealing the pointy black Mauser held fully extended at Tomas's forehead.

"I—I've no idea. I've no idea. All the liquor was new. I—" The man was at a loss for words as he stared at the barrel. "I twisted the caps myself. They were all new."

Bastick glanced back at Otto. "Do you smell the faint change in the humidity of the air, Otto?"

"*Nein,*" came the hollow response.

"What about the slight tinge of color? Its hue faded from violet to purple as he spoke. Do you see this?"

The albino shook his head violently.

Bastick reached gently with a hand the size of a rump roast and took Tomas's face by the jaw. He turned it delicately from one side to the other. "Do try, Otto. It's more helpful for your education this way. Breathe in."

Otto audibly obeyed.

"Breathe in once more, Otto. Do you smell the change in this young man now?" The detective carefully pulled the bartender's face upward and leaned close, sniffing. Otto also sniffed the air, but the vacancy in his eyes did not fill.

The detective dropped the bartender's jaw and stood erect, breathing in once again. "Anything?"

"*Nein!*"

The detective turned his face to the boy to look into his yellow eyes for the first time. "Hmm. You may be like everyone else, Otto. I thought you might see and smell as I do."

Otto's eyes escaped to the ceiling, and the detective shook his head.

"Men in fear for their lives rarely lie. And if they do, it's quite easy to detect." Bastick kept his eyes on the shrunken Tomas, whose whole body was vibrating from the intensity and insanity of the moment. Bastick packed his horn pipe with tobacco. "He's innocent," added Bastick, detaching his gaze and patting the man's cheek.

Tomas's eyes closed. He took a deep breath of relief, even as Otto's gun remained on him.

The detective moved to the window and struck a match to light his pipe. He stared out at Berlin's extinguished streetlights—the city was on blackout orders for fear of night bombings. "Why must it be so dark?" Bastick asked the air, and he waited for the answer.

It was the early days of flying, like the early days of voting in America. Only a few people could do it, and they had to be wealthy—the only difference was, while flying you got free liquor.

Mads Molnar just finished taking full advantage of that perk for the past several hours when the pilot announced the plane was about to land in Berlin. Reminded of his mission, Molnar's face wrinkled. His eyes refocused on the woman beside him.

She was blonde, of course, and wore a tight blue cotton one-piece pantsuit complete with a swastika on the sleeve.

"Gretchen, why not come meet the Führer with me?" he asked her in German, his ease betraying the fact that they'd been speaking the whole flight. "He's my cousin."

"Oh, you're such a liar." She slapped his arm but held on to it when she was done, looking down at it. "You're a strong liar." She too had a newly filled glass of champagne on the side table in front of her massive, cushy chair.

"Why, thank you," he said. "It's from wrestling bad guys." He leaned back to look at her appraisingly.

She fidgeted, eyes darting around. "What?" she asked.

"Do you think I'm too tan to sire a master race? Be honest. Maybe you can balance me out."

She laughed, slapping him again.

"Isn't that a profession here?" he asked. "Part of the war effort? 'You're commissioned to produce one thousand Nazi babies,'" he said in his best Hitler impersonation.

She leaned close to him. "Oh, hush. That's silly."

"It's a tough job," he said.

Molnar didn't notice the lean man two rows behind him, who had been taking a particularly keen interest in his conversation with the woman. The man could have been Hungarian. He was tall and dark. His glasses matched his features and shaded his eyes, but those eyes could very well have been pinned to Molnar.

Molnar's mind was on more important realities. He now understood the world into which he was landing on four big, black bouncy tires. It was a world in which all the young men had been shipped away to kill and be killed for the will of one man.

As he and Gretchen got off the plane together, Molnar looked around the airport. This was also a world of single young blondes. He remembered the "bird in the hand" saying and made sure to get this blonde's number before they parted ways, reminding her that he needed a place to stay. She assured him he couldn't stay with her if he paid her, but her smile disagreed.

She went off to wherever young blondes with swastikas on their arms go, and he got into a taxi to meet his summoner: Colonel Riffel.

Molnar saw that the taxi driver was a man, so he pulled his gray Stetson Whippet fedora over his eyes and took a nap.

The car stopped moving, and Molnar heard the driver's door open. He slowly removed the hat, waiting for the driver to get his door. It opened. Molnar grabbed a large briefcase—his only luggage—and moved past the driver with a nod. He looked up in front of him to see a large German manor complete with a balcony capping the entryway and stone stairs leading from the door to Molnar's feet.

The door to the manor opened. Charles held it wide so Colonel Riffel could walk out and down the stairs toward Molnar. The stubby little colonel was dwarfed by his surroundings, but he navigated them with the ease of practice. His hand stretched toward Molnar as he reached ground level. Molnar took it, shook it, and looked down at him.

"Welcome, welcome!" said Riffel, taking Molnar by the arm and helping him up the stairs, as if stairs were as hard to ascend for normal-sized people as for him. "Finally, I get the chance to meet the famous Doctor Molnar! You know English, German, French, and Hungarian; is that correct?"

"Add Swedish and Spanish, and it is," said Molnar, cresting the stairs and prying himself from Riffel's grasp. "I got around a lot as a kid."

Riffel looked to heaven as if to thank it. "You come highly recommended," he added. "Have you had a chance to review the information?"

"Yes." Molnar patted his briefcase. The two moved past Charles, down a long, ornate rug and beneath a long, ornate chandelier to the sitting room—where they sat. "I have a few questions," said Molnar, looking around at all the oak and glass.

"Fire away!" said Riffel, moving to his heavy, glass-topped desk and waving at a cushioned chair behind him. "Oh, but first: welcome to Berlin! Refreshment?"

"If you have a scotch, neat, I'd drink it," said Molnar, taking the seat and setting his briefcase beside him.

"Charles!" Riffel called. "I'll have the same but with an ice."

As Charles busied himself, Molnar got comfortable and stared down his new employer, who refused to sit.

"Who knows about this?" Molnar asked. He'd learned to ask a lot of questions of his employers. In this line of work, it was hard to know if you were being scammed.

"Just me and you," said Riffel. "And ... the"—expletives escaped his lips—"vintner. The vintner knows." Riffel lit a cigarette, offering one to Molnar, who refused. "I'll kill him as soon as we have all the bottles."

"How many dead?" asked Molnar, accepting the scotch from Charles's languid grip.

"Two bottles have killed at least three men," said Riffel, smoke coming out his nostrils. "We're not sure how many died at Troy Bastick's party."

Molnar noticed the man's hands shake a bit as he took his scotch from Charles. "OK," said Molnar, taking a drink. "The last thing I need is a list of names and addresses."

Riffel lifted a paper from the desk in front of him. "I've already prepared you that list." He brought it to Molnar.

Molnar's eyes danced over the names and stopped on one. Something in his face said he knew the name, but his voice didn't own up. "Why don't you just call them all and warn them?"

Riffel shook his head. "I sent the bottles to those I wanted to impress, not to friends. They would turn me in to the Gestapo in a heartbeat." Riffel paused as if he were realizing this for the first time. Then he cleared his throat, and his tone got serious with the detective for the first time. "No one can know that the wine is poisoned, and no one can consume the wine. And if they do, we must make it look as if they found another path to the afterlife. Every bottle came with a note from me. Destroy all the bottles and the notes. You understand ..." His ferrety fingers steepled. "We must stop them without anyone—especially the press—finding out. Now, I've already fixed things with the second bottle, which I read about in the paper. I couldn't wait. My men ran over and scraped up the evidence. And a little birdie told me that Widow Bastick isn't aware of the bottle and the wait staff cleaned everything after the party." Riffel used the smoldering butt of his cigarette to light another.

"If we can't call them, the odds are against us," said Molnar, taking another drink.

"Nothing's easy!" snapped Riffel. "I hired you to work a miracle, and I expect a miracle."

"I didn't say it was impossible." With the pleasantries stabbed and bleeding out on the floor, Molnar added, "Did you get my estimate? Who pays that?"

Riffel pulled a check from his breast pocket, already filled out. "Here it is, doubled."

Molnar took the check and his brows went up. He folded it and put it in his own breast pocket.

"Just sign right here," added Riffel. "This is our contract." He held out a paper in German. Molnar looked down at it. The only thing he noted was the number of Deutsche Marks paid. But then he paused and looked up at Riffel.

"I have one condition of my own."

Riffel stared at the Hungarian.

"Before I left Budapest, I ran awry of Hungary's Arrow Cross party. They're associated with you all. I'd prefer to avoid another encounter. So, if this goes off, then I go to Sweden for the duration of the war. My mother's side of the family is from Gothenburg."

"Fine by me," said Riffel.

"That means I'll need exit papers," said Molnar, removing a pen from his breast pocket. "Can you arrange that?"

Riffel smiled from ear to ear, his cigarette hanging under his mustache. He walked up to Molnar and reached for his hand again. "If this goes off, I'll give you Gothenburg!" He took his pen from the table and added "with signed exit papers" to the Conditions section of the contract.

Molnar signed the paper. "I suppose that means I'd better get to work," he said as he stood.

"Another thing, Molnar," said Riffel, folding the contract in half. "You will need clearance to get in and out of our German military encampments. Take this." The colonel handed Molnar a die-cast metallic oval that looked like a flat, silver belt buckle. The front of the oval depicted an eagle holding a wreath with a swastika in it. The reverse read, "*Geheime Staatspolizei*" with the number 705 beneath. "This Gestapo identification disc will get you into wherever you need to go. It should help in retrieving the bottles."

Molnar looked at the disc, pocketed it, and nodded. But inwardly, he laughed. If only he'd had this at the border crossing in Hungary! But there might be other borders, more milk bottles.

"My final word is to encourage you in your work." The little man's wretched smile parted his face. "Remember, even if you're not a part of our military, this is a military mission. And as such, there are military consequences."

Riffel had his attention.

"If you are to fail, I will be removed from my position at the very least; and more likely"—his voice lowered to a whisper—"I'll be hanged." The man's little hands nearly went to his neck, but stopped at his collarbone. "If I am implicated, you will, I'm afraid, be implicated," he said, holding up the paper. "Under military law, your punishment would likely rival my own."

Molnar's eyes landed on the contract in Riffel's hand, and he realized he'd made a deal with Satan's little servant.

His very little servant. At least he had good scotch. Molnar finished his. "Riffel, you hired me because I don't fail. This won't be different. I'll get the bottles and save your name." He put the glass down on the table.

The men shook hands. Molnar took his briefcase and turned on his heel. Riffel called for Charles, who got the door. Molnar exited and jogged down the stairs to the waiting cab below. Riffel saluted him, all smiles and sunshine. The cab turned in the horseshoe driveway. Molnar removed his hat and stared at the list.

"Where to?" asked the driver.

Molnar pointed at an address beside a Hungarian name and looked up at the driver. "To the airport. And step on it."

The car lurched forward, and they flew down the street. A few minutes later, another car overtook them in the opposite lane. A lane for advancing traffic. The car's horn was held down. Molnar looked over and saw Charles's flapping arm.

"Go ahead and pull over," Molnar told the driver.

The taxi pulled into a farm driveway off the side of the road. The view was all crops. Charles pulled in behind them and exited the car. He rushed toward the taxi. Seeing the boy move quickly for once, Molnar jumped out as well. His hand went to the revolver in his shoulder holster, and he stared down the advancing young man.

Charles plowed forward and stopped just short of Molnar. "I've some-thing to confess!" he said.

Molnar, seeing his face, released the gun. "Slow down," he said. "Take a breath." He gestured for Charles to sit on the prominent chrome bumper.

"Will you promise not to tell him?" Charles's face was fear itself.

Molnar mulled this over. "Sure, kid. Shoot."

Charles took the seat and looked up at him, surprised to hear the af-firmation. His body straightened, and cigarettes appeared in his hand. "I told her," he said, lighting one with a flick of a butane lighter. "Riffel told me to warn them all, so I called Major General Heideling's secretary, and I told her about the wine. Just after that, Riffel got back and called it off. He doesn't know I called her! I thought, if anything, my call would only hurt Colonel Riffel." The boy took a drag and couldn't hold back a sneer. Then his face became serious again. "But now it's you too."

"What'd she say?"

The boy related the conversation.

"OK," said Molnar, and patted his shoulder. "Don't worry about it. Your secret is safe with me."

Charles tossed the cigarette onto the road. "I just wish I could get out of here." He looked off to the horizon, sure there must be greener pastures somewhere.

"You and me both, kid," said Molnar. "You and me both."

———

A dark man with sunglasses and a narrow face had watched as Charles sped off after Molnar. Now, he walked into Riffel's office.

Riffel, thinking he was alone, was sitting in front of a large piece of choc-olate cake topped with a heap of delicate and slumping crème. It was his reward for commissioning Molnar. Just as he reached for his fork, he heard a light rapping on his doorjamb and looked up to see the tall, dark man.

Riffel started. "And who are you? Charles?!" There was no answer.

"My name doesn't matter, my dear fellow," said the man, his thin ap-pendages moving lithe and slow like a scaleless snake shaped into a mid-dle-aged man. "I represent Hungary's Arrow Cross party. We are concerned with Mads Molnar."

Riffel stood and took his napkin from out of his collar. Few things upset him like being interrupted during dessert. "How in Hades did you get in here?" He stepped around the desk toward the man.

"Molnar murdered my brother in Budapest. When he's finished your work, I want him." The man couldn't help but lick his lips as he said this. His tongue didn't luxuriate; it darted: in, out, gone.

The gesture was revolting to Riffel, who kept picturing the tongue as he tried to continue the conversation. "To hell with your brother! I've just given Molnar my word to help him into Sweden." He unsnapped the holster of his Mauser.

Instead of backing away, the man slid closer. "We can help," he said.

"How?" Riffel's hand stayed on the gun.

"We had Molnar's phone bugged. We know about the wine. We know what you did." He let Riffel take this in. "But we are, of course, friends. This is a small secret to keep between friends."

Riffel sat down. "OK, I'm listening."

"If Molnar fails, we can make sure there are no loose ends—including him."

Riffel's squinting eyes moved around as his mind worked. "You mean, you won't turn me in. And if he fails, you pick up the pieces and sort it out?"

"Please, my dear fellow. Don't speak of such vulgar things as treachery. But, certainly, we will act as insurance for you. We only want Molnar in exchange," said the man; and again, the thin pink tongue darted out.

Riffel tried not to show his revulsion. "OK," he said. "That sounds reasonable. But let him work. If you slow him down or interfere too soon ..." He stood again, moving toward the man and placing the Mauser beneath his chin. "You will suffer the same treatment I will."

"All right. But we cannot wait forever."

"Neither can I," said Riffel, liking the power that the gun made him feel. "Give him a week."

"OK, until the end of the week, then. He has until Sunday to finish."

"Fine," said Riffel, lowering the gun. "Come on, I've a contract you can sign. We can sort out the details. You need to have something to lose too, my dear fellow."

The dark man moved after Riffel and into his office.

Molnar sat in the back seat and looked at the list of names for a few moments before he shook his head and told the driver to take him to Major General Heideling's address instead of to the airport.

On the way, Molnar noticed a massive portrait of Adolf Hitler adorning the top of a building. There was also a flag of a faceless German man who held a rifle and waved his compatriots onward, up a hill. The translated text read, "Ever upward! Building Greater Germany, the Third Reich!" Molnar raised an eyebrow at these.

The cab pulled up to a large office building in the middle of downtown Berlin. The rain was back on, and only a few umbrella-less masochists were on the sidewalks, grimacing against the onslaught. Through the haze of rain, Molnar saw the outline of a loudspeaker painted on the side of the building. It was one of the locations of Berlin's air-raid siren system. Molnar leaned up to the driver.

"I'll be back in five minutes. Things might get loud, but just stay put," he said. The man turned to him, questions on his face. "Just stick around. I'll explain later."

Molnar turned up the collar on his gray cotton trench coat, pulled down his hat, and got out of the car. He walked up the stairs to the blocky entrance of the Ministry of Defense.

There was no one to greet him at the front door, only a list of names and suite numbers. Molnar found his man up two flights of stone stairs and past three large swastika tapestries. He looked in through the fogged and ribbed glass of suite 305 and saw the attractive outline of a woman at a desk. Must be the one Charles had been talking about.

Then Molnar kept climbing. He reached the sixth floor, the top. There, he encountered the mechanical room, complete with a big, heavy silver padlock.

Removing a small leather case from his breast pocket, Molnar took out a tension wrench and lock pick and got to work. After some time and some looks over his shoulder, there was a satisfying *click,* the cylinder turned, and the padlock opened.

Inside the mechanical room, Molnar found the air-raid siren system and flipped a switch. Cables ran out the wall and to the roof, where an air-raid siren began to crank. It started slowly and built into a wail. Molnar opened the window and looked down in time to see the cab driver toss Molnar's briefcase onto the sidewalk, skid off down the street, and fishtail around a corner.

"That's one way to skip out on a tab," mumbled Molnar, and cursed under his breath. He kept watching and saw Berliners pour into the streets, looking to the sky. Another siren in the distance picked up his wail, and Molnar smiled. From the furtive movements and running, it looked like they hadn't heard the siren sounded before.

Molnar exited the mechanical room and locked the padlock, leaving the siren on. Then he trotted down a few flights amid sharp cries of panic from retreating office workers. He peered down the stairwell at suite 305. A dangerously voluptuous blonde with shoulder-length hair was getting hurried out of the door by a hatless white-hair. Must be the major general.

They had left the door ajar.

Molnar jogged into the room and closed the door behind him. He looked around at the all-brown, all-boring affair. There was a name tag on the secretary's desk: Marilyn Ghetz. He moved past that to another frosted-glass door. It was unlocked.

Inside, Molnar saw a major general's hat and another name tag. Atop the silver metal filing cabinet stood a bottle of wine—a 1935 French wine from Alsace. It read *pinot noir*, and it was empty. Molnar, puzzled, pocketed it. He was about to exit the office when he stopped, went back to the secretary's desk, and wrote a note on her typewriter. Then he pulled the paper up a bit so it could be read and left the room.

The alarm was still blaring when he exited the building, collar pulled up against the heavy rain. The streets were barren, the rain cold for early September, the afternoon bleak.

Berlin wasn't making the best impression.

Molnar saw his briefcase on the sidewalk. He picked it up and tried to shake off the water.

After a few blocks of getting wet, Molnar dove into a nearby metal-and-glass telephone box. He told the operator to connect him to Colonel Riffel.

"One down," he said, shaking the water off his coat.

"You make quick work," said Riffel, his smile audible. "How'd it go?"

"We have either a very active corpse or some funny business." Molnar looked down at the bottle to affirm that it read 1935. "Your wine is a 1934, isn't it?"

"Yes, why?" said Riffel.

"I'll report back with more later."

"I hang on your every utterance, like a wolf at its mother's teat."

Molnar pulled the phone away from his head and stared at it. "I have to go," he said, and slapped the telephone prongs to ring off. But he held on to the receiver and put more change into the machine.

"Operator."

"Put me through to *Sturmbannführer* Miklós Skorzeny, please."

"Hold the line... ."

Molnar looked out at the sheets of rain.

"I'm putting you through," the operator told him.

"Major Skorzeny's office," said a voice.

"This is Mads Molnar, Skorzeny's nephew. Can you put me through to him, please? I have an important message."

"I'm sorry, Mr. Molnar, but Major Skorzeny has been out of the office for several months. He's operating at an undisclosed location in the front of the war," she said. Her voice did sound genuinely sorry.

"Did you get any packages for him recently? I'm trying to see if mine went through."

"We've received two in the past week, but we forwarded them on right away. They both should be on the way to him now."

"Miss ..." Molnar turned on the tears. He sniffled. "Can you ..." His voice went weak and cut out.

"Mr. Molnar, are you OK?"

"Skorzeny's sister ... my mother," said Molnar. "She passed." He sniffled more. "I just have to get the message through to him. Is there any way you could ..." He sniffled again. "Could give me his address for this one personal note?"

"Oh dear. We're not supposed to give out his address," she said. "But I could send it for you."

"It's most urgent. I can drop it in the mail right here to save time if you wouldn't mind giving the address. I won't tell a soul."

There was a pause, and Molnar pictured her looking over her shoulders. Her voice lowered. "OK, do you have a pen?"

"I do."

Molnar took down the address and hung up, grinning. He pulled out the phone number of the blonde from the plane and looked at it. Then he looked at the bottle in his hand. He shoved the number into the trashcan and put the bottle in his soaked briefcase. Then he walked out into the rain.

————

A few hours later, Molnar sat in a dark bar surrounded by polished surfaces. Brass bar, marble counter, chrome shaker set. As if the shine could make up for the lack of light. A mirror behind the bar tried to amplify the few sconce-covered Edison bulbs at the ends of the bar and over the mostly empty tables. Molnar sat with a glistening champagne flute. It looked as if it expected to break in his hand. He stared at the tiny bubbles rising in the glass, wondering about their grip on his species.

Alcohol.

Through millennia of human society—the rise and fall of empires, the ebb and flow of languages and skin colors and tsars and prime ministers— one constant remained: alcohol. It was as married to the human condition as blood and bile, but it remained mysterious. It was too powerful to go unwatched, so it remained relevant. It was the mute member of conversations, though it spoke more than all tongues. Some enjoyed it, some abused it, some abhorred it, some feared it.

Mads Molnar stared at it, swirled it in the glass, and pulled it into his mouth. The liquid with its delicate, bubbling sensation brought pleasure and poison. It helped and hurt, and Molnar wondered at it. He respected it. To him, it remained the highest form of art—eclipsing all the paintings and sculptures in Paris or Rome—because its form was interactive. Its consumers could appraise its nuances with all five senses instead of one. And, like all life, it would expire.

As Molnar paid for another dose, he silently swore he'd never return to a museum of art.

He waited for his glass, and his eyes looked up to see an Aphrodite standing in the doorway. Her shape, like those painted on the noses of fighter jets on both sides of the war, was draped with a simple white cotton dress cinched around her waist by a simple red satin ribbon. She was the gift every 16-year-old boy wanted for Christmas and no 16-year-old boy ever got. From the neck down, she spoke through her dress to the entire room, and her language was understood. From the neck up, she was all golden face and blonde hair, and her blue eyes locked with Molnar's to confirm her deep and confident awareness of the body that she piloted.

She piloted it to the barstool beside him as the room cleared its collective throat and tried to resume its previous composure. But Miss Marilyn Ghetz, like an airliner flown into a still pond, had inextricably changed the face of the dark bar; her all-cotton figure rippled into the minds and some of the conversations of the room.

Molnar recognized the form of the woman he'd seen in the stairwell earlier that day, though her demeanor had shifted to something more impish—delightful but dangerous. It was Miss Ghetz after hours. Standing beside him, she looked at him and didn't look away.

Molnar remembered the power of the liquid in his glass, and he took a drink. Nuns and priests and the Pope himself would need a shot after seeing Marilyn Ghetz walk through the door—and Molnar only had champagne.

"Mister … Molnar, I presume."

He nodded.

"I got your little note," she said, holding up the piece of typewriter paper from her office desk.

"Like a drink?"

"Only if it costs you."

"Bartender, let's have a table and a champagne that'll get rid of all this moldy old paper in my wallet."

The bartender gestured to a two-seat table in the exact middle of the bar with a single light over its center, then disappeared. Molnar finished his drink and freed up one of the seats for Miss Ghetz. All eyes but his watched her take it. As Molnar sat down across from her, the bartender returned with two flutes and a silver pot that held ice and a week of pay in the shape of a bottle. Pouring, Molnar spoke.

"Your boss got some poisoned wine, and you got a phone call. The wine got switched and your boss is still vertical and *heil*-ing. What happened?"

"Boy, you come out swinging."

"I just want you to show your cards."

Miss Ghetz took her glass and held it out. Molnar followed suit, and the crystal tinkled together at a slightly more eloquent vibration than ordinary glass.

"A lady can't show her cards, Mr. Molnar," her mouth said as her body reacted to the champagne. It was a good reaction.

"I'll need to see at least one, or I might have to show your boss."

"Who said he hasn't already seen them?"

"I never tell a lady how to handle her cards," said Molnar, "unless my hand depends on them."

"I have very important boys who all want to see my cards, Mr. Molnar, and they don't mind squishing a private dick to keep me—and my cards— safe and warm."

Molnar finished his glass and poured them both another.

"What'd you do with the wine?"

"I got rid of it, of course," she said, putting her teeth on the rim of the flute. "Wish I could do the same to you."

"I'm not sure what we're talking about anymore, but I kind of wish you could too." He couldn't contain a smile now. It was catching, but she was fighting. She closed her eyes to take the drink, and Molnar thought he saw the corner of her mouth go up for a second. But when the glass leveled, the corner was flat.

"You're not as bad as a lot of these," she said, gesturing to the room and greater Berlin with her eyes. "And you don't sound like them either."

"My father's Hungarian and my mother's Swedish, so I've got one foot on the dance floor and one foot in the stands."

"Sounds like a difficult move."

"It is a very difficult move."

Now she did smile, and Mads Molnar was quite happy to be Mads Molnar.

He had succeeded in turning the conversation's tone, and as they prattled on, he watched her face change from coy to pert to something more trusting and, finally, to bubbly.

Molnar did one of the things only a born psychologist is capable of doing: He made the girl feel as if she were back in her parents' home and he'd just come in from the kitchen, where he'd been having a conversation with her mother about blueberry muffins. He was the attractive and un-threatening family friend, and she could be left alone with him.

The bottle was nearly empty by the time Molnar locked in this role, and he asked if he should order another. She looked at a delicate watch on her delicate wrist and said it was late and she should go.

"I might have to cry, but my wallet is relieved," said Molnar as the waiter cleared their table.

"I bet it'll survive."

"With the right medication. One more cigarette?" He held out a silver case with his initials, a large M over a small m.

She took it and smiled her first real smile. "So why am I really here, Mr. Molnar? What do you really want?"

"A night of brazen love with a younger woman," he said. She giggled, and he looked up at the ceiling as if thinking hard. "Two million marks. A place in the country with a house staff and a butler named Heinz. A golden boat that sinks when you put it to sea. What about you, Miss Ghetz? What do you want?"

She laughed, and he saw her eyes change. Now her eyes belonged to a different Marilyn—and his bizarre therapy session reached its climax. She'd become a girl of 10 who woke up every morning to the scent of baked bread and melted butter and didn't know the heat of burning books or the colors of S.S. uniforms. "I really want," she said, looking to the ceiling and putting one thin and fragile finger to the side of her mouth, "a big golden dog. A strong house … also in the country." She smiled at him and looked back up. "… That's safe. A pair of totally impractical high heels. An icebox full of food. Freedom …" She took a final drag, and her torch started to burn out.

Molnar smiled at her. "Thanks for coming."

"You don't want to say anything else?" Their eyes met.

"You can't imagine what else I want to say. But that ring on your finger keeps blinding me when I try. So I'll only say: Whatever plans you have for the wine, don't let anyone find out. Especially not the press. It'd be my hide."

Her face tried to cycle back to its previous state, but she gave up and smiled. "OK," she said, shrugging. "Just for you."

"Promise?"

"Promise."

Later that night, Marilyn Ghetz arrived back at her Berlin apartment, alone and full of a champagne fortune.

When she closed the door behind her, the look on her face shifted once more, showing its range. She'd done the edge-of-eruption bombshell and the innocent little girl; now there was something new. Her face showed something like fear as she moved through her own home. She reached for the light but stopped, as if remembering something, and left it off. The edges of relief started to creep into her eyes with every room she glanced into. The final glance was the kitchen, and she gasped.

"It's only me," said a massive, shadowy figure leaning on the sink in the dark kitchen.

Marilyn stumbled back but, recognizing the voice, forced a smile. Yet deep fear hadn't left her eyes. She kept moving backward and readjusted her face until it again spelled alluring. "Ohhhh, you!" she said, and, moving forward to the shadowy kitchen, lightly slapped the figure's shoulder.

The figure allowed the slap and smiled. "You smell as if you've been enjoying yourself."

Detective Bastick's face was illuminated by a match as he lit his pipe.

"I better have," said Marilyn, feeling in the icebox for a block of ice. "It cost him his life's savings."

"Normal men could be jealous at their fiancée's going out with other men," said Bastick, drawing the smoke into his being.

"Normal men aren't engaged to Marilyn Ghetz," she said, tossing the ice block at him. "Be a doll and break that up."

He somehow caught it in the nearly pitch-black room and fired off his shotgun laugh. It was there and loud and gone. A rectangular metal tin on the counter glinted in the light of his pipe. It was to serve as an ice tray, and Bastick put the block in. He glanced around for a meat mallet or ice pick. When nothing was readily apparent, he punched the block with a mammoth fist, and it shattered. He punched it again on the other side—precise with his blows.

Marilyn returned with the shadowed outlines of a bottle of gin in one hand and tonic water in the other, but you'd have to be a bartender to recognize them in this light. She looked at him and the ice. "Come on." She gestured with her shoulder-length hair for him to follow. "You didn't get any blood on it, did you?" she said over her shoulder.

Still in the kitchen, he peered close at the ice, pulling on his pipe to light it up. He was shocked to see one dark drop and removed that piece. He threw it into the sink and looked at his hand by pipelight. A knuckle bled. He sucked on it, appraised that it wouldn't drip, and then followed her. "No," he said, in the voice a child uses when it lies.

"Well, try not to get it in my glass, at least," she said, handing him two tumblers as he came into her living room. "Unless ..." She looked up at him over the glasses and under her lashes. "Would you rather have wine?"

"I hate wine," he said.

"I know, but I don't hate wine," she said, and a hardly perceptible tinge of bitterness clung to the word *hate*. "And remember that you promised you'd have some at our party."

"Yes, yes, I'll have some at the party. We'll have anything you want at the party." He put the ice in the glasses, making sure to draw from the clean side of the ice tin for her.

"Good boy," she said, moving to the shadowed mass of man and kissing him on the cheek as he poured the other ingredients into the glasses. "I can't wait." He kept mixing, and she took a seat. "What are you in-*ves*-ti-gating?"

"I can't talk about the details," he said to the glasses. "But it's still the case from my father's ..." He kept mixing. "My father's case is what it is."

"Any leads?"

"One came up empty," he said. "That's why I had to come see you." He looked over at her in her white dress and her ribbon, and he smiled the kind of smile you smile when you're crying. But he wasn't crying. Her white form was outlined by moonlight through the window against the pitch-black city behind her.

"Sometimes things are so dark in these blackouts," he said. "I need your light."

She looked as if she'd slap him for being such a boob. But then she relented. "I don't have any decent shutters, so I don't have a light at all!" she said. "Where are those drinks?" He crossed to her with the gin extended. "That's something you could get me, Wolfie: shutters. Really nice, dark shutters, so no S.S. officers run into my house in the middle of the night and shout at me 'cause I'm reading a comic in my nighty."

"If any S.S. officer runs into your house, just let me know."

"It might be too late by then," she said, patting the seat beside her.

He was silent and sat. He felt the heat of her, the light of her, and he leaned back and closed his eyes. The drink stayed on his thigh, untouched, and he basked in her aura, like a tanker refueling. She knew this was what he needed, and her eyes bounced around, looking to focus on something as her nervous energy built. She drank the gin to calm herself.

By the time her gin was finished, he was almost asleep.

"You can't sleep here, Wolfie," she said. "What would the girls say? Klara lives right across the hall!"

"Oh!" Bastick exclaimed, jolted from half-sleep. The full gin and tonic tumbled from his leg, and Marilyn caught it.

"Come on, big boy," she said, helping him up by the shoulder. She moved him to the door and he smiled groggily. He kissed her on the mouth like he was consuming her flesh. He put a porterhouse hand on her shoulder and pulled her toward him. He smelled her neck.

In his groggy state, he mumbled in her ear, "I imagine our offspring, endowed with my gloriously advanced abilities and your physical appeal."

"You're so good with words, Wolfie, it's a wonder I don't give in," she said.

"One more week," said Bastick. "One more week, and I'll have you. And then we can craft the next step in the evolution of mankind."

"Exactly," she said, patting the side of his melon-size head. She opened the door. "But I'm not Mrs. Bastick yet." Her dove hand pushed him lightly out the door, and he complied. He smiled at her, and she closed the door.

Marilyn leaned her back against the door, and her face remained pert until she heard his heavy steps move out of range. Then she let all of her faces fall, and relief poured over her like Niagara Falls. She shook her limbs out as she moved back through the hall into the living room, where she lifted a lighter from the table. She lit a cigarette with shaking hands and picked up Bastick's untouched drink. She drank most of it in a gulp, and her eyes went up to a bottle of wine on her liquor cabinet. It was difficult to make out in the dark, but if you had good eyes and squinted, you could still see the puckered red kiss mark on its label.

BOTTLE IV

T hanks to an official notice from Colonel Riffel and his Gestapo disc, Mads Molnar was the only man in civilian clothes aboard the six o'clock *Deutsche Luft Hansa* flight from Berlin to Paris.

The same dark, narrow man with sunglasses who had met with Riffel watched Molnar's plane from the gate. He clutched a different ticket in his hand, cursing to himself.

As the soldiers got settled in, Molnar pulled his hat down over his eyes to sleep.

There was a stopover in Frankfurt to drop off some soldiers and pick up others before the plane took off again. Molnar slept through all that. When the plane touched down in Paris, his eyes reopened and he readjusted his hat as he waited.

A young soldier sitting beside him, who had a tight haircut and creased clothing, leaned over. "You look like some kind of Schoble ad," he said. "The only fedora on the plane."

"And you look like a walking piece of propaganda," said Molnar, straightening himself and looking over at his neighbor. "We all have our destinies."

"And we're both going to Paris."

"It looks like it," said Molnar, who wasn't a morning person. He turned away to face the seat in front of him.

"I'm just curious about what you're doing there," said the boy. "A man like you."

"I'm curious if you'll be alive next week," said Molnar, looking back at the boy again for a moment.

Now the kid looked away, out the window until the plane rolled to a stop.

Molnar reached over and shook his shoulder. "Keep your chin up, kid. Everyone knows there's no action in Paris."

The kid turned back to him doubtfully. "Yeah?"

"The whole country folded like a coloring book. Play nice with the French, and you can be the boss. They probably wouldn't mind fighting, but first, they all want one more drink."

The boy grinned. "Me too," he said, unbuckling himself. "You know, it's my first time on a plane."

"You're probably glad it landed."

The boy nodded as the soldiers in the front began lining up to get out. He leaned close to Molnar's shoulder. "How long do you think it'll last?"

"It just started, kid," said Molnar, standing. The boy followed suit. "So we all better get comfortable." He offered the boy a stick of spearmint gum. The boy looked twice at it and then took it. Molnar took one too, and they stood beside each other, chewing, waiting their turn to disembark.

Minutes later in the back seat of a taxi, Molnar reached up to a thin French cabbie and showed him the address where he was headed.

The man balked, waving his hands to say he wouldn't go there. "*C'est trop loin!*"—*It's too far!* He motioned at Molnar to get out of his car.

Molnar looked out his window and saw nothing but military trucks. This was the only cab at the airport.

"Hate to have to emphasize my point," said Molnar, taking his revolver out and using it instead of his finger to point to the address. It was amazing what a prop could do to language barriers. The driver let loose a string of French profanity but put the car into first gear and buzzed out of the airport.

As the car exited Paris and headed west, the driver was still shaking his head. At a light, he pivoted his face on his thin neck back toward Molnar to reestablish his complaint. Molnar was spinning his hat on the end of his revolver.

"Yes?" said Molnar. "Would you like to say anything, *mon cher?*"

The man turned his Adam's apple back to the road, and his head resumed its shaking routine. Molnar watched it for a while to see how long he could keep it up, and then he started reading through a file he had on his uncle, Major Miklós Skorzeny.

It was three hours later when the cab approached the Dordogne River, near the western coast of France. They crossed what used to be the demarcation line separating the Nazi-occupied northern portion of France from the "independent" southern half. That line had been pushed south to Spain a few days prior.

The cabbie continued on to Bordeaux, and Molnar reminded him where to go. The cabbie's head had stopped shaking at this point, and the two were both smoking—Molnar, a cigar; the cabbie, a cigarette.

They pulled up to a large French château. The façade was flat white, its prominent windows rendering it artful, its simple geometry mysteriously pleasing to the eye. It was surrounded by a wrought-iron fence. The fence was adorned with a swastika, which looked out of place. A shock of red against the ancient face of the building. The cabbie parked outside.

"It's right in there," said Molnar in English, pointing to the gate.

"No," said the man, also in English but with a heavy French accent. "I will not go in," he added, pointing at the swastika.

Molnar shrugged, reached over the man, and took the keys from the ignition. The man shouted.

"Get yourself something to eat. I may be a while," said Molnar, pocketing the keys. The man restarted his string of profanity and got out of the car, slamming the door behind him. Molnar started it up and drove through the open gate. He drove up the semi-circle gravel driveway and parked outside the impressive château.

Molnar surveyed the area. Beyond the gate, the property was surrounded by 60-year-old vines as far as the eye could see. Molnar couldn't know that they were all replanted, grafted onto American rootstock after the phylloxera outbreak there in the 1860s and '70s. But the size of the stalks should have told him.

Molnar took out a map of Europe and circled a dot on Bordeaux. Eight other dots adorned France, Germany and Denmark, the northernmost encircling Copenhagen. Molnar put the map back into his breast pocket and walked up the stairs. A soldier opened the door.

"I'm here to see Major Miklós Skorzeny," said Molnar. "Tell him it's his long-lost nephew, Mads." The private raised his arm to the sky like a Nazi caricature and left the room. Molnar looked out the row of windows. It was a working château turned temporary German headquarters.

Molnar saw a team of Frenchmen in the fields, harvesting vines. The vines would wait for no one and the field for no war. Life continued to produce life and to grow, whether guided by the vinedressers or left to its own devices. So, the work went on. A week after the Germans had moved in, it was already business as usual in Bordeaux. Only the government and some of the customers had changed.

The private returned with a large, dark man wearing an eye patch who looked too relaxed for his *Wehrmacht* uniform. His eye patch wasn't pirate-esque; it suited him so well that you'd prefer to see him with it than whole.

This olive-skinned man saw Molnar with his eye, and a wide smile slid across his face. He moved around the private to Molnar and hugged him tightly.

"This is the best week of my life!" the man shouted beside Molnar's ear, beating him on the back. He lifted Molnar's heavy form off the ground and grunted. "We advance without impediment. The French surrender. And my nephew comes to visit—all in one week." He took a step back to appraise Molnar. "You seem bigger. Is it possible?"

"I doubt it," said Molnar. "I've been full grown for a few decades."

"Well, let's make you that way. We're going to drink," Skorzeny said. "Come on. Let's have some French liquor." He laughed a mighty laugh and grabbed Molnar around the shoulders, pulling him along and outside.

The two men sat drinking afternoon aperitifs at a sunny cafe. They were on the patio of a yellow stucco building surrounded by dainty diners. Skorzeny was the only one in uniform, and he wasn't getting a ton of smiles.

One other diner looked out of place, and he caught Skorzeny's eye. It was a Hungarian-looking man who strangely wore sunglasses indoors. "Tell me: what brings you to Bordeaux?" said Skorzeny, eyeing the dark man behind Molnar.

"You," said Molnar.

"I'm honored, but I fail to catch your point," said Skorzeny, swirling his gin and tonic.

"That's because I haven't made it. I'm here to stop you from killing yourself." Molnar drank a kind of spritz—champagne with a dash of Campari.

"Why would I do that?"

"Can you keep a secret?" Molnar leaned close.

"Of course."

"I'll need your word."

The big man consumed his liquor. "Yes! Of course, you have my word. My nephew! There are no secrets between us. Speak."

Molnar leaned even closer to his uncle. "A friend of yours sent you a bottle of wine. He didn't know it, but that wine is full of poison—the French vintner's last laugh."

Skorzeny's face turned pale. He grabbed his stomach and moaned. "My God, Molnar! Why didn't you call? Why didn't you send a wire?"

Molnar stood from his chair like a gunshot. "You drank it?"

"I wondered what the pain was. This awful pain in my stomach that comes and goes. Oh, it's spreading, Molnar," said the man, his face screwed up tight, rubbing his hand up to his heart. Molnar stood there, frozen.

"We have to get you to the hospital," he said, rushing around the table to Skorzeny, trying to pry him out of his chair.

"Let's finish our drinks first," said Skorzeny. "For Führer's sake! We have to have priorities in this life."

"Are you ... ?" Molnar saw the smile creep across Skorzeny's one-eyed face.

"Do you think I'd drink a pinot from Alsace, nephew?" Skorzeny laughed an all-consuming laugh that resonated like a bomb to the surrounding tables. Some of the other patrons looked up from dainty entrées to silently disapprove. "We're in Bordeaux, Molnar! Why would I drink Alsatian wine?" His laugh grew by the moment, and he stood up and grabbed the shocked Molnar around the shoulders.

As the shock cooled, Molnar started to smile, and a laugh followed. Soon, they were both laughing almost uncontrollably. Other tables took notice, giving side glances. The waiters wondered if they should intercede, but didn't approach.

The two men recovered and took their seats. They washed away any lingering formalities by finishing their glasses.

Skorzeny's finger went up to the waiter. "Two more!" he boomed so the kitchen staff could hear. "So, you're still in the private dick business?"

"Yes, but I'm working for your bosses now," Molnar said. "Whether I like it or not."

"It's nice to be on the winning side this time around," said Skorzeny with a smile. "A greater Germany means a greater Hungary ... like it used to be."

"You think it'll be that easy?"

"You weren't part of the advance. We took France in a month and a half," said Skorzeny. "Officially. It fell much quicker in reality. And that's after Poland, Denmark, Norway, the Netherlands, and Belgium. It's over. There's only Britain now."

"But"—and Molnar paused so the waiter could set down their new drinks and take away the empties—"what about all the rest? The *übermensch und untermensch?*"

"Hitler's racism? We all know it's the banking system that's the real issue, Molnar; I've talked about that for years. Who cares what he calls it? These usurers are getting their comeuppance." Skorzeny wagged his finger at Molnar. "I'm not saying they're all Jewish, but some of them are. And the funniest thing is"—the man's laughter tried to creep its way into the sentence, rolling beneath the conversation like subterranean thunder, but he held it down—"this was foretold in their sacred book! 'The nations will be astonished,' it said. 'Israel will be a byword.' Well, those times are here, Molnar, and we are the punishing arm of the Jewish God."

Molnar's brows went up, and he leaned back in his chair and took a drink. He rubbed his chin and shook his head. "Heavy stuff to say, Miklós," he said. "You know we won't agree on this. I think secret jealousy motivates this 'ethnic cleansing.' It's an excuse for thievery."

"It's good you don't wear the medals then, Molnar," said Skorzeny, pulling on the gin and tonic. "You were pretty useful the last time around, though."

"I was younger then. And that one was different," said Molnar, leaning forward. "That was assassinations and gentlemen and alliances. It was at least practical. This isn't. This is a spoiled brat"—Molnar held his two fingers to his lip to denote *Herr* Hitler—"playing in a sandbox of his own twisted ideology and with very dangerous toys."

"Maybe," said Skorzeny. "But at least we're on the side of the sandbox with the biggest guns, Mads. And as a soldier, if you philosophize too long, it kinda takes the punch out. I'm in it one way or the other. Against my will, at first. But if you live like that …" Miklós lit up a cigarette. "You can't live like that. I've seen men who do it, and even in this preschool fighting we've been doing so far, they fall apart."

Molnar shook his head. "Whether you dwell on it or not, Miklós, it's a war of ideology—for him, at least, and you're one of those toys." He took a drink of the red liquid.

Skorzeny shrugged. "Then I'll pick up as much loot as I can along the way. But I'm fighting for the main things." His voice rose, and his fingers counted off, irreverent of the surrounding diners. "We'll expand Hungary closer to what she was. We'll pull her out of the depression forced on her shoulders after that atrocious treaty, and we'll run out all the Bolsheviks." He smiled. "If that happens, Mads, then I'll be a happy man, and the war will be worth my life and your life and others."

"It's not worth mine. We lost the war; our fingers got rapped. I'm going to Sweden."

"Really?" asked Skorzeny, again eyeing the thin Hungarian man behind Molnar, who seemed to be listening in.

"Yes, really," Molnar said, pulling out his passport with the now-coveted word SVERIGE printed on the front. "Mom wasn't Swedish for nothing."

"So you're going neutral."

"Yes, and so would you, if you had this," Molnar said, waving the passport. "I think the war's wrong. I don't want any part of it."

Skorzeny leaned in closer. "Don't you remember the feeling, Mads? Where Death is your companion, and you not only shake hands with him, but stay the night?"

"I remember him taking Ilsa," said Molnar. "And I remember chasing him into the trenches and into hell to wring his neck. But all I ended up doing was helping him in his work. I became his salesman."

"You sold hundreds of tickets," said Miklós.

"But I retired."

"I didn't." Skorzeny stamped out his cigarette and stood up. "And it's time to get back to work."

Molnar didn't stand. "Where's the wine, Miklós? That's why I'm here."

"I'll show you. Come on."

Molnar got up, and the two men pushed their way toward the exit. On the way, Skorzeny bumped into the man with sunglasses.

"*Elnézést*," he said in Hungarian. *Excuse me.*

"*Jól van*," muttered the man. The moment the man automatically made the correct response, the barrel-like Skorzeny grabbed him by the collar and lifted him out of his seat. He carried him bodily off the patio and into the street as Molnar watched. Then he held him against the wall.

"*Vegye ki a napszemüvegét,*" Skorzeny said, and the man complied, reaching his hand up to his face and removing his sunglasses, revealing too-thin pupils that gave his eyes a reptilian cast.

"What's going on?" asked Molnar.

"This Hungarian was watching you the whole time. Look at his evil eyes," said Skorzeny, tightening his grip.

"I was only intrigued by my mother tongue, my dear fellow."

Skorzeny eyed him. "I don't believe that." He looked over to Molnar. "Always judge a book by its cover," he said. "Come on."

Skorzeny dropped the man to his feet, but held him tight at his side by the scruff of his jacket. A cab responded to his snapping fingers. When it sidled up, Skorzeny let Molnar enter, then shoved the narrow man in and followed him.

"You will tell us what you're doing here," Skorzeny declared.

After that, all of them were silent for the ride.

Back at the barracks/winery, Skorzeny herded the man out, and the three of them entered the majestic building and descended into what used to be the cellar winery. Skorzeny sat the man down and stared at him for a moment before walking to a rack of wine bottles. He took a bottle down, and struck it precisely against the cobblestone floor so that it broke in two, staining the floor.

Holding the broken bottle by the neck, Skorzeny walked up to the man. He put the bottle against the man's throat and pressed it in until thin rivulets of blood ran with the wine inside his shirt. The man gurgled out a protest.

"Why are you watching my nephew?" asked Skorzeny, leaning close to the man's thin face. "I'll turn this bottle red again. I've nothing to lose, and I rather enjoy murder."

Molnar stood with his eyes wide, staring at the scene. Should he intervene, or did Skorzeny know something he didn't? He let it play.

"I've nothing to hide. You're my brethren," the man said. "I work for the Arrow Cross. We are on the same side in this, my dear fellow."

Skorzeny let up a little on the bottle. "Keep going."

"Your nephew is wanted by them. They've given him some time for the sake of the Nazis. If he isn't finished with his job on Sunday, I must take him back to Budapest. I'm only following him to make sure he doesn't get away."

"And what will they do with him?"

"Try him and hang him."

Skorzeny thought this over. He looked at Molnar. "This true?"

Molnar nodded. "They caught me trying to smuggle Jews out of Hungary."

Skorzeny shook his head. "I told you to quit letting your politics interfere with your health." He lowered the bottle, looked down at the man, and saw his slit-like pupils narrow.

The man shrugged, feeling the new scratches in his neck with thin fingertips.

Molnar shook his head and turned back toward the steps. He started walking up them. "Let him go, Miklós. Let's get that bottle. I'll fight the charges when I'm back and sort it—"

The crack of a gun echoed in the cellar like a bomb, and the thin man's head lolled onto his shoulder. Molnar spun to see Skorzeny's arm lowering. He looked at his uncle for an explanation.

"Had to be done," said Skorzeny, holstering his gun. "You're dead in a Hungarian court; I had to throw them off your trail. Besides"—Skorzeny eyed the sunken body—"he looked like a Bolshevik. Now, go finish your work and get to Sweden. No one likes the Arrow Cross up there."

"Now they really aren't going to lay off," said Molnar.

"Come on, they won't find you," said Skorzeny, holstering the gun.

Molnar shook his head and slowly walked up the stairs.

Skorzeny followed him and sent some soldiers to clean up the man's remains. Then he took Molnar to his room. He opened up a green wooden trunk full of clothes and equipment, reached in, and pulled out the bottle of wine. It read "1934 Alsace," and, at the bottom in small letters, "pinot noir." Above that was a red kiss mark on the white label. Molnar nodded at it, confirming that it was not the same as the one he'd seen in Marilyn Ghetz's office.

When his mind thought of her, it stayed there for a moment too long. He blinked her away like water in the eyes and said, "Was there a note?"

"Ah, yes." Skorzeny reached under the clothing and pulled out a note. He handed it to Mads.

"Thanks."

"So, is that it?" asked Skorzeny.

"That's it." said Molnar. "Now it's back to Paris. I'd better move quickly."

"Well … it's good to see you. It wouldn't be a visit if we didn't disagree about something."

"Or many things. Don't stick your neck out for these, Miklós," said Molnar, tapping the medals on Skorzeny's chest. "*Ciao.*"

Molnar walked out of his room and started down the stairway, running his hand along a thick, carved, and polished hickory banister.

"Mads!"

Molnar turned back to his uncle.

"Thank you," boomed the big man. "One day my thirst might have overrun my snobbery. Get the rest of the bottles back. You'll be a hero. You might even get some more dreaded medals." He moved to the top of the stairs to look down at his nephew. "There is one more thing," he said, removing another letter from his pocket. "I wasn't sure I'd bring this up, but …" He held out the letter, and both men closed the gap between them. Molnar took the letter and looked up at Miklós when he read the front.

"Where did you get this?"

"Ilsa sent it to you when you were working as a shrink for the soldiers. It arrived after you were moved forward, after you knew she was dead. I thought it'd be too painful for you to hear from her then. But it is yours, and I've been meaning to give it to you."

Mads stared down at the aging envelope, folded it, and put it in his breast pocket. "Thank you," he said. "It's been a long time."

Skorzeny tipped his hat to Mads, who did the same and then headed down the stairs.

Molnar's hand felt the slick wood, and his heart felt a dark squeeze, reminded of mortality. It was as if he were back in the employ of an old and dreaded commander. He felt the clean and creeping bone-white fingers of Death. The invisible fingers gripped his shoulder as he trotted out of the building. They reached into his breast pocket beside the envelope and pulled out Riffel's list of names so he could see it. The finger pointed to one name after the next. The accompanying voice said, "I'll race you."

Molnar kept walking toward the car and glanced around. There was no one there. He removed the paper and a pencil from his pocket, and he crossed off Skorzeny's name. "Deal," said Molnar, to no one visible.

Much earlier that morning, Bastick stood on his balcony, hands on the railing. He didn't notice the clear sky spattered with stars or the half-full moon. He stared off the balcony and into the darkness.

He pivoted his body in a quick motion and moved his bulk into his home. He crossed the room, floorboards moaning in resistance, and picked up the phone. A round, simple clock on the wall read 4:15. Bastick began dialing.

The phone rang a few times.

"*Jawohl.*" said Otto's voice on the other line.

"I want you to get every popular French, German, and British newspaper for the last two weeks and comb them for these words. Write them down. Are you ready?"

"*Jawohl!*"

"Poison, murder, Troy, and Bastick."

"*Jawohl.*" uttered Otto's pubescent voice.

"Good. I need a report right away. In the meantime, I'll be paying a few visits before coming into the office."

"*Danke, mein Kommandant.*"

Bastick hung up.

It was still before dawn when Bastick pulled into his parents' cobblestone driveway. He parked beside his mother's blue Mercedes-Benz 320. At the door of the Bavarian-style manor, Bastick closed his eyes and stopped to take a deep breath of the cool September morning. The light was airy and new. He felt something, remembered something. Maybe it was the smells of childhood; maybe it was the smells of his father or the scent of the chase. He was about to knock but then decided to walk right in.

Bastick opened the door and saw his mother at the kitchen table, which was set for two. She looked at him and quickly wiped her eyes.

"Wolfie!" she said, getting up. "How are you?"

Bastick moved to her and kissed her on the cheek.

"I can't get used to cooking for one. Please, sit down, Wolfie," she said. "Have something to eat." She held back the tears as she said it.

"Thank you, Mother," said Bastick. "With the rationing, you'll eventually want to ..." He didn't know how to finish the sentence. "I'm still working on the case, Mother. I need to find something." He cut a piece of sausage on the plate. The skin popped as the knife pressed through, spraying little bits of fat and oil. He stabbed the sausage into a fried egg and consumed it and some of the toast.

His mother didn't reach for her breakfast.

"I'm so happy you're here," she said to him. She wiped her eyes and pulled her long gray hair back into a bun. Her skin, though aging, was plump and strong, and wrinkles hadn't laid waste to her face—only added orderly creases around her eyes like buttons on a leather couch. She was doing something right.

Bastick continued to attack the food. It disappeared as she watched. He glanced up at her, and she handed over her sausage and eggs. "I haven't eaten much since the party," she said.

"You'll need to start up once you can," said Bastick. "Otherwise, how will you survive?"

She was silent.

"I know it's hard," he said. "If someone poisoned him, I'll catch him. I'll find who did it, I promise. Nothing will stand in my way, Mother." He finished most of the egg-covered sausage in one bite. "And I'll make him pay." His mashing of food was more quadruped than human, as if Bastick were preparing it for a second stomach. "What do you think happened?"

She was quiet for a moment. "I don't know …"

"It wasn't the bartender," said Bastick. "I know that for certain. Who was in charge of the food? Did we have a caterer?"

"I made the food, Wolfie," she said. She looked up from her plate and their eyes connected. When she saw his reaction, her face turned putty-like, shrinking away like a slug from salt. Unbeknownst to Bastick, when his mother turned from ally to suspect, he underwent a transition that hollowed out his cheeks and darkened the lines of his face. He seemed to have internally changed the lighting in the room from sunrise to midnight and the location from kitchen table to butcher block.

"Wolfie! I'm your mother." She said it as if reminding a dog not to bite its master.

Bastick's mind churned. He smelled for lies—a rise in blood pressure or other bodily chemical releases. Would his mother benefit in any way from his father's demise? Did she love someone else? Was this breakfast made for another? Maybe some closet-hiding old man? Was she a sympathizer? Was she a weak point? Bastick's senses reached around the room and the house for the scent of a warm body. His ears listened for a third beating heart. But all queries returned void.

"Of course, Mother," said Bastick, his face returning to its ordinary state of heinous relaxation. The morning light was once again allowed to shine. Bastick's hand crossed the table. His mother tried to pull back, but he engulfed her wrist and gently pinned it down with the heel of his palm, patting it with the rest. "Nothing will get in my way, Mother," he said as he looked at her. Then he released her hand. "Has all the trash been removed since the party? Is there anything left that can help?"

Something in her eyes said that she'd seen him like this before, that this was a side of him she couldn't control. A side that she feared. But she was still his mother. "I think the staff cleaned it all," she said, "but you're free to look around if you like."

Bastick didn't like her choice of words or tone. "The staff," he said. "I must speak with them."

"Gaston is in the garden, I believe," she said, watching him consume the last of the sausage.

"How many others died? Have you heard?" he asked.

"I hear from Mrs. Reinhardt every day. The late Mr. Reinhardt is one of the others besides your father who was poisoned. All of his closest friends, Wolfie." She put her face in her hands again.

Bastick looked down at the now-empty plate. "Thank you, Mother," he said, shoving his chair back and exiting the room.

In the back yard, Bastick saw old Gaston, the butler, on his knees in the middle of a brick path, pruning some shrubs. Bastick took a deep breath as he descended the stairs and walked up to the kneeling Gaston. The dome of the head was bare, surrounded by a circle of hair, like an ebbing tide—revealing a smooth rock, once hidden.

"Hello, Gaston," said Bastick. The man looked up at him and got to his feet, hands on his knee to leverage his way back to vertical.

"Master Wolfram," said Gaston. "How may I help you?"

"You can tell me how my father was killed, Gaston," laughed Bastick, abrupt. "That's how you can help."

Gaston didn't betray his thoughts. He just shook his shining pate. "I don't know who did it, but I've given that night a lot of thought."

"Go on."

"If I may, sir, I believe we should remember it was his birthday. There were many gifts. Wouldn't they be the first place we should check?" Gaston looked up at Bastick, who nodded for him to go on. "I've kept them all aside. I can take you there."

"Yes, Gaston," said Bastick, surprised at his ingenuity. "Please do so."

The two men walked past an outdoor brick fireplace and followed a well-worn track through the dark-green grass and into the depths of the garden. Gaston's cottage was stone-walled and tile-roofed, and vines grew up the sides as if embracing the building into the garden itself—fighting the inanimation of the stone and mortar and infusing life into the structure.

"She told me to get rid of everything," said Gaston, looking back up at Wolf as if confessing. "She didn't want to see it." Gaston removed a large, heavy skeleton key and unlocked the door. "Just this way," he said, walking through the cozy living room and into the dining room behind it. "We'd already taken away the waste, but not the bottles. I can get a penny for them, so I save them."

Wolfram stared at the old man and then grabbed his head. He pulled the shining egg toward him and kissed it. "You did well, Gaston," said Bastick. He glanced at the presents on Gaston's maple-wood table. Most were wrapped. Wolf ignored these, knowing the unopened ones wouldn't have done harm. He saw a horn pipe at the front and picked it up. "Is this yours or one of the gifts?"

"It's one that he opened, sir," said Gaston.

"And used," added Bastick, giving it a light smell. "Did he open any others?"

Gaston shook his head. "He hated to in front of guests." The saying of it made Gaston's eyes start watering, and he wiped at them with a handkerchief.

Bastick looked at a pile of empty bottles on the ground beneath the table, and he smiled. "There was one I know he opened." Bastick moved to the pile and started searching through. Most bottles were mass-market liquor or beer, but there were a couple of bottles of wine. One brought a smell back to Bastick's nostrils and a memory to his mind. He saw the puckered kiss mark on the label and remembered staring at the dregs in the bottom. He held it up to the light. It was empty, but he remembered the bottle.

"There used to be dregs," he said, not noticing the morning summer sunlight shining into the bottle and throwing green-shaded shapes on the wall behind him. But that was what Gaston was noting.

"Yes, Margarette had already rinsed all the bottles and bagged them up, but I took them back out when I heard ..." Gaston's voice ran off an invisible cliff.

"No matter," said Bastick. "This is very helpful, Gaston."

"I only wish I could help more, Master Wolfram," said Gaston, still wiping at his face with the handkerchief.

Bastick smelled the bottle, but the scent was gone, rinsed down the drain by Margarette. He looked at the rest of the bottles and didn't remember them in particular. He smelled them all. "This is a start," he mumbled to himself. "Bag the rest of the bottles. I'll take them with me."

"Yes, sir."

Bastick took the pipe and the pinot and moved out of the room, no longer acknowledging Gaston, who watched as the huge figure left.

"I hope you find him, Master Wolfram," said Gaston to himself as the door closed, leaving the bald old man alone in his dark living room.

BOTTLE V

By evening, Molnar was back in Paris and on a payphone, listening to the French operator take her sweet time connecting him to Riffel. Through the glass, he could see the unfortunate taxi driver whom he'd forced into service taking off down the street, leaving a black line of rubber and a string of obscenities loud enough to pierce Molnar's glass encasement. The sun was well set, and the streetlights of Paris painted cool-yellow circles on the pavement. Some few pigeons hopped in and out of the light. One was bisected by it, making for a haunting half-image.

"This is Riffel," came a sleepy voice on the line.

"It's Molnar. I've another one in my hand. Sent to Major Skorzeny."

"Very fine!" said Riffel's voice. "And he was alive?"

"Yes, the bottle is unopened, and your letter is in my hand," said Molnar.

"Lovely! I'll sleep well tonight. Where to next?"

"I'm in Paris. I'll be stalking Klaebisch in the morning."

"Good," said Riffel, who finally seemed to be waking up. "Ah, yes: Heinz Klaebisch. That blowhard. I thought he could help me retain my position in France, but he didn't lift a shriveled, ratty finger. In fact, only the day after I mailed him the bottle he chided me for my conduct.

"It was war, Molnar. Loot a little here, buy a little there. He didn't understand. If I couldn't be incriminated, I'd let him drink the thing and laugh him all the way to the morgue."

Molnar's eyebrow lifted. "Want me to save him for last?"

"No, you're already there," said Riffel. "But as long as no one can link this thing to me, I don't care what happens to the fool."

"Anything else?" said Molnar.

"Just be careful. The man has a temper like a fire plug. Uncork him, and he'll explode. I cannot stress enough that Klaebisch can't know a thing. One clue, and he'll find out what happened. He has a squirming little mind that wheedles its way into every dark corner."

"Don't fret, Riffel," said Molnar. "This is what I do."

He hung up the phone and hung his hat on top of it. He took a deep breath and picked up his briefcase, then opened the door of the phone box to the raucous tones of a German beer-hall song. They came from a building with a brightly lit sign that read *Hotel Fruehauf.*

Molnar felt the weight of the briefcase with his shoulder and turned his feet toward the hotel entrance. He crossed the street, forgetting his gray hat in the phone box. The room was full to brimming with mostly German figures. All seemed to have liquid in their glasses and gleams in their eyes. A large man with a gray beard, wild white locks, and a face that seemed to emit light crossed the room to Molnar. He put out his hand and started speaking perfect German.

"Good evening! May I get you a table?"

"Sure. And I need a room."

"Ah!" said the deep voice. "Of course we have a room for you, *Herr* ..."

"Molnar," he said.

"Pleased to meet you. My name is Knut Fruehauf. Welcome to my hotel." He tipped his hat at Molnar. "I can take your briefcase to the room and bring you your key. Allow me to pull you up a chair in the meantime." The man escorted Molnar to a little table near the front door, with a full view of the dining room. Molnar nodded and handed over the briefcase. His eyes followed the bright figure as he disappeared.

Molnar took a seat and instinctively reached for his hat. When his fingertips felt his thick hair, he remembered leaving the hat in the phone booth. He got up and trotted across the street. The hat was still there, shadowed by the booth in the harsh light of the streetlamp. He grabbed it and lit a cigar. But as he crossed the street toward the hotel, something caught his eye. It was the shrouded figure of Fruehauf, darting across the lawn behind the hotel to an old barn. Taillights in an alley behind the barn splashed a hellish hue on the cobblestone street.

Molnar strolled down the sidewalk and past the hotel toward the alley behind the barn, smoking nonchalantly, proud to wear his hat. He heard muffled shouts. When he reached the corner of the barn, he squatted low, removed the hat and peeked around the corner, down the alleyway.

A massive mound of blond man with hair to his collarbone threw wooden cases into a milk truck. By the burning taillights, Molnar could make out that the crates were cases of champagne. What was going on? Molnar realized that even on an off night, he couldn't quit detecting. It was in his blood.

He kept watching, and saw Fruehauf handing the cases from the barn and through a small door to the Viking. The door was low, square, and meant for shoving hay bales through. It was barely big enough for a man to crawl into, especially one the size of the Viking. Molnar quit peeking and strolled back around and into the hotel and to his seat.

He sat down with a sudden interest in the operations of Hotel Fruehauf. His eyes took in the room. The beaten, wooden bar was packed with uniformed soldiers and moneyed Frenchmen. All were drinking and talking in degrees between cheerful and uproarious. Swinging wooden doors pivoted in and out of the kitchen as waiters flowed back and forth. As the doors swung open, a skillet-wielding, silver-haired woman caught Molnar's eye before disappearing again. Each time the doors swung wide, like a rolling shutter, he saw another frame of her cooking dance: knives shining, food flying. She bobbed deftly around the large kitchen, delivering orders to the staff all the while.

Fruehauf's burly shoulders burst through the front door. He smiled at Molnar, who nodded at him as he passed. The man flew into the kitchen, his brown face shining under his beard.

Molnar sat back and continued his survey. He noted that both beer and champagne were being drunk out of steins. It didn't look as if rationing had sunk in yet. A waiter visited Molnar, who ordered a bottle of '37 Taittinger champagne.

As the waiter returned to the kitchen, Molnar caught a glimpse of Fruehauf sautéing kilos of onions alongside the aging woman who must have been his wife. She kept up her quick succession of movements.

The kitchen doors burst open again, and Fruehauf rushed out of the kitchen to Molnar's table with the Tattinger. "I almost forgot, my friend," he said, placing the key and the bottle on Molnar's table. With a wink, he hurried to the reception podium to welcome more guests. He moved with the lilt of one who feeds on the presence of others. The waiter, flustered, came by to pour the champagne.

Molnar's brain turned. It was something more than the delicate scent of vanilla from the Taittinger that made him remove a new cigar and carefully clip the end. Maybe it was his gut warning him—that sixth sense that detectives call a hunch—or maybe it was plain old curiosity. But Molnar resolved to stick around the bar for the evening.

As time passed by and the bottle emptied, uniforms funneled out two by two. The short hand of the clock moved higher and higher; the exiting boots stumbled more and more. Molnar ordered dinner and a second bottle of Taittinger. The kitchen closed, and the gray-haired woman cleaned up and eventually left—but Molnar retained his seat. He watched Fruehauf, filled to the brim with energy. He saw him sneak a nip of a clear *eau de vie* several times throughout the night. And he also saw his pen dive down quickly onto a few abandoned receipts, adding something here or there. What was the man doing?

Molnar poured himself another glass as the final customer left. Fruehauf surveyed the room, satisfied, and removed his chef's apron with a flourish, showing Molnar that he was hanging it up for the night. Then he came back around the bar with a nice bottle of French cognac. His air of joy said his work was over and he was going to relax, and that this dark straggler in the back might as well benefit.

Fruehauf approached Molnar's table with the bottle in one hand and two glasses pinched together in the other. "Would you care to join me in a drink?"

"I've never said no," said Molnar, pushing out the opposite chair with his foot. Fruehauf dropped the tumblers onto the table, filled them too full, and shoved one at Molnar, who nodded. As he began to take a seat, the telephone rang.

This occurred just as Fruehauf's knees were crouched halfway between standing and sitting on the chair. He was in a stoop. The resolve it took to go from stoop to stand must have come from the deepest part of the man's character, but stand he did. And he gave a slight bow to Molnar, who hadn't missed the superhuman effort of will.

Fruehauf plucked the cold receiver from the cradle, and Molnar tried to politely ignore the conversation ... but failed. He couldn't help but notice the call began amiably but took a hard left, where Fruehauf's voice became distant and indistinct.

Fruehauf hung up the receiver and stood. He looked at it a moment before crossing the room. He sat in his chair across from Molnar, but his light had dimmed. The man imbibed half his cognac in one gulp.

"Tough call?" asked the detective.

Remembering he was not alone, Fruehauf forced a smile. "Not the best," he said. "Maybe life was going too well." He shrugged. "But let us discuss more pleasant affairs."

"I don't think you'll be any good at that right now. It looks like someone hit you in the gut with a crowbar."

Fruehauf smiled a weak smile. Seeing this, Molnar eased off.

"We can talk about my business," said Molnar, and Fruehauf nodded with relief. "I'm trying to find a guy named Heinz Klaebisch. Ever heard of him?"

If Fruehauf looked crowbarred before, now he looked shot. "What?"

"That's a yes. How do you know him?" asked Molnar, getting intimate with his brandy, sniffing at it as he watched the man.

"That was him," said Fruehauf in disbelief, pointing back toward the office. "On the phone."

"So he's not your best friend," said Molnar with a wry grin. "Mine either. It's strictly business with us." Molnar tested the cognac, but kept one hand clasped on the Taittinger as if it'd escape. He felt tension from Fruehauf's eyes.

"Where are you from?"

"Hungary ... Budapest."

Fruehauf tried to read something into that but failed. "What brings you to Paris?"

"Heinz brought me," said Molnar. "What brought you here?"

"I've been in France since I was 12," said Fruehauf, sweat starting to stand on his brow. "And Paris for the last 25 years. It's my home."

"Fought on this side in the last one?"

"Yes."

Did he say it proudly? Molnar wondered.

Neither man touched his drink. Molnar'd seen a lot as a psychologist, and even more as a soldier. And he still saw the brightness hiding in Fruehauf's eyes, a deep and truthful brightness—and his instinct said to trust him. Molnar'd seen the final moments of this light in the eyes of men before they left a moat-like trench for lead hail. He'd smelled the stench of 90-day-old corpses being used to buoy soldiers over mud the consistency of custard. He'd watched a man who'd been cut in half by a shell hang from the seat on his crashed plane … while continuing to shoot his handgun at the advancing enemy. He'd summered at Death's and stayed for the fall. And he could see Death's brand on Fruehauf—because after the soul of a man is burnt out of him and his spirit is a blackened eggshell, he often loses the ability to lie with his eyes. Molnar knew this and saw the truth nestled in Fruehauf's brown irises.

He also knew that the Gestapo disc wouldn't help him. So he went the other way and removed his pocket watch. He placed it on the table. It bore the Hungarian coat of arms. On the left side of the shield—the sinister side, as it's called—was the Cross Lorraine, the sign of the Free French Forces. Molnar pointed his thumb to the cross. Fruehauf looked at it and then up at the detective, questioning.

"You're for the resistance?" asked Fruehauf in a hushed voice.

Molnar nodded. "I'd rather everyone run his own country," he said, staring down at the coat of arms, and then back into Fruehauf's eyes to drive the point home.

"Most people haven't done much so far," said Fruehauf. He took a drink of his cognac and lowered his voice to a whisper. "I haven't done much." He paused, thinking on this and scrutinizing Molnar's eyes. "What business do you have with Klaebisch?"

"His life is in my hands," said Molnar. "Is he a good man?"

"Are any of these Nazis good men?"

"They can be," said Molnar. "Some are forced into it by summons or conscription, like yours truly. Some are helping undercover. But all of them have had it hard since the last war and have been told this is the way to salvation. Most of us humans do as we're told. You know that; you were in the first war." He looked up at Fruehauf, who was grave. "We've all had an instinct to obey beaten into us. It's how we succeed in school. It's how we succeed at work."

Fruehauf swallowed, and said, "Klaebisch is not a good man. But I've been forced to work with him for the past few months. He calls me a friend. I call him necessary." Fruehauf leaned back in his chair and sighed.

"What's the trouble?" said Molnar. "Maybe I can help."

Fruehauf dove deep into Molnar's dark-blue eyes, and he felt the pain of loss and the thickness that must develop around the walls of a heart so it can keep beating under such pressure.

But none of that really mattered to Fruehauf. If he didn't have a miracle, he'd hang. So he related to Molnar story of paper bottles that he added to his guests' abandoned receipts after they left. Those represented real bottles that had been pushed out of the back of his barn and sold on the burgeoning black market, bringing in double the price.

"There simply isn't enough good champagne to go around, and the Germans get first draw," Fruehauf explained. "And they buy by the truck-load because the cheap *franc* is only worth five German *pfennigs*. And now Klaebisch is about to find me out!" Fruehauf released all his air. "Maybe even tonight."

Molnar mulled this over and finished his last glass of champagne with his eyes closed. His hand went absentmindedly into his pocket and felt the Gestapo disc. The pause lasted so long that Fruehauf began to shuffle in his seat.

Then Molnar reanimated. "I've got an idea."

———

Heinz Klaebisch opened his eyes at precisely 6:15 every morning. He stood, lifted his bedroom window, and let the weather determine his mood for the day. He stared at the square his window cut into the sheet of the world before going to the bathroom, drinking a pitcher of water, and sitting at the table where his breakfast always awaited him with the *Paris-Soir*.

With the paper, variance began. Not before.

But this morning, Klaebisch's eyes opened, window opened, bladder emptied, throat swallowed—all in perfect succession—and then there was an interruption. Atop today's *Paris-Soir*, his beady eyes landed upon a letter sealed by a large oval of pressed wax that was remarkably similar to the imperial eagle on Molnar's Gestapo disc. Klaebisch glared as he stooped to lift the envelope. It was a decided change of schedule.

The night before, Klaebisch had had another surprise. Shortly after his call with Fruehauf, his secretary came in with word that Knut Fruehauf was the original recipient of the bottles of champagne now being discovered on the black market. Klaebisch, in disbelief, had studied the documents that condemned his friend Fruehauf. He felt as if his own name were on the paper.

Today, his surprise upon opening the letter came with relief. The letter was from Berlin, and its cover page read:

"*STRENG GEHEIM—TOP SECRET*

For *Gauleiter* Heinz Klaebisch's eyes only."

Behind that, the letter read:

"Dear H. Klaebisch,

"It is important you know that one of the men to whom you supply champagne is serving a dual purpose for the fatherland. His name is Knut Fruehauf, and he works as an undercover ear in France for the Gestapo.

"His newest commission is to work with our headquarters in Berlin to pinpoint the heads of a black-market smuggling operation we believe to be operating within Paris.

"His orders are to speak to no one about this affair, as it is considered TOP SECRET. You are privileged with clearance for this information so as to continue your duties without impeding Fruehauf. We ask that you burn this letter upon reading and speak of it to no man, upon penalty of death.

"Yours sincerely,

Pils Kloy, *Kriminaldirektor, Geheime Staatspolizei*"

The moment Klaebisch's eyes reached the last word, they returned to the top to reread the letter. A noise came from the kitchen. The eyes paused.

"*Fräulein* Dana!" Klaebisch yelled. "Do not enter this room until I call for you! Do not allow anyone to enter! Do you understand?"

"Yes, *Herr* Klaebisch," piped a muffled voice through the kitchen door.

Klaebisch's eyes again reached the bottom of the letter. He folded the paper, removed a brushed-metal lighter with a black swastika from his pocket, and walked to the fireplace.

There was a knock on the door. "*Herr* Klaebisch, there is another package for you when you finish eating," said the muffled feminine voice.

Klaebisch watched the last of the paper go from white to red to black, turn petal-thin, and finally crack under the heat, dissolving in the fireplace. Klaebisch walked to the door, opened it, cleared his throat, and took the package from the delicate, thin arms of a girl dressed in an apron and bonnet. Then he shut the door in her face and sat down at his table.

The box was wooden, long, and rectangular. It had an insignia signifying it came from a colonel. Klaebisch used his fork to pry the lid off the box and reveal a dark bottle of wine with a pink ribbon tied around its trunk, holding down a note. The note obscured a red, puckered kiss mark on the bottle's white label.

The note read:

"A *wineführer* must at least try the best of the wine in the country he runs.

"Sincerely,

Your faithful servant,

Colonel Riffel."

Klaebisch raised an eyebrow. He smiled so wide it hurt his sunken cheeks.

Then he glanced at his watch. "Is 6:35 in the morning too early to have a drink?" he asked no one in particular. Glancing over his shoulder and getting no response, Klaebisch put the bottle back in the case and sat down to breakfast.

That afternoon at Fruehauf's bar, an effervescent version of Mads Molnar sat beside the stringy Heinz Klaebisch. They were in particularly high spirits. The clattering of pots and pans punctuated their conversation. The poor Fruehauf was back in the kitchen, sweating amid a frenzy of activity—which Molnar knew was keeping his mind from the precipitous plummet of pure panic. But Klaebisch had something else in mind.

"Knut!" rang out Klaebisch's voice. "Knut, I have something to say!"

The pots paused their clanging. A moment later, Fruehauf entered the room and leaned heavily on the counter, a drop of sweat clinging between his brows. His eyes went from Molnar to Klaebisch.

"There you are, friend!" said Klaebisch. He too leaned on the counter. One shoulder was raised especially high, the other sunken low to hold a glass of Gewurztraminer. "I just made such good acquaintances with your lodger." Klaebisch nodded at Molnar. "I invited him to a royal dinner, and I'd like you to come as well."

"A royal dinner?"

"It's a dinner with some very important people—officers! Tonight," he said. And he leaned in closer. "It's for some … officials from the *Reichstag*." And now his voice lowered to a tipsy whisper. "Word is that the … Führer may attend."

"How could I say no?" said Fruehauf, smiling against his will.

"You can't!" said Klaebisch, leaning heavily again. He stared at Fruehauf for a moment too long to be normal. Then he cocked his head a little and kept staring. He opened his mouth as if to ask a question and closed it again. Then he smiled. "You're a good man. I'm proud to know you. One day, we'll have a lot to talk about." He took a glug of wine and turned on a heel back to Molnar's smiling face and open arms.

Molnar stood and held his glass out to toast the return of Klaebisch's attention. The wine *Gauleiter*'s hand extended, and a broad smile stretched across his tight face. He almost stumbled to ensure their glasses touched, and he gazed into Molnar's eyes as they toasted. Klaebisch looked as if he were a schoolboy given attention by the town bully.

Klaebisch's being eased into its true form, only revealed after it contained enough wine. He took another drink, looking out the window, lifting his elbow daintily and imagining himself very Otto Von Bismarck-esque. The elbow was a bit high and caused the wine to dribble down the corner of his mouth. He quickly wiped it away.

Molnar didn't react but kept grinning. Klaebisch didn't realize it, but as he sat, he was sharing a table with his savior or executioner. The evening's conversation was an invisible chess board between Molnar and Death. And they were playing for Klaebisch's life.

"Heinz," said Molnar, "I'm curious."

Klaebisch looked at him, hanging on his words.

"How'd you get where you are? You're in an enviable role."

Klaebisch saw Molnar's grin and returned it. He took a sip. "I love wine, my dear. I love wine. The root, the vine, the grape, the juice—" He hiccupped, and looked around as if it had come from someone else. "Once it's turned—shown its true form."

Molnar nodded and took Death's queen-bishop pawn with his knight. "True form," he said. "War does to humans what fermentation does to grapes. Shows their form once pressed."

"That's clever," said Klaebisch, thin neck bobbing sagely. "And true."

"That's one thing I love about war," said Molnar. "What do you love about the war, Heinz?"

"Power," said Klaebisch. "I have …" And he interrupted himself with a high and grating laugh. "I have power, my dear. Do you know what ah mean?"

Molnar kept the smile on and nodded affirmation. Death took Molnar's king bishop with his king.

"I know you do," Klaebisch said. "I remember walking into snooty wineries. So snooty. I couldn't afford a bottle with a million Deutsche Marks then. And now they bow to me. 'Welcome, monsieur,' they pipe. 'Try this wine or that wine or take a cellar tour. Remember us when you're buying, monsieur.' Blah, blah, blah."

Klaebisch finished his fourth glass and poured himself another. Molnar was silent. "But another thing I love," Klaebisch said, thinking he was lowering his voice as he leaned forward. "All the young Frenchmen are fighting for us or hiding." He almost spit. "And all their little, helpless girls are only too happy to trade themselves for a place in the bed of the Wine Führer!"

"When the cat's away …" said Molnar.

"Klaebisch will play," chortled the man. "But you know what I love most?" he asked, on a roll. "I love how we're doing Darwin's work. It's so good for everyone."

"Go on," said Molnar, as Death moved his queen bishop to cut off Molnar's escaping king.

"I'm going to butcher this," Klaebisch said, slapping the detective on the shoulder. Then he closed his eyes as if to splash his brain with ice water. When he opened them, he seemed to have sobered himself up by a considerable degree. He began: "It isn't logical to agree with Darwin's natural selection and imagine it relegated to beasts alone. If mankind's common ancestors are beasts, then why would the process end now that we're in a more advanced state?"

Klaebisch's wits seemed to have returned entirely. He went on: "Only modern societies would be so haughty as to undermine evolution … but we have. I quote the late Darwin's perfect work: *The Descent of Man.*" Klaebisch's eyes closed again as he recalled the text. "'The weak members of civilized societies propagate their kind. No one who has attended to the breeding of domestic animals will doubt that this must be highly injurious to the race of man'—and I'm forgetting something here. It's

something like, 'hardly anyone.' Yes! That's it! 'Hardly anyone is so ignorant as to allow his worst animals to breed.'" Klaebisch's eyes reopened
and he took a gulp of wine. "The Führer, you, I—we are truly Charles
Darwin's soldiers! Oh, and he goes on to commission us and give our
rallying cry: 'Looking to the world at no very distant date, what an end-
less number of the lower races will have been eliminated by the higher
civilized races throughout the world.'"

Klaebisch's wine-glass-holding hand smashed down on the table as he
finished the sentence. The bottom of the glass cracked, causing his thin fist
to drip red drops on the table. He carried on. "And this man and his son
were some of the last honest Brits! So ... we do their dirty work.

"I remember my first few months in the S.S. when we made a long line
of the gypsies and Negroes lie shoulder to shoulder in a trench they dug.
I saw the looks in their eyes. We walked down that line. And I did—I did
it; I put my weakness to the side and ended their lives for the greater good
of mankind. It cost us two *Reichsmarks* in lead to improve the race. And I
truly felt like Darwin's hands and feet."

Molnar flicked his king over, looked at Death, and said, "He's all yours."
He got to his feet, ignoring a puzzled look from Klaebisch, and walked up
the stairs toward his room.

"Where are you going?" called Klaebisch.

"I'm all in," said Molnar, pausing on the steps.

"See you tonight," said Klaebisch.

"Don't forget that wine you mentioned," said Molnar as he continued
his ascent. "I'd love to give it a try."

"But of course!"

The Führer did not attend the ceremony that night, but there were enough
metal bars in the room to smelt a Panzer. Molnar couldn't help but notice
the bottle-shaped package under Klaebisch's arm as the man introduced
him and Fruehauf to officers around the room. As dinnertime commenced,
the butler escorted the men to different seats around the long dining table.
The name cards were separated by alphabetical order to encourage new
people to meet.

As they passed Klaebisch's seat, Fruehauf looked at Molnar with panic. The seat beside Klaebisch held an elegant white note card with a cursive silver script that read: Pils Kloy. Molnar saw this and tried not to sweat as he and Fruehauf were escorted to their separate seats across the table from Klaebisch and Kloy.

How could Molnar have known the Gestapo director himself would come to Paris that night and be seated beside his man?

To Molnar and Fruehauf's horror, Pils Kloy walked in and shook hands with Klaebisch. All Molnar could do was try to regulate his digestion as he watched Klaebisch drink heavily. Soon, his conversation with Kloy started to crackle. Molnar glanced at Fruehauf, who looked like a rabbit in a snare.

By the time the main course came, Klaebisch and Kloy had finished the table's wine. Molnar saw Kloy look around for another bottle. Klaebisch's hand went up for a waiter, but after a while with no luck, he dropped it. As his hand landed at his side, his eyes lit up, and Molnar smiled deep within his soul.

Klaebisch's twiddling fingers came back with the bottle of pinot. He presented it to Kloy, and his mouth moved as they looked at it. One found an opener, and the liquid entered their glasses.

The detective smiled over at Fruehauf, who stared back blankly, unaware. But Molnar's appetite suddenly grew, and he sliced into his filet mignon.

Klaebisch and Kloy drank deeply from the evil draught, and Death began his work.

After Molnar's last bite of *crème brûlée*, the pinot was gone.

Molnar stood and walked over to Fruehauf's seat and leaned low to his ear. "We might want to make an exit," he said. "But I need that bottle."

Fruehauf looked up at him and nodded.

Molnar headed to the coat room. With his trench coat over one arm, he made his way back to the table. Halfway there, he intercepted a waiter and forcibly relieved him of an expensive bottle of Moscato *Strohwein* that the waiter was bringing around for dessert. The waiter looked as if he'd swallowed a cayenne pepper and followed in Molnar's wake.

"I come bearing gifts," said Molnar as he approached Kloy and Klaebisch with the thin bottle in his hands.

The men rang out an applause as Molnar poured them too much of the wine.

"Sir, please allow me," said the waiter, now at Molnar's side and trying to remove the bottle from his grasp. With a subtle twitch of his hips, Molnar knocked the man into an oval dessert table with a crash. Klaebisch and Kloy stood from their seats amid the ruckus, and Molnar used the moment to slip the pinot bottle into his deep jacket pocket.

Then he righted himself and looked down at the man as if he were an innocent bystander. "You really must watch your step," said Molnar, holding the dessert wine out as a peace offering. The fuming man stood to his feet as his face continued to redden. But some remembrance that his employment hinged on his composure clicked in his mind. He cleared his throat, slicked back his hair, and accepted the offering.

Klaebisch and Kloy began bubbling with laughter that percolated into a boil as the man walked away. They slapped Molnar's back and grabbed their wine.

With the laughter hanging in the air, Molnar bowed to Kloy and said, "I'm sorry to say, but I must be going, *Herr* Klaebisch. It's been such a titillating evening; thank you for inviting me."

"How can I be upset after such a generous pour?" said Klaebisch. "I'm sure I'll be seeing you again at Fruehauf's."

"You never know," said Molnar, who tipped his hat to the men and exited before Klaebisch could introduce him to Kloy.

Molnar reached the coat room and saw Fruehauf. "You may have saved my life, Mads," whispered Fruehauf, donning a scarf.

"Let's hope Klaebisch doesn't start spilling secrets!" said Molnar with a laugh.

Fruehauf tried to smile, but it didn't work. "I need to stay busy. Can I be so forward as to invite you to give me a hand tonight in moving my champagne? I'll give you a few bottles for your time."

"How could I say no?" said Molnar.

———

The party was nearly over, and two particularly overjoyed Nazis were standing from the table to leave when a waiter handed them a card to sign for the beloved man who'd missed the event. Kloy reached into his breast pocket, feeling for a pen that wasn't there. His hand came out with a similar-shaped device: his personal seal.

"*Trantüte*! I lost my pen," he told Klaebisch, blinking at him like a sheep. "I was about to try to sign with this!" His thin laugh dribbled out as he held up the seal.

"Use mine," said Klaebisch, holding out a black and ornate fountain pen. Then he noticed Kloy's seal, and his jovial expression melted like mozzarella on a steam engine. "Wait—what is that?"

"It's my personal seal," Kloy said. "*Dummkopf* that I am, I thought it was a pen." He took the fountain pen from Klaebisch's limp hand and signed the card, then passed it along to the man beside him. The whole while, Klaebisch stared at the thin, pen-shaped seal. When Kloy reached to return the seal to his pocket, Klaebisch grabbed his hand and stared closer at the penny-sized end of the seal. It only bore Kloy's initials: PK. There was no eagle, no wreath, no decoration of any kind. It bore no resemblance to the seal that had closed the Top Secret letter sent in Kloy's name.

"Do you sign everything with this?" asked Klaebisch.

"Of course!" said Kloy. He pulled his hand away, cringing from Klaebisch's clawing arm. "What's wrong with you?"

Klaebisch stared at the man's face. "I have something to say! Normally I'd never disclose this, but … I feel compelled."

"Say it, Klaebisch! There are no secrets between Nazis," said Kloy, trying to right himself after the half-dozen glasses of wine.

"But by law, it is a subject I cannot breach."

"In that case, keep it to yourself," said Kloy, returning the seal to his pocket and turning away from the man, who was becoming stranger to him by the moment. He took a step toward the coat room.

"Yet it involves you and your seal," said Klaebisch after him.

Kloy turned back to the man. His voice lowered. "Then say on, man!"

"Here?"

"Here is fine. Say on."

Klaebisch related the morning of the strange letter in Kloy's name and the story of Fruehauf.

Kloy turned dark-cherry purple.

Molnar was standing outside Fruehauf's barn in the alleyway behind the hotel, sipping a glass of black-market champagne. "Is he always late?" called Molnar, leaning low to yell through the barn's little hay door.

Fruehauf called back through, "No. He's never late."

"Oh, I think I see headlights now," said Molnar, finishing the glass and setting it onto the cobblestone street.

"Get down behind the dumpster. Let's make sure it's him!"

The sound of a screaming engine and a string of profanity came down the alley as a Horch convertible screeched around the corner of the barn and toward the front of Fruehauf's hotel. Molnar stared into the cab of the passing car and saw two red and enraged faces in the front and, in the back, two soldiers—their eyes wide, knuckles white, gripping anything fingers could grasp as the car slid around the corner.

"It wasn't him," said Molnar. "But I know who it was."

"What do you mean?"

"Wait! There are more headlights coming."

"Stay down," said Fruehauf.

"What?"

"Stay down!"

"I am!"

A milk truck skidded to a halt in front of the hay door. The enormous blond Viking of a man whom Molnar had seen the previous night leapt out. He looked down at Molnar. "Who are you?" His voice sounded like it came from inside a barrel.

"I'm helping Knut."

"Who told you to come?"

"I did!" yelled Fruehauf from inside the barn. "Now let's go." He shoved a case through the hay door, and the men began to load. "Who was in that car?"

"Take a wild guess."

The men worked furiously. Cases were tossed from one to the next and into the truck. With only a few cases left to shove through, Fruehauf heard gunfire.

Crack, crack, crack! came the quick report of a Mauser outside the barn. The work paused, and Klaebisch's squeaking voice yelled from outside the barn door: "Open this door!" The final case was tossed into Molnar's hands.

Molnar handed it to the Viking, and the two men crept into the truck. The Viking put a key into the ignition.

"Don't start it," said Molnar, grabbing the man's arm.

"Don't tell me what to do!" said the Viking, twisting the key. The truck's engine stuttered, shuddered and sputtered, but didn't light up.

Klaebisch and Kloy heard the truck trying to start. "Break down this door!" commanded Klaebisch. The two soldiers with him began smashing into the barn door with their shoulders. It heaved on its hinges.

"Hurry up!" shouted Molnar, and Fruehauf climbed out of the hay door and into the alley just as the soldiers crashed through the door.

"No!" screamed Klaebisch, seeing the disappearing form. "They're in the alleyway! Get back to the car!"

The four men raced back through the barn to their car.

The Viking's massive fingers held the starter on, but the engine only sputtered.

"Push!" said Molnar. The Viking looked like he was about to balk, but then nodded and jumped out. He and Fruehauf began to push the heavy milk truck as Molnar slid into the driver's seat. The powerful Viking propelled the truck forward at an incredible rate until it got going down a decline. Molnar shoved it in second gear, turning the engine over just as Kloy and Klaebisch screeched into the alley.

Fruehauf ran up and climbed into the passenger's seat, and the Viking scrambled onto the rear bumper as Molnar motored away. The officers started firing, and the Viking dove into the bed of the truck with the champagne. The door smashed open and closed as the truck bounced down the cobblestone road. Bullets rained on the Viking, who hid behind the crates as best he could. Champagne popped every few moments. Deciding to die drinking, the big blond opened a bottle himself.

Kloy's face maintained its tomato tones as he reached over the convertible windshield to blast round after round at the dodging blond form. Klaebisch maintained an unbroken string of profanity that made the soldiers behind him stop firing from time to time in awe. Kloy aimed at the rear double tires and blew one out.

Molnar kept the gas down and blew through stop lights trying to escape, but the convertible stayed on his tail. The truck rounded a corner and nearly sailed into a police cruiser, which proceeded to add itself to the chase. The cruiser's powerful engine carried it past Klaebisch, and soon it was neck and neck with the truck.

"Knut!" yelled the cop—or *le flic*—to Fruehauf, recognizing him. "*Qu'est-ce que le enfer se passe?*" *What in hell is going on?*"

"These Nazi bastards are trying to catch us!" Fruehauf yelled, leaning out the door. "You'll have all the champagne you can drink if you get them off my back." A light came on in the officer's eyes, and Fruehauf knew he'd dialed the right combination.

"OK. The moment I turn on my siren, stand on your brake," instructed *le flic* over the roar of the engines.

"OK," said Fruehauf, looking at Molnar. Molnar nodded, keeping his eyes on the road.

Both of the rear outside tires on the truck were gone, and Kloy aimed at one on the inside. The Viking got an idea and tossed a case of champagne at the convertible. It smashed the face of one soldier, knocking him into the street. The police cruiser swerved to miss his tumbling body.

"They're wasting your wine!" said Kloy, and Klaebisch responded with sputtering rage. The Viking stepped on the bumper and threw another case out of the truck, missing the convertible entirely. Then he threw a third. The second soldier crumpled under its weight.

Le flic followed behind, waiting until Klaebisch got close enough to give his signal. The Viking stepped out to throw another case, but lost his balance. Before falling, in a panic, he leapt off, aiming for Klaebisch. Klaebisch swerved, but the Viking still hit the hood and bounced onto the ground.

"We'll get him later!" Klaebisch cried. "I'll get close now, and you can climb in."

"No! That's madness," said Kloy. But Klaebisch was already closing in. He was nearly bumper to bumper with the truck when *le flic* turned on the siren. Molnar leapt from his seat, putting all his weight on the brake. A terrible screeching of tires and a rending of metal tore the air, and the profanity came to a final stop.

It took them 10 minutes to get the truck off the shattered convertible.

"You don't see that every day," said Molnar as he, Fruehauf, and *le flic* stared at the car's remains. The men pulled the crumpled convertible top over the grotesque figures inside to protect children from the sight.

The officer drove off with a closed mouth and several cases of champagne for his trouble. Molnar parked the still-mobile truck behind Hotel Fruehauf. The owner tipped his hat and handed Molnar a couple of bottles of Veuve Clicquot before stumbling off to bed.

As Molnar drank, he tossed the empty pinot noir bottle into Fruehauf's pile of hundreds of glass bottles, which were being saved for reuse in a massive, wooden crate in the barn.

BOTTLE VI

Detective Bastick's eyes were bloodshot from refusing sleep. They squinted tightly behind red-tinted goggles, and his face grimaced as if undergoing torture. His fist was fused around the twist throttle of a Zündapp K500 bike, holding it fully open. He couldn't obtain priority on a flight without disclosing the specifics of his mission—a thing he refused to do. So he had driven 18 hours across the mostly rural roads of much of Germany, from Berlin to the Rhine. Now, at 10 a.m. on Thursday, he was tearing down the highway from Colmar to the west side of the Alsatian valley. He was pointed toward a small town named Katzenthal. He sped by trucks and cars, spending half the time in the opposite lane.

Headed straight at an oncoming truck, Bastick passed the car he was overtaking and veered into his own lane. The face of the truck driver was bloodless as Bastick passed.

Bastick ramped over the center of a roundabout at top speed. He rocketed down a dirt road with a brown squirrel tail of dust in his wake. The road bisected a valley of vineyards and led to a white clock tower and the quaint village of Katzenthal. At the crest of the hill of the village, overlooking the clock tower and church and bakery, was the winemaker Neuf's own winery.

Bastick blazed into the circular driveway and skidded to a stop, sending a whiplash of dust billowing up to the very door of the house. He leapt from the bike and bounded up the stairs. Removing the empty shell of Neuf's offending bottle from his riding-pants pocket, he rapped on the door thrice with it. Then he returned the bottle to his pocket, bent forward, rustled the dust out of his hair, and stood again, slicking it back. Finally, he lifted the goggles from his eyes, revealing two clean patches in his otherwise dust-covered veneer.

Neuf answered the door himself. He was happy to be interrupted. Once again, he'd been pulled out of the cellar and into the middle of doing the paperwork that allowed his business to operate in the newly Vichy-run section of the country. He was only too willing to leave it to his wife. When he opened the door and saw the bull that was Bastick, Neuf took a step back.

Bastick entered the ceded territory and leaned down, kissing Neuf on one cheek and then the other. He started in clear French. "My name is Detective Wolfram Bastick from the Gestapo." He gave a slight bow. "May I have a word with you?"

"Why, certainly; please come in." Neuf stepped back, allowing the man to fully enter. "May I get you something to drink?"

"Tea, if you have it," said Bastick, moving into the wide greeting hall alongside Neuf. If you saw the two men walking together, you'd wonder who was leading whom. You'd wonder whose house this was, and you'd note the discrepancy between the enormousness of Bastick and the smaller, Bonsai-tree toughness of Neuf. The two men walked to the sitting room, and both retained an air of royalty belonging to a time forgotten—the blue-blooded temperament bombed out of most Europeans in the first war.

"May I offer you a seat?" asked Neuf, waving at a table and chairs.

"I'm afraid I won't take it," said Bastick, staring down at the man. "It's been a long ride from Berlin."

"You took the train?"

"I drove."

"Oh, but how the Germans embrace discomfort."

"It seems to have served us well," said Bastick, removing his gloves and slapping their dust on his pant leg.

Neuf cleared his throat. "Very well. I'll ring for the maid." Neuf walked to a bell on the mantelpiece and shook it a few times. The maid, complete in a slightly outdated housemaid's black dress and white frills uniform, came in, and Neuf told her what to bring. Bastick rested his elephant elbow on the mantel and leaned hard against it, testing the construction. Then he glanced down at the roaring fireplace before turning back to Neuf.

"To business," said Bastick. He held the bottle up to Neuf.

"Ah, yes, the 1934 pinot. A very good year. Almost rivaling our 1929," said Neuf, smiling at Bastick.

"This bottle was poisoned. It killed my father," said Bastick, pulling his father's horn pipe out of the breast pocket of his tweed jacket. He removed his tobacco and began packing. "That's why I'm here. I need records of every bottle of this vintage you've produced and every buyer who bought it. And I need it today," he said, lighting the pipe.

Neuf's face revealed nothing. "*Mein Gott!*" he said in German. "I'm so sorry, Detective. That my bottle could—!" He put his hand to his forehead, shaking his head. "*Mein Gott!* I will get the records."

Bastick snorted at him, holding his gaze, smelling for lies. Then he nodded his pipe in acknowledgment as he put fire to the tobacco in a circular pattern, pulling on it in short nips. Neuf started toward the office, but just before he exited the room he halted, pivoted half way, and asked, "Is there more information you have that may help identify the purchaser?"

"It was a gift to my father, Troy Bastick. That and the fact that it's taken the lives of several other German officers is all I know," Bastick said.

"Very well." Neuf exited.

Bastick pulled the smoke into his mouth and rotated the bottle around its base on the mantel. He cleared his throat the way a horse neighs. The maid brought in the tea, and Bastick summoned her to him and lifted the saucer to the mantel. He waved away sugar and milk.

"May I do anything for you to make your stay more comfortable … master?" she said in heavily Alsatian-accented German.

Bastick raised his brows at her use of the word *master* and shook his head. "*Merci, non, mademoiselle.*"

"If there's anything else you should require.…" She moved the little silver bell closer to Bastick's elbow, and brushed his forearm with her delicate fingers. The touch flipped a physiological switch in his nervous system, and his near-superhuman senses sprang to life. He consumed her sensorially in the blink of an eye. He smelled the tiny white wild *aster pilosus* flowers stuck in a twist of brown hair behind her ear. He saw her lack of wedding ring, her tan skin, and the light, near-permanent cracks in the pads of her fingers and palms from housework. He noted the barely visible pulse of her neck and how it quickened. Quickened. He reached out for the neck and gripped it lightly, pulling the woman's body close to him and smelling her fully. She didn't resist. His nose ran up the pulse of her neck, following it up and behind her ear.

His teeth tested the flesh of her earlobe. But after a moment, he released her.

She stood there, looking up at him, a willing victim. She put her hand on his powerful arm. Her body language told the common tale of a husband lost and a once-gorgeous past turned lonely by the decisions of other men—men in far-off halls, smoking the cigars and drinking the scotch that her husband could never afford. She was alone now. Forever alone.

She stared at Bastick throughout his sensory appraisal. When he closed his eyes and pulled on the pipe, a shudder quivered through her to the core. She turned slowly and walked out, thoroughly shaken.

His eyes opened, half squinting against his smoke. He squatted down and put a new log into the fire. Then he stared into the flames.

"What a ravaged landscape we men have made," he said.

Then he stood and started spinning the bottle again.

He consumed another cup of tea before thinking of his fiancée. He remembered her the way hounds remember quail. This Saturday, they'd be married. The life he never thought he'd attain. A picture-perfect figure of woman and success at his work.

But his father. His father's blood cried out from the ground. Bastick's fist collided with the mantel.

A moment later, Neuf entered with a large envelope stuffed with receipts. "Here are all of them, Monsieur."

"Thank you." Bastick pivoted toward Neuf.

Neuf carefully stacked the papers on the table and invited Bastick to a seat. The detective remained standing, but stepped to the table and began flipping through the papers quickly, his thick fingers turning suddenly nimble. He scanned through them one by one. The minutes passed, and Neuf tried to remain standing and at ease. Not being an official buyer, Riffel's name was, of course, absent.

After 10 minutes, Bastick looked at Neuf questioningly.

"This is all there are," said the vintner.

Bastick glared down at the man, long and hard. "Do you have a phone, monsieur?"

"But of course," said Neuf. He led him to the receiver in the kitchen to allow privacy.

Bastick asked the operator to connect him with his lackey, Otto. "Any success searching the newspapers?" asked Bastick, relighting his pipe.

"*Ja!*"

"And have you found anything in them?"

"*Ja!*"

There was a long pause on the line as Bastick waited for details. "Well! Don't keep me on pins, Otto. Tell me what you've found!"

Otto told him two officers were poisoned by the wine in Munich and another in Épernay, France. That man was still alive.

"What's the name of the hospital in Épernay? I must get to him."

"*Centre Hospitalier.*"

"Very fine work, Otto." Bastick hung the phone and leaned against the wall with his eyes closed, pulling on his pipe. He was still. So still that if you saw him, you'd start looking for rust. Another poisoning in France? This might be bigger than he'd thought. And none of the men poisoned were on Neuf's receipts. Something didn't add up.

Suddenly, Bastick's eyes popped open and movement resumed. He turned on his heel and went back to find Neuf sitting with the paperwork. He put the horn pipe on the mantelpiece and walked to the table, placing his hands on it to lean close enough to Neuf to feel his breath. He stared down into the vintner's eyes.

"We only need receipts for purchases of three or more bottles," said Bastick, still watching Neuf. "People were poisoned by two more of your bottles of this vintage."

"*Mon Dieu.*"

"I know what happened, Neuf," said Bastick, staring at him, smelling out his feelings. "I should have seen it before, but it finally hit me."

"Wonderful! Which recipient do you think is responsible?"

Bastick smelled only the light-green scent of tranquility from the man across the table. Composure. But on second smell, there was something hiding behind that: a scent that he'd missed before. Maybe it was because French wasn't his first language. The facial expressions of falsehood weren't always cross-cultural. But Bastick sensed the elevated heart rate of untruth, and a rolling rage ignited in his belly.

"How many did you poison?"

"Surely you don't mean that I had a hand in ... !"

Bastick, motionless, let the words hang between them, like the blade of the guillotine. The tones of the half-finished sentence rang "falsehood" louder and louder. And then it was over. In French, German, or Nepalese, Neuf had cracked. Bastick held his gaze, and the first drop of sweat sprouted from Neuf's absent hairline and slid over his forehead to nestle between his eyes. Neuf wiped it away with the back of his hard hand.

Bastick's rage percolated. Somehow, this small man had killed or helped kill his almost-perfect father. His more-advanced, more-powerful, and more-intelligent father had been slain by this wiry Frenchman.

"It must have been difficult for you to watch my countrymen come back to our homeland and reclaim it. But you're a farmer, a heart made of earth. You had to go down with a fight. How could you cultivate a little taste of your own pain?"

Neuf dropped his eyes, and a few drops of sweat fell on the hard cherry table in front of him. Bastick moved slowly behind him and then quickly grabbed the man's wrists, pinning them together and yanking them so high behind Neuf's back that they nearly snapped. Neuf's body was forced to leap out of his seat and dive forward to keep his arms intact. His body doubled over, pressing his face hard against the wooden surface. He grunted and Bastick leaned down beside his ear, Neuf's stubble of gray hair combing through Bastick's mustache.

"But how did you get them into the hands of your enemies? That's the question, *Herr* Neuf. You see"—and Bastick wrenched the man's hands higher, torquing them up and smashing his face into the table. And his voice rose with them: "My father's blood is on your head!" His voice lowered, and he leaned even closer to Neuf. "But his blood won't be the last. For the sins of men, the women suffer."

"Listen—" began the vintner, craning his neck so he could look back at his captor.

But Bastick's rage boiled over and his enormous fist came down like a blacksmith's mallet on the side of Neuf's head, hammering his temple into the table. "Shut! Up!"

The fist came down again, harder. Perhaps too hard? When the blow fell, something in Bastick's stomach turned. Neuf's soul had smashed through the table and out of his body, leaving the human shell far above it, lying limp.

Bastick released the form to sprawl on the table and slowly slide, with a thud, to the floor. "That couldn't have killed him," he said to himself. Then, as if to assuage his own doubts, he added, "Wait right there." Then he grunted and sprinted out of the room and up the stairs, opening every door in the hall until he reached the office. He saw Neuf's wife seated at a desk. Her curly gray hair was held loose in a careless bun.

"May I help you?" she said, surprised and indignant.

"I believe you can. Would you kindly hand me that desk phone beside you?"

She snorted at this German level of presumption, but she handed Bastick the black rotary dial phone.

"Thank you, *madame*."

He yanked the cord from the wall and yanked the other end from the back of the phone. Then, grabbing her arms, he swiftly tied them behind her and to the back of her hardwood chair.

"Cry out, and it'll be the last thing you do," he whispered in her ear. He tied her ankle to the chair leg and stood to survey his work. Her face was fury and fear.

"Don't worry, my dear. You're not my flavor."

Bastick tried to move his massive bulk noiselessly down the wooden steps and back toward the study and Neuf's body. As he entered the room, he swung his weight through using the doorjamb, like a little boy running through the house. He danced over to a pair of black wrought-iron tongs beside the fireplace and lifted a large, violently flaming log. He placed the log on Neuf's thick carpet in the middle of the room and stooped to roll the carpet up around it with a flourish at the end. He tossed that against a wall and gleefully threw the table and chairs on it. Smoke poured out of the ends of his giant cannoli fire-starter.

As flames began to crackle, Bastick moved toward the prone figure of the vintner. Just before he squatted down, his eyes caught a glint from the delicate silver bell on the mantel. He paused, staring at it, and then moved to the mantel and reached for the bell.

A few minutes later, Bastick walked back into the room where Neuf lay, futilely trying to wipe fresh blood from his sleeve. He looked up at the fire crawling up one wall. The light mantle of smoke hanging near the ceiling stung his eyes. He pulled on his goggles, stood over Neuf, and kicked him in the ribs with a heavy boot. Neuf did not react. Through the smoke, Bastick sensed the bloody maroon odor of a cooling corpse. He frowned.

Bastick smashed his balled-up hand into the vintner's back. "That's for dying so easily!" He punched the figure again, and something in it cracked. "That's for killing my father!"

Bastick gave a final blow to the vintner's corpse and stomped outside to his motorbike. Wisps of nearly invisible steam poured from the vintner's window, and Bastick stared at them. Then he donned goggles, straddled his motorbike, and sent rocks flying as he tore out of the driveway, racing at top speed toward Épernay. His face had a look of total abandon, helmetless, goggles plastered against his face, and hair flapping in the wind.

———

Earlier that morning, Molnar was on a pay phone in Paris with Eva Sandor, his secretary. He was wearing his usuals: gray hat, gray trench coat, gray trousers, and black shoes. The shoes stood out, and their beautiful leather with elegant lines made his otherwise monochromatic outfit posh. He finished biting the end off his cigar and lit it.

"The last message," sighed Eva with utter disdain, "is from some German wench."

"What's her name?"

"Of course you wouldn't know … it's one Marilyn Ghetz, and she insisted that she reach you. She said if you didn't come before Friday, quote, 'the bottle will be jeopardized.' That's it. She just hung up after that. No 'goodbye, Miss Sandor'; no 'thank you, Miss Sandor'; no 'kiss my foot, Miss Sandor.'"

"It's purely a work relationship, Eva, like ours," said Molnar.

"In that case, it's worse than I thought. She needs all the help she can get."

"Anything else?" He pulled the velvety smoke into his mouth and released it from the corners, letting it collect under the ridge of his hat and enshrine his dark hair like a wreath before slowly escaping around the sides of the brim, floating to the top of the telephone box and wallowing above his head.

"Not unless you want to hear my own girlish thoughts."

"You're a girl?"

"How quickly we forget," said Eva. "Then back to work. Keep those Nazi women warm." The line went dead.

So, he needed to be back in two days or she'd squawk? And according to the snake-like man that his uncle killed, he needed to finish the job that weekend, or the Arrow Cross would hang him. Great. He pulled out his map to start planning his route, connecting the dots of bottles of wine on the way back to Berlin.

He pushed the door open and let the billow of the smoke pour out into the sky. The chilling breeze was overcome by the last hiccups of summer wind, which warmed Molnar's body. He hailed a cab and hopped in. Then he showed the driver his map, putting a finger on Épernay, France, as his first stop on the way back to Berlin.

"Step on it."

Molnar pulled his hat down and lay back for the ride. Luckily for him, he was 200 km closer to Épernay than Bastick was.

An hour later, his cab slowed in front of a black wrought-iron fence with gold serif lettering reading *De Venoge*. It was the champagne house that employed Molnar's next target: Pierre Cardiff. The driver pulled through the intricately designed entryway and stopped in front of the flat-faced white limestone building. Molnar got out and stretched his hamstrings before trotting up the entrance stairs. He entered and walked up to a counter where a wren of a girl with big eyes and brunette hair back in a loose ponytail looked up at him like she was in a cage.

"Don't get frightened," he said. "I'm just here to see Pierre."

The girl frowned. "You aren't serious."

"Not usually. I smile more," he said without smiling, "but you caught me on an off day."

"*Non*, I mean that Monsieur Cardiff is at '*os*-pi-*tal*. He has got very sick, monsieur," she said, still looking as frightened and flighty as a puffy bird.

"Oh, silly me," said Molnar, removing his Gestapo disc from his wallet and holding it up. "Where does he live? I'd like to talk with his family or his dog—whoever's there."

If she had neck feathers, they'd be ruffling. "We don't tell this information."

"But I'm special." He placed the disc on the counter and pushed it toward her to peck at.

She cleared her throat. "I'll write it down for you."

Molnar left her to her feed and got back in the cab. In a few minutes, the taxi arrived in front of a beautiful stone apartment building with blue shutters. He held the paper up to the cabbie.

"Is that C1 or C7? Can you tell?"

"*Sept,*" said the man.

"Thanks," said Molnar. "Mind sticking around?" The man nodded his acceptance, and Molnar exited. He found his way up two flights of sandstone steps to C7. His knock yielded nothing in return, so he took out his set of picks and a tension wrench and got to work on the brass lock.

An elongated and lanky male neighbor walked up, accompanied by a Miniature Schnauzer. Both man and dog were mustachioed. Molnar went on picking. "What do you suppose you're doing?" asked the neighbor's voice, which sounded female.

"Didn't pay his electric bill," said Molnar.

"Why, Pierre would never do such a thing," said the now-flustered voice of the now-flustered body. The Schnauzer's hair stood up, and its mustache waggled.

"I just do what they tell me. The connection's inside, and we gotta turn it off."

"But you're not even French."

"They can't get you French to work for so cheap."

The man realized this was correct and snorted. The Schnauzer snorted as well, and they both stood there watching as Molnar kept picking.

"Well, how long does it take?" asked the man.

"It's not like the movies," said Molnar, trying to concentrate.

After a few more moments, the man scoffed and walked downstairs. "Maybe I shouldn't pay mine either; you'll never get in."

"If it were easy, everyone would do it."

"Not the French!" hollered up the man, and the Schnauzer yapped an exclamation point as they walked out the door.

The tumbler tumbled, and the door unlocked with a click that, to Molnar, was very satisfying. He shook his head and entered.

The apartment was beyond posh and was packed with champagne in every form: corked bottles, uncorked bottles, paintings, and racks. Molnar walked on the marble flooring through the kitchen and picked up a red apple. On the desk, he saw a stack of paper. Flipping through it, he found Riffel's note to Cardiff and pocketed it. But he didn't see the uncorked bottle he was looking for and so walked through to the balcony. It overlooked a green courtyard with a round water fountain. Molnar took a bite of the apple and stared down at the fountain. Then he started opening doors until he found a little closet. The closet contained Molnar's treasure: a garbage bin. He opened it and shook his head as he squatted to go through the garbage. He picked out half a dozen bottles before he reached the pinot noir. It was empty, sure enough, and he brought it up into the light.

"If it were easy, everyone would do it," mumbled Molnar to himself.

A few minutes later, back in the cab, Molnar stared at the bottle as the wheels of the car started for the hospital. How could such a thing—light-green glass wrapped in a white label—cause such destruction? He noted the label with its text spelling the vintage, grape, and year. Then he rolled down his window. As they passed through a particularly barren alleyway, Molnar chucked the bottle hard at the curb, like he was a teenager with his friends. The glass shattered, spraying the curb and the side of the brick building. Teenage Molnar would have yipped with glee, but middle-aged Molnar just smiled and rolled up the window. Evidence destroyed. One more down.

Molnar's shiny blue taxi pulled under the hospital carport, and the detective stepped out.

Inside, he told the nurse he was a friend, and was escorted into Pierre Cardiff's room. The room continued the hospital's sterile motif of all-white doors, floors, and bed sheets. Cardiff's shock of bright-red hair stood out against the blank world.

Cardiff managed a half smile up at him. "Do I know you?"

"No. I'm a detective. Trying to figure out what's ailing you. Any ideas?" Molnar removed his Fedora and a cigar. "Want a smoke?"

Cardiff's weakened arm reached from under his sheets, and he gestured for the cigar, nodding. "I'd love one."

Molnar removed a cutter and snipped Cardiff's cigar with a sharp *click*. Then he put it in his mouth for him, opened his lighter with a *snap*, and lit the thing.

Cardiff pulled smoke in. "Maybe it'll heal me," he said.

Molnar crossed to the room's single window and opened it. Then he closed the front door gently. "Who knows?" he said.

"I've no idea what happened to me," said Cardiff. "That is the strangest part. I'm on so much morphine at this point"—he gestured to his IV drip—"who knows what's going on in my body? All I know is it doesn't hurt." He held up the cigar. "And this is nice."

"It better be. It's not a cheapie. You got no idea what happened?"

"Maybe bad food?"

"Got enemies?" Molnar pulled on his own cigar.

"Not really. Only a man at the champagne house who wants my job, but I can't see him putting me down for it."

"Got friends?"

"You wouldn't know it by the empty room"—the man looked around it—"but yes."

Heavy steps approached the room at a quick clip, and there was a shout from a nurse.

Molnar braced himself, turned to the door, and put his hand in his pocket, fondling his snub-nose .45. "Hope you were right about the enemies," said Molnar.

The two men bore witness as the door was flung open, testing its hinges. The doorway filled with the exhausted but unforgiving body of Detective Bastick. He pushed his way a meter into the room and stood there, staring at Molnar and Cardiff. He closed his eyes and breathed in the sterile, sickly scent of the hospital. The moment lasted long enough that Molnar raised an eyebrow at Cardiff.

"Ah! The varying and intricate nuances of death and dying," said Bastick, opening his eyes. He glanced at Molnar and moved to Cardiff's side. Seeing the cigar, he removed it from the man's mouth and threw it out the open window.

"Hey!" yelled Cardiff. Molnar raised the other eyebrow.

"It gets in the way," said Bastick, crouching low over the man, fanning away the remnants of smoke and sniffing the air.

Molnar's hand was still caressing the .45, but he allowed this gross infraction. Cardiff gazed up at him pleadingly, and Molnar shrugged. "I can't teach everyone manners," he said.

Bastick took a second glance up at Molnar from his crouch. "And who are you?"

"The guy who gave him the cigar. Who are you, besides the guy who took it away?"

Bastick's eyes went back to Cardiff. "I'm Detective Wolfram Bastick. I'm here to find out how this man was poisoned, and where he got the bottle."

Molnar mulled this over. These were the things that he didn't want Cardiff to think about. In fact, these were the things that he didn't want anyone to think about. "On second thought, I'm not so happy about you throwing out that cigar," said Molnar. Then he stepped back and slugged the crouched beast in the side of the head, putting the weight of his whole body behind his fist. Bastick sprawled on the floor with a heavy thud, and Cardiff smiled weakly at Molnar.

"And I'm not so happy about your riling up our friend here." Molnar took out the gun to show it to Bastick, who looked as if he were about to spring from the ground and choke out the man's life. "I'll give you to the count of five to get up and run back to the cage you crawled out of this morning, or you'll never get up again."

Bastick was being confronted. The thing was a rarity. His body rebelled against his mind, and he remained crouched, internal battle raging.

"One."

"I'll have your life for this!" Bastick spat at Molnar, his bloodshot eyes berserk with rage.

"Two."

Bastick's body slowly rose from its crouch on the floor and stood. "I'll split your liver in two."

Molnar smirked. "Three."

Bastick turned and stamped across the room, turning at the door.

"Four."

"What's your name?" Bastick shouted.

"Five," said Molnar and, without raising the gun from his hip, shot Bastick. The ogre cried out and fled the room. Even lions run when wounded.

"Quick trip to the hospital," said Molnar, looking down at Cardiff for a reaction. But the man's eyes were no longer focusing. They were soft, and his mouth was twitching from final nerves. White froth collected at the corners. Molnar threw the blanket over the man's face and leapt out the open window. It was only one story up. Molnar landed softly in the grass at the side of the hospital and turned toward his waiting car.

Something on the ground caught his eye, and he reached down to pick up Pierre Cardiff's still-smoldering cigar. It wasn't the first time he'd shared a smoke with a dead man.

"The fiend shot me!" said Bastick to the nurse who was wrapping up his shoulder. He was not in the Épernay hospital anymore; he was in a cell with barred windows and standing drops of moisture on its stone block walls. "I can't believe that he would shoot an officer of the law." The prison nurse nodded at him as she tried to wrap the last turn of the bandage. "The sharp shot of pain. The smell of my blood. They were ..."

"Traumatic?" she offered.

"Exhilarating," said Bastick, wide-eyed, looking at her. "I've never been shot," he added. "Even in the war."

She shook her head at him.

As his awe passed, he gritted his teeth in rage, remembering how he'd sensed the direction of the bullet and tried to dodge, but it had been so fast. He'd felt the power of the bullet try to spin him as he darted out. He'd run halfway down the hall, the rust-colored smell of his own blood overwhelming his senses. And then the instinct of flight had succumbed to concern for his arm. He'd looked at it. The bullet had only pierced the outer deltoid muscle and missed the bone. Realizing as much, Bastick had bellowed at himself in rage and rushed back to the room, only to find the gray man gone and the patient dead. He'd grabbed the body and pounded on the chest with his good arm to try and restore enough life to get a word. Just one word. Meanwhile, he was bleeding on the corpse with his injured arm. As he was thus engaged, a male nurse had seen the scene and called several others to convince Bastick to stop.

After throwing the nurses about the room, Bastick had tried to explain why he was there—that he'd been shot by an intruder, that the patient had died of natural causes. But the panting men didn't seem to hear, and once a quorum of a dozen white-coated bodies was reached, the nurses rushed the monster and wrestled him into a straightjacket.

Now, Bastick sat in this dark cell, waiting for the warden to get through to his superior officer at the Gestapo to vouch for his actions.

"You're not badly hurt, detective," the nurse said. "You'll be fit as a Frankfurter soon enough."

"My wedding is this Saturday," said Bastick, mostly to himself.

"Oh really?" The nurse perked up the way women do at the mention of one of their kind attaining a new and sought-after way of life. They reappraise the man and their faces seem to say: *So you were worthy of one of us?* Their mouths ask details: "Where?"

"In Hamburg, where my mother's family is from," he said. "My fiancée has no family left. They all died in the war."

"I'm sorry to hear that," the nurse said. "Hamburg will be beautiful."

———

It was Thursday afternoon, and Molnar was standing in a large church in eastern France and staring at the stage, where twenty human skeletons hung by stockyard hooks laced through spine and ribcage. The bones were clean and white, and every set had a label with a number tied to the third rib on the left.

"Do you ever get the feeling you're witnessing one of the truly horrific pieces of human history? That people will be counting these corpses and inscribing these names on plaques in a far-off and future world forever marred by these events?" Molnar looked down at a Wire Fox Terrier sitting beside him.

The dog cocked its brown head against its all-white body. Its little white mustache sniffed the air. The dog then seemed to nod and look down sorrowfully.

"Me too."

The door in the back of the church opened with a creak. "Ah, my dear Professor Molnar!" said Dr. Lothar Fleischhacker. His lanky body carried a blond, boyish haircut, which framed a youthful face. All of which lurched toward Molnar. "Welcome to Natzwiller Church! Thank you for requesting to view part of our collection. No one seems to have the time nowadays, especially psychologists!"

Molnar nodded at him, and the doctor noticed the dog. "Max just loves our experiments, don't you, Max?" He rubbed the dog's head. It stood at dutiful attention. "You see, Professor Molnar, there are important collections of skulls of nearly all the races and peoples. Except for the Jews, of which science has so few skulls, so it is not possible to draw any meaningful inferences. The war will hopefully give us the opportunity to acquire a tangible scientific document by procuring the skulls of Jewish-Bolsheviks who embody the unappetizing but characteristic subhuman."

"I see," said Molnar. He and Max made eye contact for a moment before he followed Dr. Fleischhacker down the rows of pews and then up the few black side stairs to the stage. The doctor removed large metal calipers like thin-rounded lobster pincers and approached a skeleton. "We don't have many of the Bolsheviks yet, but hopefully we'll get some." He took a measurement from the bottom to the top of the eye socket. "To be honest, we haven't found much difference in the western Jews and French skulls. I posit we need to explore the eastern peoples."

Molnar leaned in close to the doctor and looked at the number on the calipers. "What do you hope to find?"

"Hard evidence of the evolution of species, of course," said the doctor, looking at Molnar as if he'd asked him the color of grass. "Evidence for the evolution of mankind, to be exact."

"Exemplified in the size and shape of the human skull?"

"Between the *übermenschen* and *untermenschen*," said the doctor, looking at Molnar as if he needed to bring him up to scientific speed. "Natural selection?"

"I see," said Molnar.

"Do you?" asked the doctor. "Many people don't. If we can demonstrate through the size and shape of the brain the order of the racial evolution of man, we can help guide that evolution—creating the true übermensch." As the doctor said this, his passion was emphasized by his bouncing golden locks.

"What if you find no difference in intelligence between races?"

The doctor hid his eyebrows behind his bangs.

"To play the devil's advocate," said Molnar. "Look at the '36 Olympics. We Hungarians did pretty well, and so did Germany—but look at Jesse Owens."

"You said intelligence, not physical capacity, my dear professor! It's all made quite obvious by the decisions of societies of varying races. Which are more advanced? Which are locked in constant civil wars? Which seem unable to claw their way out of primitive life?"

Molnar perused the skeleton forest as the doctor continued. Bright stage lights made the bones stand out in stark contrast against the heavy black stage curtain behind them. Their shadows added a horror-show effect to the stage floor, casting unnatural shapes—angles of light and darkness that should never be seen.

"The more advanced races and cultures are more capable of satisfying the basic human needs in life," said Fleischhacker. "The less-evolved races aren't. It's that simple."

"Don't you think it's possible that all races evolve intellectually at the same rate?"

"How would that be logical, Professor Molnar?" asked Fleischhacker, turning to the detective and letting his long, caliper-gripping arm fall to his side. "If all species evolve based on survival of the fittest, then by virtue of natural, geographical, and societal challenges and constraints, one region of the world must evolve at a quicker mental clip. Especially if the majority of that people group stay in that location. Even one society or country will outpace another. Many modern Western societies are already undermining evolutionary advancement by allowing all humans to reproduce. That's why we're carrying out sterilization of the mentally retarded. Is it not obvious?" Fleischhacker pivoted a step and turned his palms to the ceiling. "This is the mental dishonesty I don't understand about many Western societies. You can't have your evolutionary cake and eat it too! They don't think through to the logical conclusion."

"Maybe because it all sounds so ugly."

The double doors of the church bounced open and a very short, bald man in shirtsleeves and a waistcoat entered, dragging an even smaller, limp body through the door and down the few stairs that descended into the sanctuary. The shoed heels of the body knocked against the wood with each step. The head lolled. The bald man pulled the body to Fleischhacker's feet, like a dog with a duck, and dropped the torso and head with a thud onto the wooden stage.

"Life's not pretty," said Fleischhacker, allowing his smile to crescendo into a climax of condescension. It was a secret face only taught to those thoroughly tenured in the halls of tertiary education.

"Neither is Death," said Molnar. Fleischhacker saw Molnar's eyes look up beside him as if there were another person standing at his side. But there was no one there.

"A fresh one, doctor," said the little man, looking up at the two men to see if he was interrupting.

"Good work, Remus," said the doctor. "You see how physically sub-par specimens like Remus can prove useful when sterilized?" he asked Molnar.

Remus was silent.

"His undersized body hides a sharp mind," said the doctor, patting Remus's head.

The doctor knelt and began measurements of the face and cranium. The figure was of a small, hatless boy with dark hair and pale skin. His eye sockets were sunken in from what looked to be malnutrition. His clothing was old and worn. "Where is the Jew from?"

"Romania."

"Yes! We're moving further east," said the doctor in a fit of excitement, looking up at Molnar. "I can tell by his temples. This may be a good addition to—"

The boy's body convulsed in a cough and then resumed its limp form. The doctor turned to the little man, who shrank away in fear.

"I thought he was dead! I checked his pulse," said the wide-eyed Remus.

"Don't fret," said the doctor, removing a syringe from the long pockets of his white frock and plunging it into the boy's neck. Molnar lunged toward him, but the doctor depressed the plunger, and the syringe returned to his pocket before Molnar could reach him. "This specimen is too good to let go," muttered the doctor to himself. He looked up at Molnar's hand, now gripping his shoulder. "My dear professor, I treat every specimen with respect, just as I do my collection of butterflies. They are important, unique, and they must be kept intact."

The boy's mouth opened, releasing a final breath and staying ajar.

Molnar released the man, removed a cigar, snipped, and lit. His hands weren't shaking, but they weren't steady.

"Do you enjoy wine, doctor?" he asked.

———

That evening, Molnar and Fleischhacker sat at a circular marble table. The room was bright, the floor was pink marble, and the roaring fireplace retained a bone-white façade from the dedicated attention of the cleaning staff. Overly rich German and French couples sat at similar tables set in a doily-shaped pattern. Waiters wearing waistcoats wove in and out of the doily, placing bits of color here and there as they moved, splashing the yellows and reds of appetizers and entrees onto the all-white tablecloths.

"No, I don't like wine, professor, to answer your question," said Fleischhacker, brushing his blond hair behind his ear. He reached into a bag at his feet. "But I brought along one that was a gift from the mutual friend that you mentioned: Riffel. It just came in this week. It's"—he squinted at the label—"Pie-knot No-ear or something such. I wouldn't know." He spun the bottle's white label and feminine puckered mouth toward Molnar. "Maybe you'll make better use of it."

"It looks delicious, but I don't want to drink alone."

"Well." The man made a disgusted face, flaring his nostrils with an abandon available only to those incapable of hiding emotion. "I'll have a small glass if you will."

"Deal," said Molnar, waving for the waiter.

The waiter had just entered the kitchen and received a rejected chicken roast. He had taken only one bite before coming back out to bring a peppermill to a large woman wearing too much fur. That his chicken was in the kitchen cooling—the streams of steam thinning—was forefront in the waiter's mind. But with the professional fortitude of a circus performer, he took the bottle from the men and began a flagrant, over-accentuated dance of his simple task: un-corkery.

His face disturbed Molnar. The pale skin and dark strands of hair reminded him of the dead child from a few hours prior.

"Do you wish to continue our conversation about natural selection?" asked Fleischhacker. "You seemed shaken in the amphitheater. I don't mean to encroach on your understanding of mankind."

"I don't know." Molnar pulled his gaze from the waiter and stabbed it into the doctor. "I always thought it made sense that diet, lifestyle, and environment were what formed us into different colors and shapes."

"Yes. That's true. And it's those same influences and others that give us varying IQs," said the doctor. His Husky-blue eyes watched the boy flay the aluminum neck wrapper up the center and peel it back like he was skinning a mouse. "Enough high IQs bred together produce higher IQs; more intellect, larger frontal lobes; and smarter humans. Some races are already woefully behind our own, Molnar. I didn't make nature do this; I'm just the observer."

The doctor shrugged and smiled the smile of intellectual pity at Molnar, a being not yet ready to allow the full, terrible truth of reality into the delicate oyster flesh of his mind. The smile said: "I understand that you can't release your grasp on emotions long enough to work from a place of honest and ruthless logic, but *we've* done so. We call it science, and we're acting upon it."

The long man unfolded his appendages, spider-like, and capped the conversation. "If you don't like the messy side of evolution, there are other theories on the development of man out there. Germany is just sold on this one."

The waiter was finally through, and he presented the cork, resting on his fingertips, to the doctor, who smelled it and made a face. Despite the grimace, he nodded at the glass. The young man poured the wine, and the doctor sniffed it and kept his nostrils flared. "I don't know, there's a strangely familiar smell about the bottle that reminds me of my work, but ... I can't put my nostrils to it." He looked at the liquid as if it were an affront to his diploma. "Professor." He looked at Molnar. "Would you prefer to test it?"

"I'm no wine expert, Fleischhacker. It's your gift."

"I think it smells distasteful." The young waiter was still standing there, awaiting the sign that he could flee back to the kitchen to finish his fast-cooling chicken. The idea swelled in the back of his mind as this lanky man pussyfooted with the wine. The waiter inched backward and was about to turn and leave when Fleischhacker leaned toward Molnar. "Maybe we should just have some beer and toss this trash into the garbage. Or you can drink it." A long finger went up to keep the retreating boy near as the decision was reached.

"I thought you said you'd have one with me."

"Well, now I don't want it." The Husky eyes looked to the boy. "Bring us two glasses of beer and take this away."

The boy delicately pinched the glass and bottle and moved toward the kitchen, to add a free drink to his free—if cooling—dinner.

"Wait a minute," said Molnar, but the waiter was just far enough through the doily-pattern maze that he could feign bad hearing.

Molnar looked at the professor, and the man shrugged. "Life is too short to drink wine," he said, and laughed the loud gasp of a laugh he reserved for his own quips.

The boy sat at a small wooden stool in the alley behind the kitchen. The bottle of wine was on the ground by his ankle, and Fleischhacker's glass on a small wooden table in front of him. He hovered his hand over the chicken and smiled. Then he took a bite and lifted the glass to his lips to let some of the liquid into his mouth to start digesting the protein in the meat, changing the flavor and adding depth. But just as the rim touched his lips, the door behind him burst open, almost hitting his arm. Molnar entered to the shout of a prep boy whose pumpkin soup he'd upended.

"Hey!" Molnar yelled down at the startled young man, who dropped the glass from his mouth. Molnar grabbed the glass and threw it into the street. Then he saw the bottle and did the same with that. The waiter looked at him, stunned, as did the prep boy who followed him out.

"Did you drink any?"

"No—no."

"Good." Molnar thumbed a thumb at the pile of glass and liquid. "Bad wine." He looked at both young men but added no more. Then he turned back into the kitchen and tipped his hat at the angry chef. At the front of the kitchen, he told a waiter to send a bottle of beer back to the kid in the alley and put it on the doctor's tab.

"I was wondering when you'd return," said Fleischhacker. "You surely are an enigma, leaping from the table. I'm so glad you're here! You must come and really see my work at Natzweiler-Struthof. We've much to talk about. Just tell the guards I sent for you."

Molnar took his seat, and beer was served. He ordered champagne for himself and sat back to endure the rest of the doctor's thoughts while he silently devised a new way of killing the man.

———

A few hours later, Molnar was lying on the folded comforter of a hotel bed in Natzwiller with his jacket and shoes still on. He was staring at the ceiling. Without moving his head, he lifted his wristwatch into his field of vision. It was getting late.

His fingers played a drumbeat on his chest and then crawled their way into his breast pocket. They felt something and pulled it out.

The letter.

He stared at his wife's handwriting. He remembered pieces of a once-happy life.

His first peer-reviewed paper for *Psychological Bulletin* had been published. It had been acclaimed, even, and he had done a few interviews with a few disinterested journalists and had given a few speeches to a few interested psychologists. Several papers later, he was working on a book. And his wife had a second heartbeat.

Her hair was blonde and her face soft and easy on the eyes. Molnar had thought of that saying, "easy on the eyes," when he'd first seen her, and it had made his mind churn. He wondered if it was literally possible that the eyes could relax more when locked onto a soft-textured surface than a hard one—just as some colors were more restful for the eyes. But could a woman's cheeks do even more? Would their viewing rejuvenate the souls of men at war? Molnar'd believed it was a good hypothesis, but wasn't able to come up with a proper theory about it, so he'd crossed the dancehall and started talking with her.

The conversation would've furthered his theory, except that he'd forgotten all about that by then.

It wasn't two weeks before the two of them were married and wasn't two years before she was pregnant. Molnar had been happy. Though the country was plunged into war and he'd been called to serve as a clinical psychologist for the men at the front, he'd counted it all joy. He'd returned to see his wife every chance he got.

The phone in his hotel rang, shaking Molnar from his thoughts. He crossed to get it.

"I hope it's not too late, Dr. Molnar, but your coat is here from the cleaners. They rushed it, like you asked."

"Thanks."

He hung up and stared at the phone, resting there on its generic brown hotel desk. It looked so lazy he wanted to give it a job. Besides, his wife was gone. He put the letter back into his pocket and thought of another blonde with a face that calmed his eyes.

He reached for the phone.

———

Against all odds, and resulting in many disappointed Berliners, Marilyn's figure lay like an abandoned hourglass on her couch at home on Thursday night ... alone. Swing music emanated from her phonograph player, and her hand held a bottle of whiskey beside her rounded hip. The other hand hung from the couch, wrapped around a spray bottle of soda water that rested on the carpet. Without moving her form, she sprayed the soda in her mouth with one hand and added a shot of whiskey with the other. She let this mix around before swallowing it.

The phone rang with a jarring rattle. Marilyn slowly put her instruments down and moved to it, lifted the receiver with a flick of her delicate wrist. "Feel lucky. You caught me."

"Marilyn, this is Mads. Did I interfere with your beauty nap?"

"Mads ... Mads. I can't for the very life of me recall a Mads," she said, stretching the phone cord to the couch and lying down. "I've heard of a dashing sleuth who fills women with champagne and dissolves into the night. But he's Mr. Molnar. He's out fighting crime. Who is this?"

"You have such a way with words. It's a true blessing," said Molnar, adjusting the phone.

"Thank my mother."

"Everyone should thank your mother. My secretary said you called. She didn't say why, but that there were tears."

"What do I have to cry about? I'm engaged to a man who wants to marry me on Saturday. He also wants to roast my liver. I'm not sure which he wants more."

"Which bothers you most?" asked Mads, picking at the cheap wood of the hotel desk.

"Is this my heart or my liver talking?"

"Whichever's less calcified."

"They're both charred, but the liver's had it worse," she said, glancing down at the bottle and cringing.

"My advice is an iron girdle," said Molnar, leaning back in his chair. "If it's big enough, it'll solve one problem and complicate the other. Or maybe it won't do anything about the other—I need to brush up on my anatomy."

She giggled. "Aren't you going to come and stop me? My heart and my liver will thank you."

Molnar leaned further back in his chair and smiled up at the ceiling. "What about the rest of you?"

"We'll see about the rest of me."

"There's important work here—kids to save, wine to drink."

"But you have to ask yourself," Marilyn said, smiling her devilish smile at her own reflection in the dressing-table mirror, remembering the mantle of power she'd been given at birth. "What's more important to you? You're a psychologist."

Molnar was silent for a moment. He rubbed the top of his head, messing up his thick, dark hair. "'Should I marry this man?'" said Molnar. "When I was growing up, these were the sorts of decisions that women made on their own—or they consulted a daisy. 'Does he love me? Does he not?' They didn't ask the private eye."

"I'm supposed to marry him. But you need to come and convince me that I'm wrong. Besides, the party is going to be outrageous."

Molnar'd played these games before, and his face said so. "I must regretfully decline, my dear," he said. It took guts, but he had guts.

"I didn't become Marilyn Ghetz by letting men decline. Or by begging. Your secretary has the address." She twirled a piece of her hair around her finger and watched the golden curls twist round and round. Little perfect threads of gold popped up one by one as her finger reached the ends of individual strands. "Oh, and there's an open bar. We'll even have your favorite wine." Before he could say anything else, she added, "Toodaloo!" and rang off.

Molnar hung up the phone and looked up at his own desk mirror and his own blue eyes, shaking his head at himself. "She's a bad girl, Mads."

The bad girl was back on the couch, doing her mouth-mixing routine. A new record was playing in the background.

———

Newly washed coat and shoes on, Molnar lay on the bed and stared at the ceiling. He looked down at his feet and remembered the dead kid's shoes. He remembered how small they'd been. And, as he once again felt the outline of his wife's letter in his pocket, he remembered... .

"Terrible," she had said, shaking her head and staring down at the Sunday paper.

"What?" Molnar'd asked. They'd just finished dinner, and he was nursing a brandy.

"An altar boy stole from the church. They let him take up the offering every week for years. He was just a kid then. Now, an old man, he's confessed." She kept shaking her head at the paper. "No one is good."

"What's that supposed to mean?"

"You're not good. I'm not good. None of us is good." She said it emphatically, laying the paper down on the table.

"Everyone is good in his own mind."

"You told me that's just a self-protection mechanism."

He smiled at her. It was a time when it was easier to smile. "Yeah. We don't want to live with the admittance of our faults. Sometimes, we change memories."

Her angel face formed temporary grooves between her eyes, trying hard to wrinkle. She pointed at her belly. "He's good."

"It's a he?"

"He kicks that way," she said, smiling and looking down at her belly.

"Yes. He's good. For now."

She reached over and slapped the top of Molnar's head. "We need to keep him good," she said. "They don't stay good unless you protect them."

He laughed at her concerned face. She was too young to make that expression. She was almost a kid herself.

His wife moved behind him, put her hands on his shoulders, and leaned close to his ear. She breathed warm breath on his neck. "Promise you'll protect him? Promise you'll protect all of our kids."

"OK." He held his right hand up, à la Scout's honor. "I do hereby vow." He laughed and took another drink.

Back in the purgatory of now, in his cardboard-colored room, Molnar remembered the dead kid's face with its open mouth. His scalp broke out in goosebumps, and he got up and walked out the door.

Soon, he was sitting in a dark cab. There was no moon. The cab's ally-yellow headlights cut two circles ahead of them in the blackness as the car moved down the road. Molnar was glad of the dark. When a streetlight passed, he tried to keep it off him as if it'd singe his flesh. Molnar felt the presence of Death sitting beside him, equally adept at avoiding the light.

"Dark men do dark jobs."

"How's that?" asked the cabbie, who chewed on a stubby cigar in the side of his mouth, trying not to look like Porky Pig.

But Death had heard Molnar just fine. "I've never understood men's feigned revulsion of our work."

"Our work?" asked Molnar.

Death grinned. "Yes. Glad to have you back." Molnar wondered how Death formed sibilant sounds without any cheeks.

"I'm sure you keep busy."

"Fella," said the cabbie. "I can't hear what you're sayin'. You gotta speak up."

"It's high season," said Death. Molnar could hardly make out his face. He did a better job than Molnar of avoiding light; his face seemed to eat it. "But I enjoy working with you. You amuse me."

"Speak for yourself," said Molnar. "Think I'll make it out of this thing alive?"

"Chances are slim."

Molnar stared at the sheen off Death's skull. "We had some close scrapes."

"Speaking of which, I wouldn't stay in this car if I were you."

There was a long pause in which Molnar stared at the back of the seat in front of him. "You're trying to scare me," he said.

"Maybe I just want to keep you around a little while longer."

The cabbie didn't say anything more, but Molnar saw his eyebrows in the rearview mirror. They were doing the dance of concern.

"Just keep it straight, cabbie," said Molnar. "I'm only talking to myself."

After a few minutes, the cab pulled up to the entrance of what looked like a prison. Lines of barbed wire glinted in the light of a single bulb at the front of the guard station.

The bulb flickered on and off, casting light onto the wire wall, making the metal go from matte to sheen to matte. A wooden sign above the gate read, "Natzweiler-Struthof."

The guard leaned out to talk with Molnar in the back seat. Molnar held up his Gestapo disc. "I've got an appointment with the doc."

"Oh, official business, I see." The man looked at his watch. "He's still in there. He was excited about something. He almost dropped his badge in his rush. First building on the left."

Molnar nodded at the guard, who waved at the others to open the gate. The whole compound looked recently and hastily built: fir logs hewn from the surroundings and stitched together with chicken wire, barbed wire, and nails.

They drove down a dirt road naturally formed in the grass by repeated use.

"This gives me the creeps, Mister," said the cabbie. He looked back at Molnar as if a thought had crossed his mind. "Hope you don't mind me saying."

Molnar ignored this. "Pull up to this first building." In the middle of a large brown field stood a brown wooden cabin in the chalet style. It stuck out from the slightly inclined hillside like a broken nose. Further up the hill stood a long row of fenced-in wooden houses slapped together without insulation. The only decoration was the geometric shapes that the white-dirt paths cut into the brown and green hillside, but it was too dark to see all that. The cabbie pulled up in front of the building.

"I need you to wait here in the car for me," Molnar said.

"Well, I'd like to, but I have to—"

"I'm not asking." Molnar held up his Gestapo badge.

"If you put it that way," said the cabbie, chewing harder on his cigar.

"I do. And turn around so you're facing the gate."

The man looked at Molnar a second time but did what he said. Molnar pulled his trick of taking the keys just in case the cabbie got a bright idea. The cabbie made the usual noises and faces at this, but a dark look from the man who talks with Death shut him up.

"I won't be long."

As Molnar walked toward the little house, the cabbie rubbed his eyes. He thought for a second that the man was holding a scythe. When he looked again, Molnar had disappeared into the house.

The cabbie removed a shiny metal flask from his breast pocket and drank from it for several seconds before getting back to his cigar chewing.

Molnar entered the house without knocking. It was pitch black, and he moved silently through to a wooden hallway. There was a weak white light shining through a crack in a wooden door far down the hall at the back of the building. The light cut a long white line toward Molnar's feet. He moved on his tiptoes down the hall and avoided the light like a kid avoiding cracks in a sidewalk.

A giggling came through the door, along with the clacking of two feet.

Molnar was at the door now, and saw the lanky, spectral form of Fleischhacker throwing long shadows around the room in a hopping, un-gainly dance. Fleischhacker tapped around a table with glee. The table had a young, dark-haired girl on it. She was strapped in with leather wrist and ankle bands. A single bulb cast strange lighting on her swarthy face. She was a Roma, a gypsy, probably 10 or 11. At the foot of the table, between the girl's tied ankles, was a hole leading to a bucket beneath. Rivulets in the table led to the hole, like a grill that has a runoff for grease. There was a full syringe and a string of tools on a stainless-steel table beside her.

Molnar walked into the room and stared at the pair. It was total horror, but Molnar's face said he was at an art show. Fleischhacker looked up at him with a start. Then he smiled at the look of interest from the detective.

"Couldn't stay away, could you, professor? I know how you feel. We had such a compelling conversation at dinner. My mind kept spinning afterward. I realized that I was put on Earth for such a time as this. It's so rare that while you're working, you know you're making scientific history."

Molnar stood, staring.

"It was the boy today that made me realize I've been doing it wrong. I'm in a unique position." The doctor moved toward Molnar in his excitement. As he got close, drops of sweat running down his youthful face became apparent. "For the first time in human history, we have access to everything we need to improve our race." He was very close to Molnar now, and he put his hands on the detective's shoulders. Molnar stared at him. "Who knows how long we'll have to finish our work?"

"What'd the kid make you realize, Fleischhacker?"

"I must be proactive. I've been waiting ... waiting." Fleischhacker bobbed his head as if he were looking at a clock over Molnar, watching the minute hand. "Hoping some of my favorite specimens will die in this work camp so I can do my own work." He combed long fingers through blond hair. "I've had my eye on little Miss 98840 for months now. Look at her!" He rushed to the far side of the table and put his hands on the side. He leaned close to the girl's face, a drop of his sweat falling from the tip of his nose to the tip of hers. She whimpered, but her mouth was gagged, so not much sound got out. "Her undersized temples"—he pointed with an index finger as if it were a pin and he was giving a Lepidoptera presentation—"and her brow. The boy made me realize that I don't have time to wait, Molnar! The guards don't care. You think the guards care? They didn't care if I worked with her or not. They just shrugged when I asked. And you're here, Molnar, for the final moments of light in her dull and simple eyes."

"What's the best way of ending her life?"

"The serum, of course," said the doctor, as if Molnar were back to his stupid questions again. He picked up the full syringe, a shining, clear drop hanging at the end. "It's what I used on the boy. The bones must be intact, you see."

Molnar moved up to the side of the doctor and looked down at the girl. Her large brown eyes pleaded, and their water freely spilled down the young, sunken cheeks. Molnar leaned to her ear and whispered something.

The doctor looked at him when he righted himself. "Oh, don't do that. Don't bond with them. Don't communicate. Even if they aren't the same level of human, it may haunt you."

"I doubt it," said Molnar.

"What did you tell her?"

Molnar took the syringe and the elongated man's ten fingers in both of his own hard hands and squatted down lightly before springing up, quickly and deftly shoving the long syringe vertically into the soft flesh of the doctor's neck under the jawbone. Molnar's rage-fueled strength was so great that the syringe disappeared entirely, and the plunger depressed to the hilt.

The doctor stared wide-eyed at Molnar and took a step back. He bled down his white frock and tried to gurgle a sound or two from his punctured windpipe, punctured nasal passages, punctured eye, punctured frontal lobe. Molnar stared at the man as his face sprouted a new, thicker, red sweat, and he slowly dropped to his knees.

"Natural selection, doctor."

The doctor's body resumed a non-rhythmic dance similar to what it had been doing when Molnar had walked in. But now he was lying down for it.

Molnar put his finger to his lips and looked at the girl. He spoke in German and then French, telling her it was OK and not to make a sound and that he was there to help. She nodded. The tears had stopped. He'd undone three of her brown-leather straps when the door behind him creaked.

Remus gaped at the now-still body of Fleischhacker. He looked up at Molnar, and then he ran from the room, howling. Molnar undid the last strap and turned to chase the figure. "Follow me!" he yelled at the girl, who did so.

Remus was wailing like a dog that hears a siren and running for the front door. Molnar sprinted after him down the hall. The little man's hand was reaching for the doorknob when Molnar grabbed his shoulder and yanked him around. His body spun toward Molnar. With horror-filled eyes, Remus shrieked, "What did you do to him?"

Molnar pulled the man back down the hallway, past the girl, and toward the grisly scene. Once back in the room, Molnar looked down at the bald man. "Why did you help him?" he demanded.

"I was only following orders."

Molnar shook his head. "Here's one more." Molnar pulled his revolver out, and the little man cowered. "Go and take that syringe out of his neck."

Remus obeyed and stared up at Molnar, hands covered in the blood of his master.

Molnar tipped his hat, closed the door, and bolted it from the outside.

The wailing came back, but it was muffled by the door. Molnar smiled at the girl. She looked at the closed door, heard the wailing, and took

Molnar's hand. His eyebrows went up, but he kept walking. The two of them entered the cab, and Molnar handed the driver his keys.

When the cabbie saw the girl, he stopped chewing. The brown stick of tobacco in his teeth looked more like mashed potatoes than a cigar by that point. "Who's that?"

"When did you start asking questions?" asked Molnar, waving the revolver at him. "Tut-tut." He gestured for the man to start driving. "Now, you get down," he told the girl, and she shrank into a ball and climbed behind the driver's seat. Molnar threw his jacket over her, and the guards didn't even glance into the car as they drove through.

Molnar told the girl she could get up. As they drove off, she looked out the window. Despite the cold air, she rolled it down and filled her lungs. A sudden rush of emotions sent tingles through her face and made the moon swim in her vision.

BOTTLE VIII

Molnar didn't usually drink during the day. And he didn't usually choose rye. He'd tried to drink only champagne since the first war. But today, at noon, he sat in a French café in Strasbourg and sipped rye and stared across the table at the 11-year-old gypsy as she consumed too much food.

"Are your parents in the camp?"

The girl didn't look up or signal that he'd made a noise. She'd gone through soup, salad, and half of a baguette. He tried another language with the same result.

This wasn't how he'd foreseen his Friday afternoon. He looked at his map and the location of the next bottle. Munich. On the way to Berlin. He took another sip of rye and carried it with him into the café, to protect it from the ravenous child. He moved to the phone box opposite the blinding sheen of the café bar, with its chrome espresso machine and wall-length mirror. He sat by the phone and told the operator the number. It took a few minutes to get through to Berlin.

"Riffel," said Riffel, sitting at lunch in his parlor. When there wasn't an immediate response on the other line, he repeated, "Riffel!...Riffel!"

Charles stood in the background, holding his serving napkin and a platter covered by a silver cloche. He waited for a signal. This was how Riffel insisted on enjoying his lunch.

"It's Molnar. I have two more bottles. That's seven down."

"Oh, thank *Gott* you're still on the case. I was starting to lose hope." Riffel vigorously waved Charles over, as if he should have already known to come. Charles set the man's place at the table with care. Riffel leaned his chin back as a sign, and Charles complied by tucking the man's white napkin into his shirt collar. "Have you destroyed all of the evidence linking these to me, Molnar?"

"Mmm-hmm."

"The bottles are gone?"

"Mmm-hmm."

"And the notes?"

"Mmm-hmm."

"So where are you?"

"I'm nearly at the French border," said Molnar, taking a sip of rye.

"You mean the ex-French border."

"Yes."

"Where are you off to next? I must have this all put behind me, Molnar. It's in your own best interest to be fast. That is, if you're still thinking of Sweden." Charles pulled the lid from Riffel's tray, revealing sausage, sauerkraut, and potatoes. Riffel began forking the three into his mouth in combination.

"Munich next. Then it's up to Hamburg. But there's something else. When I was in Épernay, I ran into a man. A real gorilla who called himself Detective Bastick. He was after the bottle. Did you hire another PI?"

A half-chewed sausage fell from Riffel's mouth onto the silver platter and made a splattering thud on the edge of his plate. Charles's eyes closed, and his mouth twitched but didn't smile.

Molnar waited, but there was no answer. "Because I shot him."

Riffel started breathing again. "Is he dead?"

"I just winged him to teach him how to hear," said Molnar, leaning over to take a peek out the window and check on the girl. She was trying to see how full she could get her mouth.

"So he's not dead?" Riffel gasped.

"Not unless Germans store their kidneys in their shoulders."

"You must kill him!" Riffel pounded the table with his hand, and its contents jiggled.

"So, you didn't put him on the case?"

"No." Riffel's eyes stared up to the ceiling as if remembering something. Sweat stood on his forehead. "I have to go."

The line went dead. Molnar hung up the phone and went back outside. He sat down across from the girl, who was still hard at it. "You almost finished?"

She ate the last crumb of her baguette and looked up at him, smiling, with her mouth full. Then she pointed at the menu.

"No more. You'll get sick."

Her face pouted.

"Sorry, it's for your own good. Let's get out of here. We still have work to do."

Molnar might not have admitted it, but it wouldn't be a stretch to say she looked like his daughter. They had the same skin tone and hair, though his eyes were blue. He paid the bill and stood, waiting for her to get up. She did so, walked over to him, and took his index finger in her hand. He looked down at her and shook his head, but she didn't let go. They walked together toward another waiting cab.

Meanwhile, Colonel Riffel sat in stunned silence at his lunch table. A tiny chewed-off chunk of potato rested in the center of his lip, shaded by his nose, clinging to the follicles of his dense mustache. The potato was peppered with green bits of dill and would look quite appetizing in a different locale.

Morning papers surrounded Riffel's table. He'd been scanning the headlines of four popular European newspapers every morning since the bottles had gone out.

One article read:

"Wolfram Bastick, the Gestapo's premier detective, investigates his father's death. 'He was poisoned!' Bastick told our reporter, but refused further comment."

"Wolfram," muttered Riffel. His eyes were pinned to the ceiling, and his napkin was pinned under his collar, but his mind wasn't so securely fastened. It floated into the past, carrying him back to a Bavarian beer hall 20 years prior, where he'd been drinking with Bastick's father: Troy.

The long tables and benches in the room had been made of rough-hewn wood, replete with notches and imperfections. The tables had held heavy glass mugs of heavy German beer. The benches held heavy ex-officers from the first war. Many were missing some bit of appendage, so their sleeve or pants leg hung loose at unnatural points. Some were missing eyes.

The too-few lights hanging from the ceiling made it look like a meeting of pirates. But these pirates hadn't found any treasure. They'd only survived horrors to end up here: disillusioned and reparations-poor.

So they nursed the mental wounds of destroyed honor. They'd grown up playing soldier, and all rules of sportsmanship they'd learned lay shriveled and twitching on the field of modern warfare. War was no longer a gentleman's game of Bridge. It was the torture of the soul. It was a new psychological torment not known before the trenches and mortars and months of stalemate suffering in literal blood pudding abodes where every moment could contain a whistle in the air that spelled your death, or worse, maiming. Maybe war always had been this bad but they'd been looking from a different angle.

And now, all these men sat in a room. They'd lost battles and friends and legs, but more preciously, they'd lost the unwritten code they knew. So they drank and joked and tried to redraw life. Some managed to make rough sketches, and some kept drawing and erasing, drawing and erasing.

A younger version of Riffel, with thicker hair, sat beside Troy Bastick. They clinked their glasses together and drank off their Dunkel beer. Riffel saw Troy's son, Wolfram Bastick, sitting on another bench at a table full of officers of his own rank. Riffel couldn't later remember why he asked it, but he did. "How did your son make out?"

Troy took another drink before putting down the mug. "Wolfram's alive!" He shrugged, waving at the boy across the hall. "So am I. Thank *Gott*. You know, he really was special. Peculiar, yes, but evolved. He was the *übermensch*, truly." And then he leaned across to Riffel. "But his mind"— he shook his head—"is different."

"So is mine," laughed Riffel.

Troy didn't laugh. He looked across the table at his son, sitting alone amongst dozens of men. No beer in his hands. No light in his eyes. "He was on the front lines of Verdun for months. He got stranded."

Riffel thought he understood what this meant: months of mud and standing on the corpses of your friends and using your helmet as a latrine and living in constant fear. And then there were the rats.

But he didn't understand.

Riffel looked at Wolfram Bastick: powerful shoulders sunken, eyes locked on some non-existent point. A man beside Wolfram spilled beer on the table, and it cascaded onto Wolf's lap. Wolfram looked up for an apology, but the man drunkenly shouted a jeer at him and laughed. Wolf rose slowly from his seated position, and a light came back on in his eyes. He yanked the man from his seat, smashed him into the table. Using his own forehead like a mallet, Wolfram battered the man's face repeatedly and precisely until it began to change shape. The men around him finally found the capacity to move and tackled Wolfram to the ground.

Riffel remembered helping Troy pull enraged men off his son and seeing the two shades of blood on his face. One from Wolf's own bleeding nose—the other splashed across his face and smiling mouth. But it was his eyes that stuck in Riffel's mind. Wolf's eyes were cold and filled with an ecstasy that made Riffel look away.

Charles saw Riffel's face undergo the same contortions it had two decades prior. And even with the wedged bit of potato resting in Riffel's philtrum, the look scared Charles.

The assaulted man didn't die, but it still took some of Troy Bastick's political sway to keep Wolfram out of prison for the egregious assault. His detective badge had been suspended for several months, but it was returned. And there hadn't been such an incident since. But there were rumors. Rumors of a far worse encounter on the front lines.

A shiver ran down Riffel's body. He looked down at his lunch and, for the first time in years, considered not finishing it. The pause was long and painful. But then his arm began to move with the tenacity of habit, and he placed another bite of potato in his mouth.

———

They'd kept him overnight. How could he have been caught off guard? It must have been the lack of sleep. He thought about his not having a gun on him. Next time, he would be ready.

A hard-looking French guard walked in and stared, as if Bastick were a caged animal. The guard didn't get too close. "The Gestapo called and sprang you. Come along," said the man.

Bastick waited as the door opened. He moved past the guard and into a room with his effects. Then he pried his massive physique out of his prison garb and put on the blue suit he'd been wearing when he'd come in. He noticed his own blood still on the shoulder and checked his watch. He had a wedding to catch.

———

Mads Molnar and the little girl with the dark hair sat in the back of another taxi, this one driving through the streets of Munich. He saw her fingers rub the brown leather seat, feeling the ridges of the stitching with her tiny fingertips. She seemed to do it absentmindedly and hummed a tune that Molnar didn't recognize. "What are you singing?"

She kept humming but didn't say. The cab came to a halt, and Molnar climbed out. The girl started to follow him, but his dark hand kept her seated in the car. "You'll have to stay."

The humming stopped, and quiet tears instantly welled in the corners of her eyes.

"I'll be right back."

The tears spilled down, but he didn't crack. You had to be firm. He stood up straight and started to close the door on the adorable face. But as soon as he released her, she was out after him and standing at his side. Her eyes were going like faucets, and he shook his head and closed the door behind them both. "All right. But stay next to me. And don't talk so much."

She grabbed onto his finger again, and the streams stopped running. The two of them walked together down a cobblestone street, past ancient brick houses. Molnar saw the address he was looking for, and the two climbed up white stairs. Molnar grabbed a heavy brass knocker in the shape of Satan's head and rapped it against the black door that was thick enough to stop a tank.

A few moments later, an old man with an impressive and upturned mustache pried open the door. From the look on his face, it wasn't easy. And from the second look, it used to be.

"Are you General Fitzdorff?"

"That depends on who you are," said the old man, ruing the interruption. Then he looked down at the little girl, and his militant expression melted. "I see you at least have good taste in friends." He smiled and tried to pat the girl's head. She made like a rubber doll and bent away from his hand and behind Molnar, moving herself to his other side. It was a move most adults weren't able to pull, given societal norms. As if in rebuttal, the old man coughed a cough that'd make you wince. It looked like he didn't like doing it.

"And she's normally so friendly," Molnar murmured. "The name's Molnar, and you can call her whatever you'd like unless she says otherwise." They both looked at her for a response, and she closed her eyes but remained frozen. Molnar pulled out his wallet and produced his Gestapo ID disc. "I'm in town investigating a case in Munich."

The old man smiled and opened the door wide. "Well, why didn't you say so? Please come in." He opened the door to a dark oak hallway for which Molnar's yearly salary couldn't buy matching drapes. The little girl gawked at an intricate carving covering the arched entryway over their heads. On the left, it told a story of tragedy—a little girl taken out to sea by the tide. Her parents gnashing their teeth in the waves, trying to save her. On the right, it was all bliss—an adult woman with a fishtail, swimming around with her circle of mermaid friends and too-excited fish.

The little girl couldn't stop looking at it. *Death and Rebirth*, thought Molnar, as he pulled her along after the old man.

"We don't get too many visitors anymore."

"There's a lot going on out there."

"That's what I read," said Fitzdorff, over his shoulder. They entered a shiny parlor with gold and ivory for trim. In most homes, it'd be imitation; but Molnar's gut said this wasn't. Neither was the standing general's suit from the First World War in a glass case in the corner of the room. It was in good condition, minus a tear in the left shoulder. Molnar's eyes instinctively tried to match the tear to the old man's physique. Fitzdorff gestured to plush, cushy seats, and Molnar saw the sunken edge of his left deltoid muscle through the shirt, as if it'd been bitten off.

Molnar put the girl in one seat. Her head bobbed around, taking in the room. He also sat, and the old man collapsed into a third chair as soon as he did. His weak frame was still capable of its gentlemanly duties, but not without taxing his determination.

"So, how can I help you?" he asked, trying to cover another painful cough. Even with that show of physical weakness, his question had the military tenor that expected to be answered with quick efficiency.

Molnar sensed this and wished he'd have come up with a better cover story. He looked for a moment longer at the old man and sensed something honest about him. So he decided on the truth. "Someone sent you a bottle of wine from Alsace. A pinot noir ... a *Spätburgunder*."

The old man nodded.

"It's poisoned. The sender, Colonel Riffel, had no idea that it was, but he sent me to intercept the bottles."

The old man seemed at a loss for words. His eyebrows lifted, and his eyes followed them, looking to the adorned ceiling. The face said that he'd drunk the wine already and was now trying to figure out how much he cared about dying.

"How long do I have?"

"When did you drink it?"

"Last night."

"Maybe 24 or 48 hours ...I don't know. I only saw one guy who drank it."

"Is there an antidote?"

"I don't know, but you should go to the hospital, and we should find out."

"Why didn't he call me or send a telegram?"

"He's an—" He looked down at the girl. "He wants it covered up. Didn't want me to say anything about it. Just recover the bottles—empty or full—and burn his letters and any bodies along the way."

The old man shook his head and looked at nothing in the fireplace until the girl started squirming around. He smiled a little smile. "It's not as if I'm young. But I bet it's not going to be painless. The cough is new. My stomach feels as if the lining caught on fire."

"Let's go to the hospital." Molnar stood. "It'll only get worse from here."

The man put his hand up as if to stop a car. "I've lived for a while." He stood as well and walked over to the glass case with the suit and faced it. He rubbed his broken left shoulder. "I will stay here. Better to die with two strangers than alone." He rested his hand on the glass case and looked over his shoulder at Molnar. The old man's grit came through. "Death gets you one way or the other, doesn't he?" Molnar looked around for his dark friend, but didn't see anyone. "How did you get here?"

"Cab."

"Tell him to go. I have a car that you can ... have. I'd like to take some of your time in exchange. You have a lot more of it left than I."

Molnar nodded, and he and the girl left the room as the old man stared through the glass at the remnants of his glory.

Molnar and the girl returned after a minute. Molnar had his briefcase now. The old man saw them in the glass, but he didn't turn. "Take a seat, please. I'll speak my mind now."

They complied.

"We never should have fought the first one, and now we're fighting a second. We're following a charismatic tyrant, and we're trying to take over the world on the strength of his persona. It's not right. Germany needs me now more than it ever has, but it won't listen to me anymore. I'm too old. Can't possibly help. I saw it from the start, but no one cared. They just placated me and sent me bottles of poisoned wine." He laughed at the ironic truth of this last bit and lifted a bony finger by a bony forearm toward a wooden humidor across the room. "Want a cigar—or five? I still feel passable. We may as well go out smoking. Go ahead and get the Upmanns. I've been saving them for a special occasion. Special or not, this is the one."

Molnar moved somberly across the room and opened the box. His cigar-appraising eyes did their appraisal. The contents of the box matched the contents of the room. He pulled out two Upmanns and grabbed a cutter and moved to the old man. "Thank you. Got something for her? She likes a heavier smoke."

The old man chuckled even though it hurt. "Shirley!" His voice rose slightly as he said it. Molnar took his time in cutting the cigars, looking into the old man's eyes. His once-plump and full face remained round, but it sagged with age—speckled with the mysterious light and dark polka dots of time. Molnar handed him the cigar and picked up an ivory lighter, big as a tumbler of whiskey and heavy as a bottle of it. He pressed the silver button on the thing with one hand and balanced it on the other. The old man's cigar lit up.

A plump maid walked in. She wore a blue apron and was the picture-perfect Bavarian mother: fat cheeks like apples with pink centers; blonde hair in a bun with some kind of white doily hat that Molnar couldn't figure out; and round, pink arms like raspberry pastries. "How may I help you, sir?"

"Well, you could have been here half an hour ago to get the door to send these two away. But then I suppose I'd have died alone." Fitzdorff laughed. "Do you have any sweeties for this little girl?"

Shirley looked down at the gypsy, and her maternal instincts flipped on like a circuit breaker. "What have you two put her in? It looks like she's wearing a canvas bag!" Molnar looked down at her. He'd forgotten that she was still wearing her concentration camp attire. He'd just ripped off the numbers on her back. "Is this how you dress your child? Come here, little girl." Shirley moved to the gypsy, who wouldn't have let a team of oxen pull her away from Molnar a few minutes before. But Shirley lifted her easily from the chair. "We'll give you some pastries and clean you up and you can wear some of the clothes we have, can't she, General Fitzdorff?"

"Yes, give her whatever she wants."

The gypsy was so hypnotized by this woman's overpowering emanation of apple tarts and cinnamon that she didn't make a sound as she was carried from the room.

Molnar toted the two-ton lighter back to the table and tried not to break the glass as he put it down. Then he took a seat. The old man sat in the chair beside him, staring at the crackling fireplace. They smoked in silence until the cigars were three-quarters through.

"I'd like to ask you to do something for me," Fitzdorff said.

"What's that?"

"When we've thoroughly finished these fine cigars, and a couple more—along with a few fingers of a bottle of 40-year-old scotch that I've never opened—I'd like you to drive me to a certain spot, and I'd like you to put a cigar in my teeth, and I'd like you to shoot me in the heart with that gun on the hip of that uniform over there." His long, bent fingers reached toward the glass case, pointing at the worn leather holster on the hip of the ghostly uniform. "I know this is asking a lot, but I'd need you to bury me there. It's beside my wife's gravestone. No need to give me one. I don't think anyone will come and see it."

"All right." The two of them continued in silence as the cigars smoldered. Molnar saw the third chair fill. It was his old white friend. Molnar nodded at him. Death was always smiling, so his expression remained the same.

The two men lit new cigars with the lighter, and Molnar reached his across to Death for a toke.

"I don't have lungs, Molnar; how do you expect me to smoke?"

Molnar shrugged and looked back to the general, who was eyeing him over his non-verbal exchange.

The general asked if the girl was his daughter, and Molnar told him how he'd gotten her. The old man stared into the fire after the story.

Shirley came in with a transformed little gypsy. The girl's hair looked clean and full, and her cheeks looked pinker. She almost smiled at Molnar. She was wearing a white-and-blue dress, and both men could tell she was uncomfortable in it. The old man smiled at the girl like she was his last link to life.

"She looks beautiful, Molnar!" said Fitzdorff. He crouched as low as his ancient body would allow and looked at the girl. He reached his hand out this time to pat her head, and she started to pull away, but then allowed the pat, like a cat waiting for you to give it a chicken leg and willing to undergo the torturous molesting required to get it. "These belonged to my youngest daughter. She's long gone now, but this little girl can have them all."

Shirley looked at the two men as if they were doing a truly noble thing. Her hands pressed together in a state of prayer. There was a light in her eyes from the sated desire to dress something cute. "OK, let's go look at your new wardrobe, little one," said Shirley.

The gypsy girl smiled, for the first time, at Molnar. Tears came back into her eyes, but they had a different sheen.

Shirley and the girl left the room, and Fitzdorff looked back at Molnar. The old man too was near tears. The tortured waif's wish-come-true was stirring starving hearts. Molnar wondered if there was a way he could sell tickets. "Shirley gets all my belongings when I die," Fitzdorff told him. "My wife and children are gone. They are all dead." The fire flickered, throwing shadows of the old man's wrinkles over his face and making the ghostly, impassive face of Death hollower. "But if you will carry out my wish, then before we go, we'll open my vault, and I'll write a line in my will. It will say that Shirley must care for that little girl until she's 20."

Molnar looked at him. "Are you sure you want to do that?"

"What does it cost me? And what are you going to do with her? You're best friends with the Angel of Death."

The old man and Death laughed at this. Molnar nodded.

The old man carried on. "I want to do as much good with these stupid things"—he waved around the room—"as possible before I exit the terminal. It feels like you're leaving a country and you have to get rid of all of your currency before the plane takes off. And now I know the exact time of my departure. I guess that's how any true German would have it." He laughed again, and his aging face filled with new wrinkles at the sound. "You'll keep me on schedule." He coughed painfully, and the smile disappeared.

Molnar nodded again.

"The final thing is to pin this all to Riffel. That dirty Nazi!" At this, the old man stirred from his seat for the first time, almost rising from it.

Molnar raised one finger. "As much as I would like to comply, if Riffel gets found out, I won't get out of the country," he said. "I'll get a German noose. Or a Hungarian one. The Arrow Cross is following me, and they want me dead. This job is the only thing standing in their way."

The old man was silent for a long while. "Then that can be your payment for doing my will. We'll let it go." Molnar and Death looked at him as if he were 20 years younger. "If I've learned one thing in life, it's that we all get our just desserts, served hot or cold. And it's more satisfying to watch an enemy eat molding cake. You'll have to enjoy the spectacle instead of me."

Molnar nodded at this too. Death was getting bored. Fitzdorff must've gotten the hint, because he stubbed out his cigar. Molnar followed suit. The old man pried his hollow form out of the chair and gestured for Molnar to follow. Death kept his own hollow form in his seat and watched the two fleshy beings move up the marble stairs to Fitzdorff's vault, which sat behind an acrylic portrait of another old man who resembled him. Molnar looked away out of courtesy as Fitzdorff opened the vault.

The general removed an aging legal paper, and began writing by hand.

———

A racing-red Alfa Romeo convertible sailed down country roads mottled by the long afternoon shadows shading the first breaths of autumn. Green leaves were edged with varying colors of red, gold, and orange. It was a beautiful drive in a very fast car, and Molnar was making that car work.

"Just after this turn, you'll see a little dirt road on the right. Take it."

Molnar and the old man were both in the single front seat. Death was finding his own conveyance. They slowed quickly and turned down the dirt road. Molnar was careful now and took it easy, to respect the tires. They drove to the end of the road, and the old man flapped a long arm to the right, where there was a turnoff. "Park it there." Molnar obliged. "It's just at the top of that hill."

The two climbed their way up a slight incline to the crest of a hill under an oak. A single half-oval stone slab stuck out of the soil with tufts of grass obscuring the base. Flowers grew, even in the cooling breaths of fall, around the back of the stone. The two men—one in the strength of youth, the other waxed old, shriveled, and wiry—stood beside each other, looking down at the destiny that awaited them both, in time.

Time.

"Time keeps passing, Molnar," said the old man, eyes on the gravestone. Then he grunted and doubled over in pain, holding his stomach, feeling like a bear trap had lodged its metal teeth in the soft pink flesh of his belly. His tough old face swallowed hard, and his tough old mind knew sure and certain that Molnar wasn't lying to him about the wine. He stuck his hand out and pawed at the air, telling Molnar to give him the cigar. Molnar handed him the scotch instead, and the old man took a swig and dropped it. It landed on its base without spilling much.

"The smoke."

Molnar produced the H. Upmann and stuffed it in between the feeble lips. They had the beginnings of the thin white film of death. And Death himself now appeared to watch his man work. Molnar lit the cigar, took five steps back, and drew the gun.

"Got any last words?"

The old man screwed up his face to the sky. His expression said he was fighting against the pain and the nearly overwhelming urge to be sick. But his mouth opened, and words spat out in bursts. "Honor. Most people won't know if you have it or you don't." He paused, and his face got tighter. "But it's one thing you can take with you from this desperate place." Silence again. Face pulled wrinkles tight. "It's stored in a place near your soul. Be honorable. I tried to be it." He grunted again and nodded.

Molnar took careful aim and fired. The round from the general's old .45 plowed through Fitzdorff's heart and knocked him back onto his behind. The cigar fell from his mouth and hit the earth, smoldering there. Fitzdorff's body didn't make another conscious sound, but it finished the processes it had been trying to get the old man to carry out. Molnar didn't watch, and he didn't take the cigar. He got a shovel from the boot end of the hot-rod-red convertible and started digging a hole beside the headstone.

The sun was well set by the time Molnar dragged the corpse in. The weightlessness of Fitzdorff's body made Molnar think of the scarecrow in the Wizard of Oz. When he got him in the ground, he took a breath. Then he started chucking dirt onto the old man. After a while, the body was covered, and darkness ruled. Only then did Molnar pick up the bottle of scotch that was nearly his age and take a long pull, rubbing the newly torn callus marks on the meaty pads of his palms. He held the liquid in his mouth as it set a controlled fire on his tongue, and he sensed the nuances of the expensive burn as it moved down his throat and into his stomach.

———

It took time and tears before Molnar convinced the little girl to stay with Shirley. He said he had to catch a wedding. When she knew he was going to leave and she couldn't stop him, she hit him and hit him and hit him in the arm. But lightly. She had been taught too well to hit him hard. He knelt there and balanced himself against the blows. She ran from the room, and Molnar got his hat from the stand. Shirley read over the will as Molnar carried out his business. Fitzdorff had spoken with her before they'd left. Shirley had fully agreed, and happily, to take the girl in. She hadn't had a child around for too long, she said. The only legal hurdle was that neither Molnar nor the old man knew the girl's name. So they decided to call her Annabelle Fitzdorff and added that name to the will.

Molnar shook hands with Shirley and walked out the door. He got into the convertible and started it up.

Annabelle came running out of the big brick house and down the steps and to the door just as Molnar was about to pull away. He looked down at her and opened the door. She leapt into the car and hugged him tightly around his chest.

"I love you!" she yelled, pressing her face into his chest. "I love you, and I'll love you forever." She pulled her weeping face away from his shirt, leaving a dewdrop imprint of her eyes, and she looked up at him, her mouth wrenched closed in stubbornness. Then it opened. "And my name is Carmella Boswell."

Mads Molnar laughed. It was a big and full and deep laugh of abandon. It sounded like he'd stored a barrel somewhere in his chest and he saved it for these particular moments. He climbed out of the car and picked the little girl up under one arm and carried her back into the house, laughing all the way. He set her down and looked at her, and her tears were still there.

Molnar kept laughing. "You're gonna have to settle for Annabelle for the next decade or so," he said. "But I'm glad you finally found your voice."

BOTTLE III (PART 2)

If poise had a pose, Marilyn Ghetz was pulling it as she stood in the triplicate mirrors of the tailor's shop. She looked at her figure, as did every pair of eyes that passed by the glass windows of the downtown Berlin shop.

The owner—an old, plump, gray-haired German woman named Gretchen—smiled at Marilyn. As Marilyn twisted in a particularly intriguing way to see the bare back of her gown, a full-grown man with a black fedora and a wife on his arm ran directly into a telephone pole outside. On his impact, Gretchen smiled again, congratulating herself on her storefront real estate and her clientele. The man didn't fall down entirely, but he stumbled. His wife looked from him to Marilyn's goddess-like form and kept walking down the street with her hands on her hips. She turned and her mouth opened, but Gretchen couldn't hear her words through the glass. The man rubbed his forehead and his brow and decided to take a seat on the sidewalk until composure returned.

Marilyn was oblivious to the scene as she ran a finger down the intricate lace pattern on her hip. "I wonder what my brothers would think about this dress. I hope they wouldn't see it as too ... accentuating." She looked up at Gretchen.

The tailor moved to her side, studying the lace. "Oh, I think it's the right balance. I'm sure they'd be so proud!"

"I was proud of them." Marilyn stared into her own eyes in the mirror, but she didn't focus on them. "I'm going to toast my brother Reinhardt at our party. I even got a special bottle of wine that I know he'd love. My fiancé knew him."

"Oh, that will be lovely," said Gretchen.

"Yes, it will be lovely," said Marilyn, and there was something frozen in the syllables she spoke.

Gretchen helped Marilyn off the mirrored stage and away from the storefront. The public couldn't handle it. Marilyn sashayed into the dressing room to wriggle out of the dress. The fallen soldier on the street sat at-ease. A thin line of blood ran down his forehead, past his nose and alongside the corner of his still-smiling lips.

———

Miss Sandor's long, dark figure stood at its full length in the office. She bent herself to one side, torquing and releasing tension in her body. Her lips parted and moved slightly as if she were counting. Then she leaned to the other side, and the phone rang. She didn't leap for it but kept torquing, trying not to rush the routine. Her lips moved. The phone rang a fourth time. Her beautiful lips formed very ugly words instead of numbers. She moved to the phone, lifted it to her face with flair, and said, "Molnar's office" as if someone had personally insulted her.

"It's me."

She called him an unprintable name and kept counting, shifting her body so she could do the side bend while holding the phone.

"It is that time of the morning, isn't it?" Molnar asked, looking down at his watch. "You're like clockwork. I just need the address of the wedding."

"Of course you're going to her wedding ... 39, 40, 41 ... Why did I think you'd ... 44, 45, 46 ... get some sense and find a new broad?"

"What's the address, Miss Sandor?"

"50!"

"Congratulations."

"You'll thank me when you get back here," she said, looking down to admire her hip. "Once you've been spurned by another blonde with another mental complex and are licking your wounds. It seems to be a theme with you. But of course, the psychologist can't diagnose himself."

"I'm afraid I missed that lesson. I had an appointment with my masseuse."

"You're a riot." She searched through her desk and found a stack of papers that had come in for him. One was made of delicate white crepe paper and had a golden border. "Found it. Looks like it's in Hamburg. It reads, 'Dr. Mads Molnar is cordially invited, blah, blah, blah, wedding of Blonde Dunce to—ooh, nice name, Wolfram. Sounds like a real winner. She's to be Mrs. Wolfram. Blah, blah, blah—"

"What's his last name?"

"You wonder how it'll sound? Mrs. Bastard. That's what it'll be. Whoops. I mean Mrs. Bastick. His name is Wolfram Bastick."

Molnar's mouth closed tightly. He remembered meeting the man in the Épernay hospital. "This isn't going to be pretty."

"Is that all? I have to get back to work, Molnar." She looked down at her waist as if it was already growing. She gave him the address, then added, "It starts at six. Be there or be—"

Her voice was interrupted by the sound of breaking glass. She sang out a string of expletives, and the phone made the sound of a rock hitting wood. Her expletives stopped.

"Sandor!"

There was silence for a moment, and then a voice came through. The voice sounded young, obedient, sadistic.

"Who is this?"

"It's Molnar!"

"Two of our men are dead because of you. You can run and hide, but your secretary can't. You have until Sunday to get back to Hungary, or we'll have to punish this fine specimen instead."

"Don't you touch—"

"I'm afraid the lady has to go," interrupted the voice. "She can't be bothered right now."

The line went dead, and Molnar slowly hung up the receiver. He stood in the phone box, hunched over. A few moments later, he righted himself, opened the line back up, and asked the operator to connect him with Miles Fekete in Kissvábhegy. The line rang several times. Sweat danced down the lines in Molnar's forehead.

"This is Miles."

Molnar couldn't have known it, but Miles was standing in nothing but plaid boxer shorts in his kitchen, holding a cup of coffee. He was a swarthy man with a full head of hair and a permanent smile. He had a beer belly, but you wouldn't know that by his face.

"Miles, Eva's in trouble! Can you check on her?"

"Sure thing, Mads. What's wrong?" Miles had the phone leveraged against his shoulder as he unscrewed the cap of a bottle of amaretto and poured a healthy glug into his mug.

"It's the Arrow Cross. Bring the big gun. And I'll owe you one, Miles. Send me a bill, and I'll square it out with you."

"Don't say such things, Mads. I'd pay to check on Eva." He took a gulp of his concoction.

"They're there right now, Miles. Hurry."

"I'm on the way out the door," said the man while he chugged the rest of his drink and looked around for his pants.

"Thanks, Miles."

———

A few hours later, in Hamburg, a strikingly handsome blond man with a strikingly thick beard, wearing a powder-blue suit and a black tie, entered an outdoor *bierhaus* terrace. The Basticks had rented it for their traditional German wedding-eve party known as a *Polterabend*. It was an informal event with peculiarly appealing traditions. The blond man walked down one of the long, rough-hewn wooden tables searching for his name and nearly ran flat into Marilyn Ghetz.

She looked into his blue eyes and made a questioning face, and then she covered her mouth to keep from laughing.

"How could you not recognize me, my dear?" asked the man in a thick Swedish accent. "It's your cousin."

She was silent for a moment as her head was bowed and her eyes were closed and her smile was tight and she was shaking a little. Then she rearranged her face and righted herself and opened her eyes—once more the perfect bride-to-be. "Hans!"

"Yes, *Friherre* Hans."

"Cousin, Baron Hans! My only living family. I didn't think you'd be able to make it." She put one hand on his shoulder, the other on his chest.

"How could I miss your wedding, my dear cousin? You told me all about the wine. Oh, there's an empty spot there." He pointed a tanned finger at Molnar's nameplate. "That sounds like a rather tough name, though. I'd hate to get on his bad side."

She nearly laughed again and took a step back to look at him. "Sure, have his spot. Don't worry; he's soft as whipped butter."

"Well, in that case, I don't mind if I do." Hans slid toward the heavy wooden seat.

But before he could take the seat, Marilyn said, "You have to meet my fiancé! Don't just shrink into someone else's chair."

"You know that's my wont, Marilyn, my dear. You know how introverted I am." He slyly pocketed Molnar's name card as he said this.

"We all must grow up someday, Hans." She took him by the muscled triceps and pulled him after her. He seemed to be trying to avoid any sudden movements of his head as he followed. She dragged him until he was directly in front of her betrothed mountain of flesh.

"May I present to you, my one surviving cousin, and honorable Baron Hans Åsström," said Marilyn, still holding Hans by the elbow. "I didn't think he would be able to make it, so I didn't mention him to you. I know how your mother gets her hopes up."

"Why! What a wonderful surprise!" Bastick moved in front of Hans and extended his hand. Their flesh encountered, palm to palm, and Hans stared into Bastick's eyes.

After a moment, Bastick pulled away. "You... ." He stepped back. "You smell like someone I've met." He knit his eyebrows. "But no, that's impossible. Do you wear a cologne?"

"No," said Hans, staring into the flat brown eyes of Bastick. "I'm afraid I don't."

Bastick shrugged. He smiled at Hans and pulled him toward himself with intense strength and hugged him to his body. "Welcome to our *Polterabend!* I'm so glad my wife has some surviving family. This is a reason to celebrate in itself!" Bastick grabbed a plate off the table and smashed it to the ground, sending shards flying for meters across the slick wood.

Hans grabbed another and did the same, shouting, "*Scherben bringen glück!*"

Bastick roared with laughter and happiness and smashed another plate on the table.

"Wolfie!" Marilyn chided. "Not so soon. Hold yourself in. Your mother will have a fit. What will people eat on? Come now, Hans." She pulled Hans away from Bastick and back toward the table. "I'll be right back, Wolfie. Don't break anything while I'm gone!"

Bastick smiled, watching them go, and stamped some of the shards of porcelain. But then his brows furrowed and he stared after Hans as he walked away.

Marilyn and Hans got back to the table, and she looked at him with questions in her glittering eyes.

"He'd snap Molnar's neck if he saw him," said Hans. "They met once before, and it wasn't pretty."

She smiled a knowing smile at him. "You're a tricky one," she said. "But so am I. When you see me give a toast, get ready."

She took a step away.

"Marilyn!" said Hans in a hushed and serious tone. "You did destroy that bottle, didn't you? You were just kidding, right?"

"What bottle?"

And just then, Bastick's mother came up to them and lightly spun Marilyn around by the shoulder. She kept turning like a ballerina so all eyes could see the twirl. "Isn't she marvelous?" said Bastick's mother to Hans.

Hans nodded. He was introduced, and the mother swept Marilyn away.

Hans watched Marilyn as she flitted around. He'd never seen her so happy, so excited. But he noticed something new in her eyes tonight. A coldness. He'd seen it once before, back in Budapest, in the eyes of a woman who'd killed her own kid. He'd always seen it in Bastick.

It made his hands sweat.

The room was filling with guests. Hans noticed many military bars on the jackets of the men, but beyond that, the dress was casual. This was a *Polterabend*, an ancient German pre-wedding tradition where guests shatter all the porcelain for luck and the couple cleans up the shards to teach them how to work together. There hadn't been enough drinking yet for the real smashing to begin.

Hans met his table neighbors and shook hands. They were delighted to hear of Marilyn's cousin. They went on about her and about how Bastick didn't deserve her, and they weren't joking. Roast potatoes and kraut and sausages and chicken were served, and beer was poured into huge ceramic steins. There was no glass at the party. "Breaking glass is bad luck," said an old woman with semi-crossed eyes who sat directly across from Hans. The beer flowed and the toasts began and a little dancing broke out on the edges of the room. Forgetting to be dour, Hans started to smile.

The party percolated. One of the younger male guests—two seats to Hans's right—was a pudgy kid with a curlicue for a haircut and suspenders. He was named Thurbert and was Bastick's nephew. He stared at Marilyn for a while after a few drinks, and then he shattered his plate and his bowl and drank all his beer, bubbles of it pouring out the sides of his mouth and down his padded gullet into his shirt. Then he shattered his stein as well. He shattered the empty bowl of his neighbor and screamed, "*Scherben bringen glück!*" The yell and the smashing were a bit too guttural to be joyous.

Hans watched and thought about the kid's being jealous. He finished his kraut and lifted his bowl and looked at Thurbert in open allegiance before smashing it into the wall. And he simply bellowed. Thurbert threw a plate like a discus, and it caught a current of air and careened into the dessert table. A very large man with a beer-keg gut yelled a German war cry and upturned an entire tray of empty mugs. They toppled in a glorious waterfall of disaster and exploded onto the floor, shooting off in every direction. It was at that point that the gates of hell were knocked in and lederhosen-clothed legs took to tables and no one kept their seats. Enormous German women with enormous German breasts gripped mugs in both fists and drank enormous glugs of beer. They smashed these together. "*Prost!*" rang out, and people cheers'd so hard their mugs shattered. Hans felt the silent pride of a person who has helped start something.

He pushed his way through the beer and the bits of ceramic until he found a Dunkel-soaked Marilyn. He lightly gripped her elbow from behind and whispered in her ear, "Whatever your plan is, throw it out. Let's get out of here."

Marilyn smiled at him. "Leave my own wedding party?" She spun away from him, looking over her shoulder as she walked. "You must have me confused with some Hungarian woman. Marilyn Ghetz doesn't flee. She wouldn't leave this party if it meant her life." Then she added, "Hang on to your beard."

Hans watched her parade through the crowd, her head held high, as guests moved out of her way. He gave his fake beard a tug and, satisfied, went back to his seat and stood beside the table. At his head height were the frolicking, dimpled knees of Thurbert's thick legs kicking ceramic-ware off the tabletop and sending it flying to parts unknown. It was too dangerous to sit down, so Hans moved back, pivoting until he found a lightly dressed barmaid with a platter of steins. He reached for one. She looked at him as if she wanted him to reach for her as well. Maybe this joke with Marilyn had gone too far. He should let her figure it out for herself. This barmaid was, if not more intriguing, at least more immediate.

"Quite the engagement," said Hans, taking a drink.

"It's lovely, these," she said, as her tray quickly emptied in front of him. She gave him the fluttery eyes and glanced at his left hand. "You single?"

"You German girls don't mince words," said Hans, realizing from the light slur of those words that she'd been partaking in her own wares. "Yeah, I'm single."

"You don't have to be." Her tray was bare now. She lowered it and moved closer to him. "I simply adore Swedish men."

Hans smelled the distinctive odor of lilacs as if she'd hidden a bundle of them in her hair. He leaned back to take a drink, if only to put some distance between them. Then he looked around for a way out. He had a bottle to find. When he glanced behind him, he saw Marilyn pulling that bottle out of a brown paper bag. She walked toward Bastick, who was talking with a guest. His back was to her. Hans spun away from the forthright beer maid and ran through the crowd.

"Marilyn!" his voice shouted, but the party was too loud. She was grabbing Bastick's shoulder, and his body was rotating around like the Titanic turning from the iceberg. "Marilyn, no!" Hans tried again. But if she heard him, it didn't show.

The look on Wolfram Bastick's face as he beheld his fiancée was the pure joy only displayed in children and psychopaths. It was a boyish, unabashed glee. But as his eyes picked up the bottle of wine, his face contorted into shock, as if he'd been shot. That stuck for a beat, and then it was horror.

Hans saw this and steeled himself for an eventful evening.

"I know how much you hate wine, Wolfie, but this is that special bottle I told you about. Let's just make sure not to break the glass." She was making a little-girl face.

"Your joke is in poor taste," said Bastick. But then his mind began to connect the dots: she couldn't have known the bottle that killed his father; he had been the only one to see it. And his mind rebelled. His enormous hands gripped her face lightly, and then harder. And then harder as these thoughts rushed through his mind. He pulled her face toward his until they were almost nose to nose and he stared into her eyes, sniffing, sucking in her scent, searching for a lie.

"Wolfie, that hurts," she said, only betraying a questioning, innocent orange odor.

He released her. There must be an explanation. His mother, who stood beside him, slapped Bastick on the face. "Don't be a beast! What in Heaven's name are you doing, Wolfram?"

"Where did you get this?" He snatched the bottle from Marilyn.

"I got it especially for you," she said, holding to the hurt look of a child. "I thought you'd like it."

Bastick reached the bottle to his face and stared at the label. He knew the kiss mark, the white label, the vintage. How could he forget it? He smashed it so hard against a marble ashtray on the table that it exploded. Some people cheered, thinking this to be Bastick continuing the fervor of the event. Other platters and dishes followed suit.

"Where did you get it?"

"I got it—"

"She got it from me," interrupted Hans, who was making his way through the crowd as quickly as he could and was now behind her. "I received it as a gift from a good friend. How embarrassing to admit. But I didn't tell her about that. She only asked if I could bring the best wine I had, and this is it. I mean, 1934 was one of the best years for pinot in France."

Wolfram's suspicion relocated. His nostrils flared and he shifted his fiancée out of his path and closed on Hans.

"Who sent this to you as a gift?"

"The elegant Count Zsigmond, in Budapest. He's a collector."

"Where did he get it?" Wolfram was now nose to nose with Hans, looking down on the blond man's six-foot frame from his own towering height.

"I haven't the faintest."

Wolfram's hands went up to grip Hans's neck. He got his fingers around his throat and was about to apply his vice-like force. But instead of squeezing, his eyes lit up as if someone had poured lit gasoline into his ears.

"Is that the way to treat a new cousin, Wolfie?" asked Hans, in the voice of Mads Molnar. In the dim evening light, most guests wouldn't notice Hans's hand, very close to Bastick and below his belt. In that hand was a thin, sharp, probing knife that tickled in ways that could ruin a man's wedding night. Bastick felt the light prick and loosened his grip. "The most polite thing would be to release me and run off somewhere to pull yourself together."

The deft, exploring blade caused Bastick to release Hans and step back as if stung by a hornet. He held himself. "Your voice!" he said.

Hans hid the knife in his jacket. "Yes, my voice is often admired," said Hans, as Hans. "But perhaps Marilyn and I should take a stroll while you decide if you'd like to behave as a gentleman."

"Yes," said Bastick's mother. "Yes, please do go for a stroll. Wolfie, you're coming with me." She took Bastick by the arm and Hans took Marilyn by the arm, each escorting the two in opposite directions. They completed a few paces.

"I remember his voice," said Bastick, looking behind him. "I smelled it!" He pulled away from his mother and ran back toward Hans and Marilyn, who were just getting to the edge of the crowd.

"Wolfie, no!" said his mother. Hans turned back toward them at this, and Bastick lunged at him and yanked at his blond beard. It came off with a sticky pop. A woman in the crowd responded with a shriek.

"The gray man!" bellowed Bastick, staring down at the fake beard in his hand.

The mincing Hans, turned rock-hard Mads Molnar, stepped in front of Marilyn and pulled out his revolver so all could see it shine in the light of the moon. He held it level with Bastick's roaring face. "Yes, the Gray Man. The Blond Man feels so much nicer to say, though—younger," he said, cocking the revolver's hammer. "Either way, you know I can use this." Mads began backing Marilyn up behind him quickly.

The crowd was in shock. No more plates were broken, and all eyes were on the three at the edge of the *bierhaus* terrace. Bastick's shock was eaten by his rage, and he leapt at Mads and batted away the gun, which went off a moment too late and cut off the top of Bastick's ear. Blood spurted as Bastick tackled Molnar to the ground with the pent-up rage of a caged gorilla. Shouts went up from the crowd. Bastick pummeled Molnar, bouncing his head off the floor. The Gray Man had no chance against the monster but tried in vain to block the blows with his arms.

Marilyn Ghetz didn't scream. Her face was blank beauty. She swiveled silently to the nearest table and looked at the standing liter bottles of beer until she found one with the cap on and a telltale ring of liquid near the brim. She lifted this from the table and moved back to the two men. She set her hips wide and pulled the bottle back over her right shoulder in a perfect baseball wind up. And with the strength of Babe Ruth, she swung into and past Bastick's head, completing the swing over her left shoulder. A sickening smack sounded as the bottle smashed into the base of Bastick's skull and snapped his head forward and out of the way of its arc. His huge being folded, falling half on and half off Mads's bleeding body.

No one made a sound. Marilyn dropped the bottle to the ground, bent her figure in two—which, even at this tense moment, was scrutinized by many with intensity—and slapped Molnar's face. But Molnar was out cold, and Bastick's body was the one that stirred. He shook his head, grunted and stood up, off Molnar, erected himself, and stared down at his fiancée.

"Someone had to knock some sense into you," she said, squinting up at him.

The crowd was still silent.

"Everyone out!" roared Bastick, pivoting around so he could make eye contact with the crowd. Blood poured down the side of his head and body from the wound in his ear. As his back was turned, Marilyn picked something off the ground. "Go home! It's over!"

It was not until now that the party gained its collective wits—it had been as if the attendees had been watching a play on a stage instead of real events. The partygoers realized their part. Stiff figures—frozen in time, beer halfway to mouths—loosened. Husbands looked at wives and gave head jerks, signaling that they didn't want to stick around anyhow. Drunks sobered. Even Thurbert—elated to see trouble in paradise and the possibility of a single Marilyn—snapped to attention and looked for his hat. Molnar stayed floor-ridden and closed-eyed as the terrace emptied. Quick figures exited amid murmurs. Older men commented aloud on the events.

Younger men went in silence. Bastick's antics had thoroughly killed any buzz his partygoers may have attained, and they all drove home safe as a Sunday afternoon. Bastick's mother tried to stay behind to sort things out, but Bastick bellowed until she left in a huff.

As the exodus began, Bastick scuttled Marilyn into his car without a word. An older man went to attend to Molnar. When Bastick returned to see this, he rushed to the old man and pulled him away. "Reinhard, he may be responsible for my father's death. Don't coddle him."

Reinhard allowed Bastick to pull him away. "What are you going to do with him?"

"If he's still alive? I'll ... interrogate him," said Bastick, staring down at Molnar. He smelled the air in his deep and dreadful way. "Yes, he's alive," concluded Bastick, and a smile crossed his lips.

Reinhard—thin, bald, and spotted with age—looked up at Bastick. "You take him to the police, Wolfram. Don't take things into your own hands."

"Or what?" Bastick's anger built. "Will you stop me?" He grabbed Reinhard by the jacket and started pulling him toward the car park, getting blood on the man's clothing.

"Settle down, Wolfram."

"Shut up! You're tiny and weak and old. What could you do to stop me? You beggar! LOOK AT ME!" Bastick roared and lifted the old man half off his feet as he shuffled him off the terrace. "I AM THE POLICE! I'M THE GESTAPO!" Bastick was roaring like the lion of a man that he was. "GO HOME!" He threw Reinhard at the parking lot.

Reinhard nearly fell to the ground as he stumbled to regain balance. Bastick followed after him, ready to shove again if he paused.

Reinhard hurried away. As he got to his car, he looked back at Bastick and shook his fist when he realized he couldn't do much else. "*Du hosenscheisser!*"

Bastick ripped off his tie and used it to bind Molnar's limp wrists. Every movement he made was meant to cause pain or break the things he touched. He picked Molnar up like a sack of grain and carried him over his shoulder. When he got to his car, he opened the back seat and threw Molnar's heavy body in, trying to smash him into the other side. Marilyn silently stared through the windshield.

Bastick yanked the driver's door open and leapt into the seat. He looked at Marilyn, hoping that she'd speak. But she knew the workings of men and was silent, keeping her eyes straight ahead. Bastick roared at the windshield and cranked the car on, smashing the gas so the engine screamed in neutral. He shoved the gearbox into reverse. Marilyn was jerked forward, and she buckled her seatbelt.

It was a harrowing ride toward Bastick's rented castle, where the wedding was set to take place in the morning. Molnar was out cold, and Marilyn didn't say a word.

Bastick's driving got more erratic as he took out his rage on the road and on the few cars making their way home in the setting sun. At a red light, Bastick revved his engine to a scream as he waited. The man in the car in front of him had had just enough to drink that night that he stepped out of his car and yelled something at Bastick. Bastick leapt from the seat. It was his first answered challenge. He rushed toward the man. The man tried to retreat, but Bastick was too quick and tackled him, lifting him off his feet and driving him into the concrete. Bastick hit his own head while doing this, but he didn't notice. He did the same routine he had to Molnar, mashing every angle of the man's head. The man's body was soon limp as a noodle. A woman rushed out of the passenger seat and shook Bastick to stop him. But to no avail.

Two gunshots went off, arresting Bastick in his assault. He got off the man, panting, and looked for the source of the sound. The woman sobbed beside him, falling to her knees to check her husband's vital signs. Bastick turned and saw the taillights of his own vehicle in the distance, with Marilyn's blonde hair blowing out the window and her smooth-skinned arm holding Molnar's gun in the air. There was a bullet hole in the road and another in the tire of the other man's car. Bastick watched it deflate. He ran to the car anyway and leapt behind the wheel, leaving the crying woman and beaten man in the middle of the street. He burnt rubber on the working rear tire after Marilyn. The flat tire socked over and over. It flopped and flopped as Bastick gave chase. But by the time he was around the corner, the rim had cut through the rubber, and the car was tilting wildly to the left. Bastick kept the gas held down and just saw Marilyn's hair disappearing off in the distance. She was going very fast.

Bastick flew after her, throwing sparks and cutting a line down the whole street with the bare rim. He took a hard left too fast, and the three tires couldn't hold the car. It fishtailed, spinning out and off the roadway. The car smashed into a ditch, breaking the front axle in two. Bastick got out of the steaming car and stared after the taillights of his disappearing vehicle.

A new wound started bleeding on his forehead from contact with the road. A line of blood ran between his eyes and along his nose and the side of his mouth. He kept thinking of the word *gone*. Gone. Gone. She's *gone*. She's gone. *She never loved me. She never loved me and she's gone. She betrayed me. Betrayed me betrayed me.*

"Betrayal!" he was screaming now and started running down the street after the taillights. Tears streamed down his face as if he'd never cried in his life. "Jezebel! Jezebel!" His voice got so hoarse and pained that he finally noticed he was screaming, and then he was back in his head.

The Gray Man stole her. He got to her and he stole her and I'll get them both and he'll watch and then I'll blind him!

There was nothing else. Bastick fell to his knees and wished it would rain—to cover his weeping and to wash away his blood. But it didn't rain.

Eva Sandor awakened to feel her wrists wrapped together with rough, fraying rope and pulled tightly behind her back. All light was extinguished. She smelled petroleum and felt the jostling of her body weight against her shoulder and hip on a hard surface beneath her. She wiggled the little toes of her left foot and felt the assuring binding of her heeled shoe against her most-recent paint job. Plum purple. Then she wiggled the toes on her right foot and felt that it was bare. Curses punctuated her thoughts as she imagined the heel lost somewhere between Molnar's office and wherever she was now. She'd refrained from going out for two weekends to save for the shoes. Molnar should pay her more.

She wriggled her right foot down and felt warm metal. She was in a trunk. The spacious trunk of some vehicle. Her right arm felt dead, and if she moved pins went through her palm. She couldn't turn onto her back or she'd crush her hands, and she couldn't turn onto her chest or she'd crush her face. She slowly rotated onto her face anyway to get feeling back into the arm. Her cheek was pressed against warm metal.

"The villains. The pissing priests," she muttered as the car sailed on and the feeling painfully returned to her arm.

Amid her unbroken string of rage, the movement stopped. She too fell silent. The sound of heavy boots crunching gravel came from both sides of the car. There was a clicking-metal sound, and light poured in. Miss Sandor squinted up at the dark silhouettes of three men looming over her. They stared down at her enticing figure laced up like a sacrifice. One man gripped the rough cord that made her wrists kiss and pulled it up. That shoved her face back into the trunk before she was lifted, painfully, into the air.

Now that she was out of the dark trunk, she could see the hairy and sausage-like Arrow Cross leader, Horváth, from whose jaws she'd saved Molnar. "You don't have the greatest boss." He paused and made a queer, smiling face as he looked her up and down like a roast lamb chop. "But I understand why he hired you."

"So do I," said one of the two lean forms behind the bloated leader.

Horváth hit him lightly in the mouth with the back of his fat and hairy hand. His eyebrows touched—which wasn't hard for them to do. "Don't speak, Pisti."

"Yes, sir," Pisti said.

Eva's heart started to race. There was something in the men's eyes that she instinctively recognized but couldn't put her finger on. It scared her. The men herded Eva into the kind of concrete-block building popularized by communist architectural design that was already common in the bad side of Pest. She felt the cold blocks under her one bare foot as they pushed her into a dark room the size of a closet and slammed a metal door on her.

"Sit and think about all the other jobs you could have gotten," said Horváth. Then they walked away from her door, and she breathed a sigh of relief. But they weren't too far away, and she could hear them talk if she strained. She missed a few lines, but heard:

"Aren't we going to get to ..." said one of the lean voices.

"Get to what?"

"You know. You saw her."

"It depends on how you two behave, you swine. But we must wait till Sunday. These Nazis are always throwing their weight around."

Her heart started beating faster, and her breath came louder and louder. She tried to quiet it because she couldn't quite hear.

"So we will?"

"We?"

"Didn't your mother teach you to share, Horváth?"

Eva had heard the expression: "her heart sank." But she'd never felt it before.

———

Molnar's face looked like a beaten blood orange, and his left eye was shut tighter than a Scottish clam. His straight nose was broken and angular—an obscure shape only labeled in high school geometry. All this made his newly dyed-blond hair look comical as it blew in the convertible wind. At least the cool air helped soothe the pulsing pain and the headache that tried to come on.

His gray hat was somewhere else. Upon Molnar's insistence, Marilyn had gone back to switch Bastick's Benz for Molnar's Alfa Romeo.

Marilyn was driving north upon his quiet guidance. Words were few. Molnar had questions but didn't ask. Trees whipped by, lit up by the occasional streetlight. The leaves were difficult to make out, but the dark green became a beautiful background for the occasional passing shots of red and yellow in this early autumn palette.

Marilyn looked over at him, and the circles of her blue eyes stood out against the blurred background—bringing the third primary color to this fading-fall picture. All of it was framed by dark-gray clouds and a creeping realization that everything would soon be consumed by darkness and only two white beams of light would guide their way.

"I really am sorry you got in the middle, Mads," she said, shaking her head and staring at the road.

Molnar managed a weak smile and leaned his head against the headrest as he did so, relaxing sore neck muscles.

"I just had to. I had to try." Her face was similar to the first time they'd met, as she'd recalled her childhood. But it was even more honest now, pulled taut by the strings of an ugly memory. Molnar stared at her and tried a nod. He didn't quite pull it off, but she got the point.

She looked at him with pity and something else that even his years as a psychologist didn't help him label. But the word "maternal" came to mind. Her blonde hair blew in the breeze, all over to one side, as she turned to look at him. Her hair was thick enough that it put up a fight, straining against the wind. Molnar kept mum. He wasn't sure how well his jaw worked. But he saw in her eyes that she wanted to talk, to tell him about something. And he wanted to know, *Why Bastick?*

But she was mum. Molnar stared at her as she looked at the road. His eyes relaxed. He remembered the other relaxing face he'd rested his eyes on. And he thought of the letter in his pocket.

By the time his mind was back, the light was all gone and the trees were still there. Her face lit up in a flash as a streetlamp did its work, and then it was swallowed by dark. In the next flash, her eyes were wet.

They were quiet for a while, driving on in the dark. "So ... to Denmark?"

"You see, there are these bottles of poisoned wine," said Molnar. "I think you know how they look."

"So did Wolfram," she said, biting her lip hard.

"Don't say I didn't try to warn you," he said. "That's how his dad died. He knows them better than anyone."

She was silent at this, biting her lip harder and trying to make an unattractive face.

"What did he do to you?" Molnar asked. "And why didn't you just shoot him over there?"

"It would be too easy a death for him."

"He'll get his," said Molnar, gingerly touching his swollen cheekbone. "Whatever he did."

She was quiet.

"About these bottles. I have to find four more. Two are in Denmark, and two here. One is about fifteen minutes north of us, outside of Neumünster. You don't have to come along, but I need to finish this. People's lives, including mine, hang in the balance." Molnar looked around for Death when he said this, but he didn't look hard, seeing how there was no room in the little convertible. Death likes his space.

Marilyn laughed. "Who would talk to you? You look like a mashed tomato."

Molnar's thick fingers went up to his face and felt around. The shapes were different than his fingers remembered. He took his trapezoid nose between the tips of his fingers, and there was a loud pop as he put it back together. Marilyn winced. The shape was better, but the swelling remained. "Good point," he said.

Marilyn's manner changed. "Maybe they'll give you some ice to put on it so I don't have to keep looking at it. Let's go. I need something to do."

"All right, take this turn."

There was not a lot of talking. Soon, they pulled up in front of a Nazi barracks. It was one of the northern outposts, here in the high German country near the Danish border. The barracks were surrounded by tall stone walls with barbed razor wire in circular bundles around the top.

"So inviting," said Marilyn. "How do you normally get into these places?"

"I just show this Gestapo badge and either make up a story or not," he said. "The thing is, my employer doesn't want them to know who he is."

"What do you mean?"

"We need to get rid of any evidence that he sent the bottle. And we need to do so without anyone finding out. That's my only way out of the country."

"Oh, this *will* be fun!"

Molnar shrugged as they pulled up to the entrance of the camp. "The guy's name is Captain Mark Klein," he said to her as a kid walked up. The kid's hair was as blond as Molnar's dyed mop. He was maybe 17 and was wearing matching brown shorts and shirt. He looked more like a Boy Scout than a soldier.

The kid saw Marilyn and righted himself to his fullest, as if a rifle had just been run up the back of his shirt. He did a flamboyant *heil Hitler* salutation and then glanced at Molnar. "*Meine Güte!*" he said. "What happened to him?"

"He tried getting fresh," said Marilyn.

The boy's eyes grew big, but then he got it and laughed. "What is your business here?"

"We have to see Captain Klein," she said. "We're here on top-secret business." She nodded at Molnar, who silently produced his flashy Gestapo ID. "Everything went wrong."

The kid was hooked. "*Meine Güte!*" he said again. "What were you doing?" he asked Marilyn, trying not to stare at the parts of her that he most wanted to see.

"I'm not supposed to tell," she said, and then her voice lowered and she leaned close to him as if there were a secret between the two of them. "But of course, I was there to seduce an officer. I needed to know if he was an informant." She leaned drastically forward so that those most distracting parts breached the vehicle.

The kid took a step or two backward. "Ohhh," he said, now fully staring. "I'll ring the captain's office. I think he's still around. It's been late nights for them lately." He disappeared for a while, and Marilyn glanced at Molnar.

He smiled, happy to hand the dirty work to her ample imagination.

"You do look like Death warmed over," she said.

Molnar's belly laugh tried to come out, but the pain sputtered it into a cough. He glanced around to see if Death had heard, but he was nowhere to be seen. The kid came back running. "OK! He'll see you!" He stumbled a step when he got closer but was able to right himself.

"Where should we park?" asked Marilyn.

After they were inside the barracks, they followed the boy—who kept glancing back at Marilyn every few seconds to see how she looked on this step or that step. Molnar's head and neck throbbed like a bullfrog's belly. The rest of him would work just fine if he didn't need his brain to run it. He forced his mind to focus and tried to keep up as Marilyn sashayed after the Boy Scout.

They walked into a large, dark room and stared at a table surrounded by standing shadowy men. A spotlight shone down from the ceiling onto the table. That table held a topographic map of Eastern Europe, complete with mountains, green grass, and a few mock trees. Skewer-like paperweights with flags marked cities. Molnar could make out Berlin and Moscow.

The Boy Scout stood at attention behind the silhouettes. One shadow waved a hand in his direction to get the attention of a tall man with a dark, full beard. The man turned toward them. Then he stood to his full height and straightened himself with his hands on his lower back as if he'd been bent over the map for the last decade. The figure of Marilyn came into his blurry vision, and he gave the Boy Scout an approving nod. The Scout saluted him enthusiastically.

The man turned back to the men at the map. "Go have a smoke!" he said. "We may be a moment." Then he slicked back his hair with his thin fingers and moved toward Marilyn. "My dear *Fräulein*, please forgive my appearance. Sleep is the dearest commodity at the moment. How may I assist you?" He acknowledged Molnar with a nod.

Molnar watched Marilyn change her face to "helpless damsel."

"Oh, Captain Klein." She said it as if it was a sentence in itself. "Could we speak with you in your office? It's a private affair I have to discuss."

The word "affair" seemed to resonate with the man, and he nodded in consent. "Certainly, my dear," he said. "Come this way."

The bearded man, hair now slick, back now straight, walked them kindly out of the room and into a tan hallway. They navigated past six identical unmarked metal doors, and Molnar wondered how they kept them straight. He wondered how anyone kept anything straight as his head continued pounding to the rhythm of his own footsteps. He hoped Marilyn knew what she was doing. As the captain opened the door, Molnar almost swooned from dizziness.

"After you," said the captain as Marilyn walked in. She made sure to move with extra fluidity. The captain went in next, and Molnar was left to grab the door before it closed and walk in with the distinct feeling that he was intruding on the man's date.

The captain took his own chair behind his generic desk replete with trophies and awards from the first war. Molnar would put him at about 55 years old. He had the crinkles of feigned humor etched into the skin around his eyes—a self-inflicted brand of falsehood. Those crinkles were all dancing as he looked at Marilyn as if she were his personal gift from Heaven. He gestured to a chair, and Marilyn almost curtsied before she took it. Molnar found a seat for himself in the back of the room, touching the wallpaper. It depicted a fox hunt. The scene seemed to have crept into the captain's subconscious, because he stared at his prey.

Molnar's hand crept into his jacket pocket out of habit and noticed that his gun was gone. He wondered if it was still at the party. He loved that gun.

"You have my undivided attention," said the captain, sitting back and putting ankle over knee. Then he rocketed forward. "How ignorant of me!" he said, sitting bolt upright. "Forgive me. We've been cooped up so long I'm not thinking straight." He opened a box of cigarettes and offered one to Marilyn. She took it and bowed a thank you. His eyes almost went up to Molnar to offer him one, but they didn't. On a normal day, the affront would not go unanswered, but today, Molnar just removed one of his own cigars and lit it up. The captain smiled at Marilyn as she tried to light her own cigarette with the desk lighter and failed. "Allow me," he said.

"Please do," she said, pursing her lips in frustration. The captain must have noticed the lips because it took him a moment to hold the flame to the cigarette. She winked at him when she saw this and he kept the flame on too long and yanked his thumb away in a less-than-gentlemanly manner. He looked at the lighter as if it had bitten him. Marilyn waited for the attention of his dishonest eyes, and then she began the performance.

She leaned forward 30 degrees. Her German peasant dress, chosen so intentionally for the *Polterabend,* worked perfectly for the occasion. "We're here on top-secret business," she said. "You received a bottle of wine recently. A pinot noir."

"Yes," said the man, and his smile disappeared. His brain became as interested as his body for the first time. "I got it from my dear friend, Colonel Riffel. I'm afraid I haven't been able to celebrate anything with it yet."

"You see, we work for the Gestapo," Marilyn said, looking at Molnar expectantly. He held up his badge. The man nodded. "You must swear not to repeat what I'm about to tell you. Not to Colonel Riffel," she pronounced the name to perfection as if she'd said it a thousand times. "Not to anyone."

The man leaned back a bit more. His brows went up, and he took a drag. There was a pause. He nodded his promise, and his false eyes squinted as if it meant nothing.

"The bottle contains a piece of a code," Marilyn explained. "Riffel sent them out to people he trusts. We must put that code together, and we need to see the bottle in order to do that."

A genuine smile appeared on the man's face, and it cut new crinkles in his skin around his mouth and eyes. "How intriguing!" he said. "What a welcome interruption." He got to his feet. "Just this way." He nodded at Molnar as well and made eye contact with his one open eye for the first time.

The three of them headed out of the room and down some stairs that descended several stories. The temperature dropped as they went. Soon they reached a large metal door. The captain opened it and walked into the darkness. There was a click of a chain, and a single bare bulb above the man's head revealed dozens of bottles of wine along the walls of the little room—like books in the shelves of a library. There were also fortified wines, brandies, and whiskeys. Molnar was a little jealous. He realized that this was the fuel that powered Nazi officers as they made decisions of life or death for millions of young men. It was the fortification they needed to pull a thousand triggers without leaving the room.

The captain moved along the wall and searched until his fingers found what they were looking for. Sure enough, he pulled out the bottle with the white label and red kiss. He looked at it closer, trying to figure out the code. Then he stepped delicately along the brick floor to deliver it to Marilyn. As he passed it off, he made sure their hands touched.

Marilyn took the occasion to squeeze his hand in rapt thrill, like he'd handed her the Holy Grail. She released his hand and asked, "Was there a note with it?"

"I threw that away. Did you need that?"

"No, no. It should all be on the bottle," she said. She held the bottle up to the light and studied the front and back carefully. She lifted it higher and higher, so her arms were almost fully extended and her back was arched as she scrutinized the label. The captain took the chance to give her a more exhaustive appraisal. "Ah, the year is 1934," she said. "There it is—" And just then, the bottle slipped from her fingers and shattered on the brick floor, sending glass and poison everywhere. Her birdlike hands flew to her mouth, and she looked at the captain as if the world were rent in twain. After his shock passed, he smiled at her and hugged her to him to show that it was OK. She began to cry.

"Oh, there, there," he said. "It's all right, it's all right. I'll have the boy clean it up." He looked over at Molnar. "Did you get what you need from it?"

"Yes, sir," said Molnar, with a grin the size of the Soviet Union.

"Good." Then he was back to Marilyn. "You see that? No use crying over it."

"Oh, but I wasted it," she sobbed. "I'm so clumsy." Her tears and shaking chest were so genuine that they rocked Molnar to his core. His smile vanished. The sheer power of this force was fearful to him, and he took note of it.

With a smile on her face and many empty promises to the captain hanging in the air, Marilyn drove Molnar through the night countryside. It'd been an eventful evening. She was flushed and full of vigor and the power of success. He was beaten and bruised and bloody and sore. After a while, they pulled into a quaint bed-and-breakfast. It was an old white-brick mansion with black shutters. It could've hosted a polo match, if it'd had a field. They got two rooms, and Molnar headed toward his without a sound. He was halfway up the stairs when he turned back to Marilyn at the bottom.

"Good work."

She smiled up at him, and he shook his head at her comeliness. It didn't take a break. He turned back to the task of mounting the stairs, and she caught up with him. They reached a hallway decked with portraits of characters so stuffy they wouldn't bow to the queen. Molnar used his good eye to squint at his white-and-black key ring and read the number 7. He fumbled the key into the door. Marilyn used her 24-carat sapphires to see the number 9 on her key ring. She opened her door while he was still fumbling with his.

She watched him, and he finally got the key in and turned over the lock. "Good night, Marilyn."

"I was supposed to be married in the morning."

He had to summon most of his manliness to remain civil and standing at this point. Every bit of him wanted to throw himself in bed and sleep for a week. He nodded at her statement. It was valid. Emotions did exist. So he needed to acknowledge that.

"It's a strange feeling," she said.

"Runaway bride."

"With a gun," she added, holding his up.

"I was looking for that." He said it without perking up. He leaned heavily on the doorknob, his body testing its strength. She noticed this—how tired he was—and knew that meant he wasn't a threat. It made her giddy, like she was spending time with a eunuch. This was a rare event. It encouraged conversation. She closed her door and walked to him, holding the gun out. He reached to take it with a mostly limp hand, but she didn't let it go. That made him look up at her. Leveraging the gun, she pulled herself closer to him. Even his beaten body responded by sending his heart rate to dangerous heights.

"I should clean you up. How can you go to bed looking like that?"

"Stick around for 30 seconds, and you'll find out," he said. She let go of the gun and pushed him into the room. She closed the door behind them and felt around the room until she pulled the brass cord of a bedside table light. Then she pulled a cord on the second. The shades were so fine they looked like gossamer. She moved back beside Molnar and guided him to the bed, laying him down on it. He complied.

As a psychologist, he knew what she was doing. Knew how safe she felt with him while he was beaten like a smashed pumpkin—but as a man who'd lost a pint of blood, all that was for the textbooks.

Marilyn left him there and went into the bathroom. The water turned on for a while, and his eye began to close. He felt her fingertips clothed by a hot towel, wiping the parts of his face that'd been nagging him for hours. She cleaned away the dried blood, bit by bit. The shots of pain were minor, as her touch was light but firm enough to do its job. From time to time he opened his good eye and took note of whatever bit of her face or body it could see. Then the sleep made it close again. He opened it to see her eyes. They were oversized and had too many sparkling facets of blue to look real—as if she were a glass-eyed doll. But the emotion they showed was real, a loving care edged by years of self-reliance. Those edges faded as she did her work. The dark-blonde brows weren't heavy, but they were enough to show concern when she saw particularly ugly parts of him. He closed his eye and opened it again to see her mouth. It was set to its task and very plump in the middle—top and bottom—before it tapered into acute angles at the corners. The color was natural and pink and unpainted. All of her seemed perfectly symmetrical. His eye closed. She wiped it with the hot cloth.

"You saved me," she said.

He tried to speak. Cleared his throat and finally did. "I tried. You succeeded."

"So you owe me."

He nodded.

"I'll have to think about how I want to be paid," she said, and he felt her breath against his cheek. "You're an intriguing man, Mads."

"I'm usually more intriguing," he said. He tried to smile, but it hurt, so he frowned.

"Why are you doing all this?"

"Sleeping?"

"The bottles. Working for the Nazis!"

"I'm over a barrel. And trying to get to Sweden." His heavy eye blinked longer than normal.

"Let's just go in the morning."

"I don't have papers …"

"Papers! What do you mean?"

"The Nazis will give me exit papers when I finish," he said, and his eye closed.

She was quiet.

"What about you?" he mumbled. "Why'd you do it? Where you going?"

"I have papers already. I had planned to go to America," she said. "But I don't think I'd mind taking a look at Sweden."

The corner of his mouth lifted and fell. He started to nod off.

She wanted to say things aloud, but for no one to hear. When he didn't move for a while, she began, slowly. "Once upon a time, there was a little girl whose mother died when she was born. But she and her two brothers and father lived in a big brick house in the countryside, and her father would sing lullabies to her when she went to sleep."

Her voice started to sing a lullaby. It could have soothed Leviathan.

Molnar's jaw was soon slack and his breathing rhythmic. It hissed through his broken nose. Her eyes went to the corner of the ceiling, and she continued her story. "She doesn't remember too much else about her father. Her brothers taught her how to make dolls out of corn husks. And they read her stories. Then her father and brothers went away. There was a war. She was only four years old.

"Much later, she found out that her father had been blown apart in the first week of the battle, as the army marched through Belgium. Her brothers survived much longer. The two of them won many medals, and there are stories about how they saved each other's lives in turn. They stayed together always. They almost survived the war. But they died honorably in the line of duty. That is what a colonel came and told her at her grandparents' house. She remembers it all. She remembers taking their medals and their uniforms. She remembers how sad it was. But she also remembers being proud of them. She grew up raised by her grandparents in the farmhouse." She looked down to once again ensure Molnar was asleep. "But years later, the little girl, now almost a woman, received a letter that told a different story about her brothers.

"The letter was from a young soldier who had fought alongside the little girl's brothers. It wrote about a group of soldiers trapped in a house that was shelled. Her brothers were with them. One was killed in the shelling and the other was injured, pinned down by his broken legs. Several other soldiers were trapped by the building. The shelling and battle went on for days, and the men began to starve. At this point, the letter warned the girl not to read on unless she wanted to know a very painful truth. Too curious to halt, she went on, often wondering later if that was the right decision.

"Her brother was trapped there beside another man—a private. Both were pinned in place. More than a week passed with no response to their fading shouts for help and they weakened, and Death hung outside the room. The private said to her brother that they must draw straws to see which one should live. And the other could eat him. It was pragmatic, but her brother refused. He'd rather die. Finally, when it seemed her brother couldn't go on living, the private slit his throat and ate his shoulder and most of his arm to stay alive." She looked down at Molnar, who was sound asleep. "Of course the private's name was Wolfram Bastick." She kissed Molnar's bruised cheek. His eye almost fluttered open but didn't have the strength. And she took off his shoes and covered him, leaving him there in his clothes.

———

Early Saturday morning, Bastick slapped his padded hand on the back of his head. Both throbbed. He'd slept atop the covers of his king-sized bed inside his rented castle in his blood-covered suit. It wore a trifecta of rust shades spouted from the veins of the Gray Man, the driver he'd beaten and himself. He'd woken with panic and sat up straight.

He'd looked at his hands. They had the same burnt-red crumbs in all the crevices. Had he killed the Gray Man? Had he killed the driver? Had Marilyn intended to poison him? Was she working for the Gray Man? And, most importantly, had the Gray Man killed his father?

Bastick felt as if he were at the center of an amazing conspiracy and couldn't see clearly. Just a month ago, he'd been so calm, so composed. He'd left all the anger behind. He'd been about to marry the girl of everyone's dreams and, coupled with his advanced abilities, produce a true *übermensch*. His mother had been on speaking terms with him again. He'd be a well-respected gentleman. But now.

He ran over to the mirror to see his damaged ear. Then his eyes went to the permanent line stitched between his eyebrows from inborn churning rage. He washed his hands vigorously with steaming water so hot it burnt, but he ignored this and kept lathering under the water with soap. A strange sensation of pain-pleasure came from the nerve endings of his burning fingers. His knees got weak, but he kept his hands in the water until the pleasure reached a crescendo. He removed his hands and bent over them, looking at the red, throbbing, and scalded flesh. Now they only felt as if they'd been burnt, sapped of power, and he ran very cold water over them to relieve the feeling.

He'd always had the problem. Mixing emotions. Mixing senses. One day in kindergarten class, he'd attributed a sex to the number four—it was definitely male. This occurrence was not unknown in children. But he'd gone on to describe a pink square as smelling of fear and swine's flesh, and the teacher had never looked at him the same again. That peculiarity became his most fearsome gift. In the war, he could see the change in plant life surrounding them before a bomb fell. He tried to describe this to one of his fellow soldiers as, "An apple-green cringing of the vegetation." The soldier told him he didn't want to know how he found these things out, but to give a shout when he did.

Bastick tore off his clothing and threw it to the floor. Naked, he showered, but not at the same burning temperature. He dried and clothed himself in his all-black detective's uniform, and took a moment to stare at his unused wedding suit. He walked down to the front desk of the castle and asked for a taxi.

"Wolfie?" said the voice of his mother from down the hallway. He didn't turn, but walked to some of the seats in front of the desk and threw his heavy body into one, listening for the squeaking of the springs. "Wolfie! Where did you go last night? What did you do with Marilyn and that man? What happened? The venue called and said your car was still there. I didn't think you'd have come back. Is that man all right? Is Marilyn? Are you still getting married?" He wouldn't look up at her, so she sat beside him and held his face gently in her hands. "Are you all right, Wolfie? Please, talk to me."

The front desk clerk raised his hand to signal that the cab was ready, and Bastick gingerly but firmly removed his mother's hands from his face. He stood to his feet and exited the lobby.

"Where are you going?" shouted his mother as he jogged down the stairs and leapt into the cab. "Where do you think you are going?!"

The cab drove off, and the driver winked in the rear-view mirror. "You really wound her up," he said.

"She's my mother!"

A good cabbie knew when to be quiet. As this one put the car into second gear, he remembered that.

———

Later that morning, Molnar woke with a groan. When you first step back into a beaten body, the pain can seem much worse than when you lost consciousness. You have to try it on and wear it around a bit before you get used to it again. Molnar knew this, and he kept his mouth shut. He stuck his clothed legs out of the bed and wondered who'd covered him up. Then he remembered Marilyn. And he remembered himself, too tired to stay awake. His wide feet hit the cold wood and he stumped over to the bathroom. He splashed water on his face. It was the kind of bone-chilling cold that only comes through the pipes of northern countries, but it felt good.

The mirror told him his face was blacker, but the swelling had subsided overnight. He read this with his right eye alone. The left was still closed.

His neck and shoulders felt as if they'd been worked over with a blacksmith's hammer. He started to rub them.

There was a knock on the door. He walked over toward it, and it opened on its own. It was a fresh-faced Marilyn wearing a white robe and holding two cups of steaming coffee in her hands. If Molnar were an older man, the sight would've induced a stroke.

"Do you like coffee?" she asked, pushing past him. "I don't even know that about you."

He grunted affirmation as he let her pass.

"With cream and sugar?"

"Black."

"Good, because I didn't bring any." She turned back to him and handed over a white ceramic mug. Then she sat on his bed. He sat beside her. She looked over at him. The face she wore was starting to become consistent—the trusting, interested young woman. It was as if she didn't have to be Marilyn Ghetz anymore, only a mere mortal. He wondered if this was her natural face or if she was putting it on. He started to take a sip but she spoke, so he lowered his mug. "Are we going to save someone else today? Capture another bottle?"

"If you want," he said, about to take a sip—

"What are you going to do in Sweden? Do you have a girl waiting for you?"

"Not in Sweden."

"How about anyplace else?"

"Only my secretary," he said, and finally took a drink of the coffee. It must have been good, because he closed his eye. "Whom I should call, actually."

"I don't like her very much," said Marilyn.

"She's not very nice."

"I wouldn't allow her around children."

Molnar had to pull his cup away again as he laughed his rolling, boiling laugh. Marilyn watched him over her coffee. Once he recovered, he stood up. "I'll be right back. Have to find a phone. We can leave soon to get breakfast if you like."

"I do like."

Molnar nodded at her and left the room. She took a drink. Then she looked around and saw his shoes on the ground and smiled.

By the time he reached the steps, Molnar also realized where his shoes were, but he kept walking. They were not worth making another exit. He wasn't sure if the clerk behind the counter noticed his bare feet, but the man's face didn't betray it. "I'd like to make a phone call."

"Here you are," said the young, blond clerk, handing over the receiver. Molnar asked the operator to ring his office. She tried and told him the line was disconnected.

"Permanently?"

"Yes, sir," she said. "We've not been able to reach the whole building."

He thanked her and asked her to put him through to a Miles Fekete in Budapest. "That one will work," she said, patching him through.

"This is Miles."

"Miles, it's Mads. Did you manage to reach Eva?"

"Mads!" This time the man was in briefs. He was still holding a mug of coffee. "No. When I arrived, the place was on fire. They couldn't put it out in time and the building is burnt down. It's gone."

Molnar was quiet as he took that in. A lesser man with a plum for a face and a business in ashes might have complained. Meanwhile, Miles's hand went out for the Cointreau; but, hearing the long pause, he reached past it for the rum.

Molnar heard the baritone thump of the cork. "Don't get too upset," he told Miles, who halted his pity pour halfway.

"I'm sorry about your luck, Mads," Miles said. "I haven't heard or seen one hair of that girl. But to be fair, she probably wouldn't run to tell me she were alive. I'll keep looking."

"Oh! I just remembered something. The man's name is Horváth. He seemed to be their leader. That may help."

Miles gurgled some kind of affirmation through the drink.

"I'll call you back later."

"Anytime," said Miles, subconsciously rubbing his hairy belly in a clockwise, circular pattern.

Molnar handed the phone back to the clerk, who was trying to grow a beard. He shouldn't have been.

If Detective Wolfram Bastick were a man equipped with average mental composure, the betrayal and probable attempted poisoning by his fiancée on the eve of his wedding might have put a crack in the structural integrity of his mind. But Detective Bastick came equipped with a subconscious switching station to deal with such atrocities. His synesthesia extended beyond his senses to his emotions. Since he'd been a boy, whenever he'd felt pain, hurt, or betrayal, Bastick's mind switched the neurological tracks to save him anguish, turning negative feelings into overwhelming determination—to succeed, to destroy. This emboldened and motivated him into a kind of mania. It suppressed his desire to sleep and eat and drink to such a degree that he could go days without such trivialities. And when he encountered humans who clung to these weaknesses, it enraged him.

Bastick, in such a state of bastardized emotions, had been a busy boy. While Marilyn and Molnar breakfasted, he picked up his car, returned to the castle, and drove to the local police precinct—all by nine in the morning. He calmly related the story of a mad Hungarian imposter who'd kidnapped his beautiful blonde German bride-to-be on the eve of their wedding.

The police wires got hot as they fired the story across the German empire. Bastick placed a call to the *Völkischer Beobachter* daily paper, related the same story, and agreed to send a photo of his fiancée. The story was slated for a column buried deep in the back pages until a special courier arrived later that morning with the photo.

A smile crept across the face of the editor-in-chief when he saw the photo, and a dusty bottle of Monopole was opened for brunch in the newsroom. The cover of the afternoon edition—shipped to every corner of the German empire—was painted with the face of "Marilyn Ghetz— Kidnapped Bride!"

Bastick was depicted as a *Count of Monte Cristo*-esque Edmond Dantès—a wronged and honorable lover who'd gotten his world snatched away by a villainous Hungarian. By Saturday evening, the public was in a fever pitch, demanding the police find this loathsome fiend only known as the "Gray Man."

Earlier that day, once they'd finished breakfast, Marilyn conceded the driver's seat to the Gray Man, and handed the keys to him across the table with a smile. "It's fun being Mads Molnar," she said. "Special gun, fast car."

"Sometimes it's even painful," Molnar said, wincing over his sealed left eye. He shook his head and went to the front desk to check out. Marilyn walked out to the car. She glanced over her shoulder before she moved to the trunk, opened it, and looked in. Her wedding gown filled it with no room to spare. She had run to get it when she'd switched cars at the venue. Her hand went over the lace pattern on the side that the tailor had changed upon her demands. She felt it between her fingers like a toddler feels silk. She heard the hotel door open behind her, and she shut the trunk and moved to the passenger-side door.

Molnar walked up with his briefcase and climbed into the driver's side of the long, single, white-cushioned seat. She slid in beside him and rubbed her hands together.

"Cold in the mornings," he said, turning on the car and the heater. It also blew cold, not helping any. "This is the bad part about convertibles," he added, grimacing against the chilling air.

"Where to?" she asked.

"That depends." He turned toward her. His sore neck kept him from making it look comfortable. "There's one more bottle left here in Germany, at a *Luftwaffe* base called Schleswig/Jagel, northwest of Kiel. We could head there. It's not far from the border of Denmark."

She was already nodding, excited as a child riding to work with Daddy.

"But I have a bad feeling about it.... Bastick."

She nodded.

"I'm betting there'll be a warrant out for me by five minutes past nine." He looked at his watch. "Maybe we skip this bottle, cross the border, and get the last two."

"But what about your exit papers? What about Sweden?"

"You're more important than they are," Molnar said, holding her gaze. "If anything happened to you ..."

"Oh, come on! Where's your sense of adventure?" Her arms were akimbo, though you'd think there wasn't enough room in the seat for it. "Be a man."

Molnar's eyebrows knit together at that, and his mouth opened in mock shock. "I'm only thinking about your safety, sweetheart," he said.

"Ha!"

"The Duchess says, 'onward,' so onward we must go," said Molnar, saluting. By now, the car was blowing a little heat. He threw it into first, and they were off. They drove for a couple of hours, stopping for fuel once. Molnar took a look at the front lines of the news-and-propaganda daily: *Völkischer Beobachter*. "Hamburg Citizen Hospitalized after Late-Night Carjacking," read the headline. Molnar read the first two lines, and they helped fill him in on what had gone on while he had been sleeping.

When he got back to the car, Marilyn was carefully cleaning the windshield in the same little Bavarian peasant dress she'd had on at the party last night. The fuel attendants were at attention, as were the customers. Molnar leaned on the soft top and joined the crowd. "You didn't tell me I missed a show last night."

"It was over in one round," she said, scrubbing a dark spot on the glass.

"What happened?"

"How much do you want?" She used her fingernail on the spot till it came off.

"Just the facts."

"All right." She bent in half to dip the squeegee into a bucket. "After your lights went out, Wolf was going to roast your toes, so he threw you and me in his car. He nearly hobbled an old man at the party for trying to help you. Then he drove off too fast and almost wrecked a handful of times and was challenging every driver." She finished the final cleaning swipe of the windshield with the squeegee and shook it off on the ground. Everyone wished she'd shake it a few more times. "A gutsy driver challenged Wolfie, and he turned his head inside out on the pavement. I wasn't keen to the idea of watching him do the same to you, so I took Wolfie's car, shot out the tire of the other driver's car, and took off."

"All while I was napping."

She nodded, putting the squeegee back into its place. "When we got to your car, you were too heavy, so I slapped you till you got up."

"Then I really do owe you one."

"Several." She smiled at him and got back into the car.

"I wondered how you got us out."

"I have my ways."

"And while I've been away, my secretary disappeared, and my office is ashes."

Marilyn thought for a while, and Molnar let her. He put the car into gear, and they took off, a dozen pairs of eyes following her, and a dozen brains imagining a dozen impossible scenarios.

They drove north, past Rendsburg and through the cropland of northern Germany. After half an hour, Marilyn insisted on having lunch.

"We've no idea when we'll be able to eat again, and I'm starving," was her reasoning.

Molnar agreed, and they stopped at a hotel in *Kropperbusch* to eat. The conversation wasn't titillating; as Molnar silently chewed, his mind was elsewhere. Marilyn glanced down at her finger and then up at the chewing Molnar. It was already afternoon. They paid and left.

After a while, Molnar saw something and pulled the car into a side road. It was a plane taking off from a runway in the distance. "So, this is the airfield," he said. "The bottle was sent to"—he looked at his list, read off the name—"*Oberstleutnant* Bartek Cermak of the *Luftwaffe*. And it should have been delivered here ... five days ago."

"Want me to play my little game again?"

"It worked last time. But if my gut is right, we'd better hurry."

Five minutes later, a hot-rod-red Alfa Romeo with the top down pulled into Schleswig/Jagel *Luftwaffe* airport. The guard leaned out and encountered a scene he wasn't expecting. Marilyn went through her paces. Molnar kept up his end. He looked a little less beaten today. He was still not pretty, but his badge worked. The two of them got to Cermak, who was a near carbon-copy of the aging, lecherous sort of overimpressed-by-Marilyn Nazi as yesterday—except for one thing. He was less of a gentleman and more of a conceited ex-pilot. Marilyn pulled her routine, and he bit hard.

"Just this way, my dear," said Cermak. His eyebrows needed hats of their own, but they had to settle with his lieutenant-colonel cap, pulled at a rakish angle to the left. His skin was just showing the beginnings of mottling. His eyes were confident slits, as if he were always staring at the sun. His smile was permanent and surrounded by clean-shaven cheeks. It wasn't a civilian clean shave but a military clean shave. You'd guess he was very handsome 20 years ago, and he'd guess he still was. "We'll be right back," he said to Molnar and the officer beside him, who resembled a bloated corpse with very pink skin. "You two have a drink, and we'll run down to the cellar." That wasn't a good sign. Marilyn kept to form without flinching, and pranced along with Cermak and out the door. But if Molnar's eyes were any less swollen, the worry would've been read in them like street signs.

The very pink officer with Molnar was sweating in the chilly pilot barroom where they stood. The room was just below the signaling tower for the airport and had all-glass walls.

"Want a drink?" asked the pink man.

"Sure. I'll have anything brown."

The man went behind the bar and chuckled to himself. Molnar followed him there and stood on the customer side. "He's always had a way with ladies."

"I guess so."

"He has a way of convincing them of things," laughed the officer again, standing with tumbler and bottle in hand. He poured some whiskey for Molnar and left the bottle on the bar between them. "Like taking off their clothes—whether they want to or not. I just wish I could be there right now." His dead eyes rolled up to Heaven—a place he'd never see.

"You do realize she's my friend, don't you? Where's the cellar?"

"The cellar is straight downstairs. And that is the perfect place for him." The pink man smiled at Molnar. "Take ice?"

"I would love some ice!" said Molnar.

The man bent down again and came up with ice in one hand and his pistol in the other. Molnar's jaw went a little slack. "You two must think that we're stupid."

"I can only speak for myself. But I don't see how that's relevant."

"Just because we live on base doesn't mean we're unaware of the outside world," said the man, nodding at the paper halfway down the bar. "Go ahead, take a look." Molnar took a step toward the paper and opened it to see Marilyn's face and the headline. The whole story played out in his mind, and his stomach sank. They'd both be arrested, but not before Cermak finished whatever evil intent he had for Marilyn. Then Molnar would be hanged or shot, depending on if the soldiers had time on their hands or not. No exit papers, no Sweden. And Marilyn ... soon, she'd be back in the arms of Bastick.

The officer laughed. "May as well finish your drink," he said, and reached to place the ice in Molnar's glass. That was the wrong move.

Molnar'd been on a hair trigger since his beating by Bastick, and had several tons of bound angst.

As the man slightly overextended his reach to get the ice into the glass, Molnar grabbed his wrist in one hand, yanked him forward and smashed his chest into the bar. With the other hand, Molnar snatched the whiskey bottle and swung it viciously into Pink's gun hand. The gun sailed against the back bar wall. Then, without releasing tension on the man's wrist, Molnar put all the pent-up rage he'd held back into several precise blows. He swung the bottle into Pink's head once, twice, thrice—pulling the wrist toward him on every swing. The bloated man crumpled. Molnar put the bottle back on the counter and peeked over it. The man had conceded consciousness at the very least.

Molnar threw back his drink, grabbed the paper, and moved through the door used by Marilyn and Cermak. He encountered a stairwell and ran down five flights to a metal door. He opened that and went down a hall. Half a dozen doors lined each side. Molnar balked for a beat and started trying them one by one. All were locked. At the end of the hall was one more door, and he heard a cry from behind it. He rushed to the door and opened it wide. Cermak was holding Marilyn in his arms, and she was crying. A bottle of wine lay on the floor with its contents spilled all over Cermak's shoes.

"You all right?" asked Cermak, angry to be interrupted.

"Peachy," said Molnar, not slowing down. He pulled the man away from her by his shoulder and clocked him hard in the jaw. Cermak smashed into the rock flooring, his rakish hat askew. But almost as quickly he sprang off the floor toward Molnar, only to encounter a magnum of wine with the side of his head. Molnar'd grabbed one from the wall. He put it back and looked down at Cermak. He was cold as a creamsicle.

Marilyn looked at Molnar with questions in her eyes.

"We're famous," said Molnar, pulling the newspaper out of his jacket pocket. He watched until her eyes got the size of cannon barrels. Then he turned to disrobe Cermak. Molnar was about the same size.

"How did this happen?" she asked the air. Molnar pulled his own clothes off, and Marilyn pretended to look away. Then he stepped into Cermak's outfit. He went back for the letter in his jacket pocket—Ilsa's letter—and tried to make sure Marilyn didn't see it.

"How do I look?" he asked. She turned fully toward him. Aside from the bruised face, he looked pretty good in the blue wool blazer with its golden shoulder patches and iron cross in place of a tie.

Marilyn stepped back to survey him. "Looks like you missed your calling," she said. Molnar smirked and handed her Cermak's automatic pistol from his belt. She took his clip of bullets too, and slipped them into a pocket of her peasant dress. Molnar grabbed her hand, and they both walked back down the hall and up the first flight of stairs.

As the two made their way out of the building, Molnar tipped his hat to a few passing pilots. The two of them got a lot of looks because of Marilyn. It's hard to be clandestine when you're gorgeous. So they hammed it up, talking and laughing as they went.

"Aren't we going back to the car?" said Marilyn out of the corner of her mouth.

"I've got an idea."

"When were you going to tell me?" she asked, keeping pace beside him.

"I just got it."

"Well, what is it?"

"You'll see," said Molnar, as he tipped his hat to a young, ogling officer.

"What if I have something in the car that I need?"

Molnar slowed his gate. "Do you?"

Marilyn was silent for several paces as they moved toward a door that read, *Die Landebahn*. There was a red light with a speaker above the door that looked as if it could be loud.

"No," said Marilyn. "I don't have anything I need. Just my very expensive wedding dress, that's all. I won't be needing that, will I?" She looked at Molnar as he pushed open the door below the red light.

"Do you want me to go get it?" Molnar asked, halting halfway onto the flight tarmac.

"I don't know. Do I?" She looked at him

It was a moment for which he wasn't prepared. He started to think about too many things. But mainly, he started thinking of Ilsa. He still felt a tie to the dead woman. As if he'd be betraying her. His hand went subconsciously into his jacket pocket. It almost felt wrong to imagine a new life. But Marilyn's stare didn't relent.

And then it went off. The red light flashed, and the speaker blared. Molnar realized he must not have done too good a job on the pink officer. He should have hit him a fourth time.

"Stay calm and follow me," said Molnar.

"We could have been to the car by now!"

"Just trust me."

She looked up into his brown eyes and saw them smile at her beneath the pilot's hat. And she thought how the Nazis got a few things right, like the cut of their uniforms, as she walked beside him. They approached a little wooden booth with a Nazi soldier in it. Beyond the booth were dozens of planes. Most were BF 109 fighter planes with single cockpits, and there was one of the 109's rejected competitors, the Heinkel He 112 V2.

At the booth, Molnar opened the little glass door and said to the soldier, "Look sharp! This is a training drill. I need keys to a plane with a dual cockpit."

"I didn't know about any training operation."

"Don't you hear that siren, you fool? It's a surprise op. They're timing us!"

"Yes, sir," said the man, and his fingers searched through rows of keys as if he used them to see. He grabbed a set, and pointed with them toward the Heinkel on the runway.

"That's the only two-seater."

"Get it started, quickly."

The man heiled and ran toward the Heinkel. Molnar chased after him with Marilyn in his wake.

On the other side of the building, the Alfa Romeo was being broken into by security guards, with a black-eyed officer at their lead. The front gate exit was being closed, and a search was on throughout the building for Molnar and Marilyn.

Back on the tarmac, Marilyn caught up with Molnar. The Nazi soldier had gotten the plane blaring. He helped Marilyn climb in, then Molnar. The man leaned in and said, "We're supposed to run through our checks now, like the fluids and equipment."

"That's part of the exercise: to see if you all have everything in order," said Molnar. "Now climb down." The man did so and heiled. Molnar saluted him and closed the glass canopy over the both of them.

"I didn't know you were a pilot!" Marilyn yelled over the engines. Molnar pointed to the radio headset. He put his on, and she followed suit.

"Live through a world war, and you can drive just about anything," he said into the microphone.

She looked out at the man running back toward his booth and at the red lights blaring. More men came from the building, headed toward the booth. "Hope you can drive it fast."

Molnar rotated the plane so it was generally pointed down the runway and yanked the throttle back. They shot down the landing strip as the security guards learned what had happened from the man in the booth. Some started waving their arms wildly at the plane while others ran back toward the building.

Marilyn felt her stomach try to shake hands with her brain as Molnar lifted them off the runway and into the sky. She stared down at the disappearing airfield below.

At 150 meters, Molnar banked hard to the left to head north.

Marilyn looked down to get a glimpse of the building's entrance. Her beautiful white dress was billowing out of the sprung trunk of the red racing machine. She watched it flap as they flew away.

Colonel Riffel sat in a maroon robe on the side of the tub. His feet were in the steaming water of the bath. His hands were held out, fingers spread wide, and poor Charles was giving him a manicure. Charles's hand slipped off the cuticle and scratched Riffel's finger.

"Ow! You pigeon!" Riffel pulled his hand back and looked at it. "Pass that glass of brandy." The phone rang. Charles passed the brandy and stood to get it—saved, for now, from further berating.

"Colonel Riffel's office," said Charles, his cropped military haircut cutting a sharp outline in a sunbeam on the wall. "He will be pleased to know—"

"What is it, Charles?"

"The Arrow Cross."

"Bring me the phone, Charles!"

Charles complied, and Riffel held the receiver to his head with one hand and the brandy to his mouth with the other. "This is Riffel."

"We have his secretary," said one of the two lean men. He was trying to relax on a metal chair in the kitchenette a room away from where Eva was trying to keep her heart in her chest.

"Let me talk with Horváth," said Riffel. Horváth, the fat one, was lying on what some might call a couch, or at least the general shape of a couch.

"Certainly," said the lean man, bringing the phone to Horváth.

"My dear Colonel Riffel!" said Horváth. "How may I help you?"

"You have her, and Molnar's office is burnt to the ground?"

"Yes, colonel."

Riffel nodded to himself and looked up at the ceiling as if he were inwardly processing the events, seeing them play out before him. "You sure it's burnt? There can't be anything linking me to the case. Not a note, not an invoice, nothing. And I can't have her contacting Molnar! He has to finish finding those bottles."

"Colonel, do not worry. I watched the fire myself. And she is in the other room, bound."

"Bound?" Riffel was quiet for a long time. "She sounded beautiful when we spoke." Riffel remembered her dirty mouth and aloof manner.

"She is."

"Did you ... do anything to her?"

"Colonel Riffel," said the fat man, "we consider her under your protection ... until Sunday."

"She is!" he said quickly. "But then again, all work and no play makes Horváth a dull boy." A giggle spilled out of Riffel's lips and into his bath.

"A true proverb," said Horváth, nodding to his men.

"Won't you save me some details of how things go?"

"My dear colonel, I would never kill your imagination."

Riffel giggled to himself. "You vicious fiends," he said. "You swine!" He giggled again. "OK. I'll get in touch if I need anything else." He hung up. "Charles! The left hand."

———

Molnar sat in the cold cockpit of his hijacked plane. His hijacked bride was in the back, trying not to be cold. The heaters worked, but it wasn't tropical.

"Where do you think we are?" asked Marilyn over her radio headset. She looked out the window to see the water below them.

"I think we're somewhere over the Baltic Sea between Germany and Denmark. Look off to our northwest. That should be the far island of Denmark. Our destination is Copenhagen." He looked down at the fuel gauge. It was still three-quarters full. Luckily for Molnar, the Germans did have all their planes full of fuel and ready to fly at a moment's notice.

"Looks like," she said, pausing to shiver, "we're saving time. Glad they didn't chase us."

Molnar raised a brow. Marilyn couldn't see that, but she looked behind her anyway. In the distance and closing in were two BF 109 fighter jets, known to the *Luftwaffe* as hunting planes. They were faster than Molnar's Heinkel.

The two planes spread out to either side of Molnar and Marilyn and closed in. Marilyn turned back to see two planes spreading out to either side of them and gaining ground. "How long have they been there?"

"The last five minutes," said Molnar. He had the throttle all the way forward to get the plane up to 500 kilometers an hour—but still, the 109s gained. "You buckled up?"

She nodded and watched the island enlarge—but the 109s enlarged faster. "Hope you said your prayers, Molnar."

He was quiet. What kind of thing was that to say at a moment like this? The engine screamed.

After a few minutes more, Molnar did gymnastics to turn back to Marilyn and smile. The expression was so genuine that she had to smile back. "Hang on," he said.

The cannons opened up. Molnar saw the red flashes before he heard anything. Then followed a *rat-a-tat-a-rat-a-tat-a*. He dropped the plane fast through the clouds, turning the nose straight down into a dive. Marilyn tightened her safety belt.

They were vertical. The Baltic Sea became more and more apparent before disappearing behind a veil of fog. Only white was visible. They kept dropping. Then Molnar pulled up hard, and Marilyn felt the force of nearly four times gravity for the first time. She lost track of that force's natural direction, and it took her vision a moment to come back into focus. The plane shook a little too much, and the engines seemed to her as if they'd stall. When the fog disappeared and she saw how close the sea was, she gasped and hoped Molnar didn't hear.

Molnar wouldn't hear an atom bomb right now. He pushed the throttle back to full speed. They cut through the air like a needle, and back up into the fog, but not before Marilyn saw land come into view about five kilometers off. Meanwhile, the *rat-a-tat* was incessant. Molnar kept the plane in the fog and the throttle open.

There was a *thunk, thunk* to Marilyn's right. "They got us!" she shouted, not sure what level of panic she should feel.

Molnar eyed the holes in the wing out the window. They looked ugly. Petroleum gushed from the right wing fuel tank. Molnar looked around for the knob to turn that tank off. He found it and closed the tank. Then there was another *thunk-thunk-thunk* to their left. Sparks flew, and petroleum dumped out of the left wing. It looked like the wing was barely holding together, with pieces of it flying off in the wind.

"OK ..." said Molnar. He pulled the plane up hard through the fog and into the clouds, trying to gain altitude. The *rat-a-tat* paused for a moment.

Marilyn wondered if they would die. Her heart was beating hard against the seatbelt, and she looked at the back of Molnar's head, which was jostling around from the shaking of the engine. And in that moment, as her life was in his hands, even within the view of Death, she felt differently about the back of this man's head than she'd ever felt about the back of anyone's head.

Molnar's hands were locked on the throttle and joystick. They breached the clouds into clear skies. Marilyn turned, looking for the planes. They hung back in the air but continued the chase, watching their helpless prey. Did they know there was no hope?

There was a sputtering sound, and the RPMs dropped. The engines were starving. Molnar had been waiting for this. He opened the right-wing tank again to let in any last bits of fuel that it might still hold below the bullet holes. The engine sputtered, the propellers almost jammed, and Molnar banked a little left to tilt any fuel to the engine. The propellers kicked back in. He'd have been sweating if it weren't so cold.

He was 2000 meters from land, and the engines held.

1000 meters. The engines started sputtering, and Molnar dropped the plane low, diving for the shore.

There, on the bank above a steep granite cliff face, he saw a narrow dirt road. He shot toward it, but they were too low. They were sailing right for the cliff side. He needed a bit more out of the plane, so he cranked the throttle wide open, pulling up. The propellers reacted, cutting the air fast and lifting him one last time. He went higher, and then the props were gone, and the plane went into a violent shaking, stuttering dance, telling him that even the fumes had evaporated. Molnar turned the key, shutting off the engines to avoid the shaking, and aimed for the road. He looked back at Marilyn, whose jaw was tight. He wanted her to be the last thing he remembered. Then he turned back and guided the plane in like a glider, using care and cunning on the wing ailerons and the angle of the nose.

They were almost to the cliff and coming in short, but he pulled up hard and got his front wheels on the roadway. The rear wheels smacked the cliff edge, and the plane bounced high off the road and came crashing down again. But the wheels held out, and the plane barreled down the road at well over 100 kilometers an hour. Marilyn gasped on the first bounce. Molnar hit the brakes as the plane careened down the roadway, which was too short and which curved at a hard right angle. He locked the brakes, and they slid down the gravel path and then shot off it and onto sand dunes. The rear wheels were knocked off, and the plane slid on its belly to a final halt.

The dust and sand began to settle. Molnar wiggled members of his body to make sure they were intact. He unbuckled himself and turned to see Marilyn. She was intact. Then he heard the buzz of two planes going by overhead. He stared through the canopy to see the 109s pass by. He waited and watched. Then he slid the canopy back and jumped out on the wing to help Marilyn from her seat. She was out in a hurry, and he pulled the canopy closed behind them as the 109s banked high in a wide U-turn.

Molnar pulled Marilyn into some nearby brush, and they both crouched, watching, hoping the fighters hadn't seen them exit. The planes dove low, and the glass of the cockpit exploded with bullets. Its riddled corpse was torn to shreds.

As it steamed, the 109s didn't turn. They held course back to Germany.

Molnar's lungs started up again. He realized he'd been holding his breath. Then he realized Marilyn's cold hand was in his own. He looked over at her. "You all right?"

Her white lips smiled at him. "You think I'm made of glass?"

"I'd have said the finest of crystal," he corrected, trying to imitate Winston Churchill.

"Don't you know I'm made of diamond, Dr. Molnar?" She said it in the voice of the queen of England, and he laughed.

"Yes, yes, I believe you are."

Marilyn held up her automatic pistol. "Let's get the next one," she said, and Molnar chuckled. He helped her stand, then pointed north, toward Copenhagen.

His stiff hand was still shaking.

————

Placing Marilyn's photo in the newspaper had worked better than Wolfram Bastick could have imagined. The paper's phone rang like a boxing bell with false-alarm sightings all over the empire. But when several *Luftwaffe* pilots called to say they'd seen the pair fly north from Schleswig/Jagel, Bastick began his deductions.

The article on Marilyn also got the attention of the Gestapo, and now Bastick was flanked by the loyal, ginger Otto plus eight *Kriminalassistents* who all wanted nothing more than to help find Marilyn Ghetz. Bastick and his entourage boarded a plane from Hamburg to Copenhagen.

Their plane landed in that city just as the sun dipped below the horizon. The propellers hadn't even stopped by the time Bastick vaulted down the steps to the tarmac below. He was followed by lackeys carrying his baggage and theirs. They were all dressed in black, with Otto in the lead. And if they'd removed their caps, they'd have revealed heads and faces as clean-shaven as cue balls. It was a requirement Bastick had made of them before allowing them to join the hunt.

The lackeys all came with automatic weapons over their shoulders. As they marched in the pattern that geese fly toward two waiting sedans, they were the very picture of military power: every muscle taut, every step in sync, every eye clear. They reached the cars, and Bastick shoved past his standing driver. He stood by the steering wheel as his men entered the back seat. Otto awaited orders.

"We're going downtown to sniff out a dog," Bastick told him.

Otto responded with his default skyward glare.

"Just drive that car." Bastick pointed to the second sedan.

Bastick climbed behind one wheel and said a harsh word to the driver outside, who'd started questioning him about taking his seat. Otto got behind the wheel of the other car and repeated the same phrase with almost the exact intonation—like a ginger scale model of the big man. They left the Danish drivers who'd brought the cars to the tarmac cursing and looking at each other in disbelief.

As Bastick and Otto drove off the tarmac in single file, the last burning wisps of orange in the clouds cooled.

Molnar saw the same clouds go cold as he bumped along in the open-air bed of a milk truck. It had taken a grand total of 30 seconds for Marilyn to wave down a ride, and she hadn't even stuck out her thumb. The driver must have thought he'd won the lottery until Molnar'd popped out of the bushes. As punishment, the driver'd quarantined him in the back of the truck with actual milk bottles while Marilyn chatted him up.

When they reached central Copenhagen, Marilyn thanked the man, and he nearly swooned. Marilyn and Molnar were soon inside the gaudy restaurant of the Palace Hotel. Marilyn insisted on luxury after facing death. Who was Molnar to argue? Both wore the same clothes from the *polterabend*, and only Marilyn pulled it off. Both had nothing but a drink in front of them so far.

Molnar listened and watched the gold-bedazzled waiters move around the room. The walls were a white diamond-pattern wallpaper with too many gold accents—chandeliers, candles, cufflinks. It was distracting.

Marilyn noticed some of the holes in her Bavarian peasant dress. "I might need to get a new one of these."

Molnar leaned back in his chair and tried not to look at anything gold. He stared at the ceiling. No luck: it was a series of gold-leaf nesting squares.

"You should take your time. Get a nice one. Get dolled up. It'll give you something to do while I get this next bottle," he said, lifting a finger for the waiter.

Air came out of Marilyn's mouth in a burst. Words followed. "You can't go without me, Mads! Anyway, I'm the one doing all the work."

But Molnar's face was stone. "Marilyn, when we were on that plane, I promised myself that if we made it out alive, I wouldn't risk your life again. I'll get the next bottle tonight. Then I'll come back for you and—"

"No."

"No?" he said, and dropped his finger to give her his full attention.

Marilyn looked at him as if he should know. That didn't work, so she spoke: "If you go, I'm going."

"You've saved my skin one too many times. I'm starting to make it a habit. You need to be here, in a golden tub, drinking golden bubbles." A waiter overheard this as he passed and seemed to nod at the suggestion. "Plus, we can't really be seen together much more." He looked around cautiously. "Remember the paper? Let me handle this one on my own. I insist."

The last words turned Marilyn's flushed cheeks a deeper red. She seemed, for the first time since Molnar'd known her, to lose hold of her masks and get overruled by an inward fluster of emotion. She couldn't speak for a moment. "If you go without me, Mads Molnar, I won't be here when you get back!"

Molnar had a hunch about this next bottle. It was a bad hunch. "Then don't be." He took his cigar out and lit it.

Marilyn didn't get challenged. It wasn't fitting. If she weren't so well-bred, she'd have slapped Molnar; but she was, so she merely stood from the table and sashayed out of the room.

The bottom half of Molnar's stomach turned to lead. He put his hand on it, and the lead crept its way to the top. He sat there feeling alone but for the trifling thought that he was doing something honorable. Something he should have done from the start. He couldn't let her get so close to danger again, no matter how dangerous she was. She was too good of a thing to be broken. That'd already happened once before, and he couldn't forgive himself. With these thoughts, his hand reached to his jacket pocket and felt Ilsa's letter.

Molnar looked into the amber liquid in his crystal glass and searched it for answers. He pondered his relationship with Marilyn. Wasn't it like his relationship with brandy? They were both beautiful, sensual, delicate, deadly. He decided that he'd rather cross the brandy, and knocked it back and lifted his hand for another. The gold-tied waiter glided over to him and gave a half bow and an expectant face.

"Double brandy."

The waiter couldn't help inwardly scoffing at Molnar's indulgence, but he moved away without a sound.

"Looks like I scared her off," said Molnar, to no one but himself.

But Molnar wasn't alone. Two tables to his right, and with a perfect view of the conversation that had just occurred, was a 63-year-old woman with a black poodle beneath her table and a copy of *Völkischer Beobachter* above it. She held the paper in her tremulous hands. Her mouth was sealed tight as her mind focused. She'd never found herself in a situation like this.

She had checked Marilyn's beauty shot on the cover of the paper against the real-life version in front of her seven times before she'd been convinced, beyond any doubt, that the two were the same woman. She knew what she must do, but her legs were still shaking. She watched as Marilyn went to the powder room, and it took all six decades of her strength of will to pry herself from her seat and walk to the front desk. She thought how she could call a waiter to do it for her, but she also fancied her name might get into the paper if she did it herself. So she stumped past Molnar, "the dastardly kidnapper," and impaled him to his chair with her glare. The poodle followed with its head down.

Molnar noticed the woman's vicious look, but his mind was stuck on Marilyn.

The woman with the poodle spilled her guts into the phone, and the message was soon relayed to Bastick and his men.

———

By 9:30 in the evening, Mads Molnar was showered, espresso'd, and in a new gray suit. His face didn't look pleasant, but both of his eyes were opening now. With the wool crepe suit, a new black hat, and a pocket full of lead, Molnar exited his room to get the 11th bottle and put this bad dream behind him. But since Marilyn's silent treatment still sat in his belly like an anvil, he stopped by her room and knocked.

"Marilyn!" he hollered through the door, knocking hard. There was no response. "Marilyn … you see, I lost someone special before …" His throat betrayed him at these words, tried to choke him. He cleared it. "I couldn't bear to do it again." He listened, but there was nothing. He pressed his ear against the door and thought he heard a rustling. Maybe the silent treatment was meant to continue. "And also if you're in there … I'm sorry for being curt."

After another moment of silence, he started walking down the hallway. The lead in his gut had melted a little from the apology.

But it shouldn't have.

Behind the door, Marilyn was wearing a beautiful new dress, but it didn't help her wriggle out of the arms of a man who resembled a human ox, and who had her mouth tightly sealed in the crook of his elbow. His bicep bulged against her face as she struggled and bit him to get free. Tears of strain and despair were in her eyes as Molnar's footsteps faded away. She emptied her lungs into the bicep, but only a muffled huff emerged.

Down at the front desk of the hotel, Molnar gave a young blond bell-hop a 10-mark note to keep an eye on Marilyn and find out if she went anywhere while he was out. The boy nodded vigorously, and his oversized hat shifted forward on his forehead.

"If you don't find out, I want that back," said Molnar, just now noticing that the kid was swimming in his outfit.

The blond boy saluted him and clacked his heels. "Yes, sir!"

Molnar trotted over to the phone to call Riffel. The operator put him through.

In Berlin, a large, unattractive German woman with baseball-bat forearms and gorilla hands was kneading the pink-skinned back of Colonel Riffel, who lay on his own couch in his study and tried not to grimace in pain. Riffel normally looked calmer in his den of leisure.

"*Sich lösen!*" boomed her voice over him, trying to get him to relax. She kept kneading and leaned forward to put more strength into it. "*Sich beruhigen!*"

The phone rang, and Riffel tried to get up to get it, but the woman's hands kept him pinned. "Let me get that," he said.

"You must relax."

"I must get that phone, Greta!" he said, wiggling and wriggling to get free. She let him go, and he sat up with relief, rubbing his aching muscles. Charles had gotten the call already, and covered the receiver with his hand. "It's Molnar. Do you want it?" he said.

Riffel looked at the massive ham of a masseuse and back to Charles and nodded vigorously. He marched, topless—his flabby, pink, and hairless belly protruding over the tight pants of his uniform. "This is Riffel," he said, trying not to sound shirtless and vulnerable.

"Riffel, I'm in Copenhagen," said Molnar. "We've all but two bottles, and I'm off to get the eleventh now."

"Excellent!" Riffel's belly quivered with joy as he involuntarily hopped. The enormous masseuse watched him with interest, like a cat watches a squirming beetle.

"I should be finished in the morning. Do you have those exit papers?"

Riffel crossed his fingers, "I have them right here on my desk," he said and looked absentmindedly at Greta, who puzzled at the fingers.

"Can you get them up here by tomorrow? I'm at the Palace Hotel."

"By Sunday or Monday, I can."

"Great," Molnar said, staring across the packed room. "Thank you."

"It is my pleasure," said Riffel.

Molnar hung up, and Riffel smiled a little smile. He turned to the massive, meaty block of woman who was eyeing him. She smiled back. He did a jig—which, as he was shirtless and in skintight military leggings, was a thing not to be described.

As he lay back down on the table, Charles asked, "Do you want me to call Horváth for you, sir?"

"And make the man miss out on that sassy morsel of femininity? Goodness, no," Riffel replied. "Besides, if Molnar messes up, they promised to recover the last bottle. Then I won't have to tell him I forgot to procure his exit papers."

Charles's passive body was shaking as he stared at the deceptive, little man.

———

Molnar's cab rolled toward Brown Briar, home of Count Gorm Olsen, head of Denmark's import and export service, and recipient of the 11th bottle of pinot. When the car neared the gated entrance, Molnar saw S.S. guards in black uniforms awaiting him. He told the cabbie to drive past the entrance. He had the sneaking premonition that his cover was too hot to stroll in the front door. Maybe it was because his mug was pasted across every paper from here to Reit im Winkl.

Two hundred meters down the road, Molnar had the driver pull over.

"Mind hanging out here for 30 minutes?" he asked, holding a bill out to the driver.

The driver shrugged, looked around at the dark forest, and gave a shiver. The place wasn't friendly looking. Molnar gave him an extra bill, and the man warmed up pretty quickly.

Molnar disappeared into the woods. The cabbie scratched his head at this and turned on the radio.

The forest would be beautiful during the day—lush with moss and old trees and near-permanent dew. But at night, it was more like an obstacle course. Molnar reached the stone wall of Count Gorm's compound. It resembled an old castle. He started walking around the wall, trying not to get his new suit caught on any thorns. By the time he was halfway around, there were a couple of scratches in the cloth, but nothing major. Then he saw a pipe that jutted out of the wall and ran along the ground, terminating into a dry creek bed with a trickle of clear water running through.

As Molnar got closer, he saw the pipe was caked with mud and filth. A thick odor overwhelmed him. The end of the pipe had a grate with a padlock barring entry. It was so dark now, Molnar could hardly see. But the pipe was repulsive. Anything but that pipe.

He left it and kept walking around the wall, searching for another entrance. Five minutes later, he was back at the pipe. He sighed and felt around for the padlock. It was an old model that took a large iron key. He took out his set of tools and set to work opening it. The newer locks took more time; this one turned over in less than a minute. He put the padlock on the ground and opened the iron hinges with a loud creak.

Molnar took a deep breath and a final look at his finery before he plunged in, instantly caking his knees in brown-and-green mud. He slogged onward.

Meanwhile, three stories above Molnar's head, Count Gorm Olsen sat behind a stone desk in a stone room with a suit of armor behind him. With his large gray beard, gray suit, and gray temples, he fit right in. He was the gatekeeper, in charge of whatever goods could enter or exit Denmark. Right now, he was looking down at a paper that showed iron ore coming in from Sweden, through Denmark, to Germany. It was a new route that'd never been run, brought on by the British blockade around the North Sea, and the recent sinking of two iron-ore-bearing ships at the mouth of the Baltic. The Nazis planned to route ore from Lulea, through the Gulf of Bothnia, to the little Swedish town of Åhus—truck or train it to Malmo, cross the strait to Copenhagen and through to Germany. It was more circuitous than a mime ordering doughnuts.

"The Führer is worried the ground shipping of my route will take too long," said a tall, thin figure with spindly appendages. He stood in a loose-fitting Nazi *Sturmbannführer* uniform that only contacted his body at the joints. "But slow ore is better than no ore, as I've told him." The major stood beside the suit of armor, strangely mimicking its pose.

Gorm looked up to see. "That is correct."

"Then we can count on you to expedite the leg through Denmark."

"Of course." Gorm nodded. "It's as good as done."

"Excellent. Thank you, count." The major heiled and exited the room.

After a few minutes, Gorm exited his office as well, almost running into his butler. The aging man was sweating.

"Count Gorm!" He paused to catch his breath. "There's a man who tried to break into your wine cellar! The guards caught him and have him downstairs. What shall we do?"

Gorm's brows went up. "Let us interview the villain."

The butler led the count down three flights of stairs to the cellar. Molnar wore manacles and a sour face. It matched his dirty suit.

"We caught this one going through your wine, count!" said a thick-headed guard with a spiral of hair on his forehead like a toddler. "He had this." The guard held up the bottle and the note from Colonel Riffel, tied around it with a piece of twine, in one hand. In the other hand, he held up Molnar's revolver.

The count took the bottle and leaned in close to Molnar. The detective stood up straight enough to appraise and be appraised. "What were you doing in my wine cellar?" Gorm demanded. "What do you want with this bottle?"

"You wouldn't believe it if I told you, count."

The gray-bearded man stared at his compatriots one after the other, then at Molnar. "You should hope that I will."

"All right. Here it is. Your friend, Colonel Karlin Riffel, sent you a bottle of pinot noir without knowing it was poisoned. When he learned it, he sent me to get it back without you getting the wiser. I got caught, but if I keep you from drinking it, that's half the job at least."

The count guffawed, and his eyebrows went up. He looked at his men again. Then he looked at the note with Riffel's name on it. "He's a joker, gentlemen. The jesting cat-burglar." The laugh continued. "I know you. People like you. Think you're smarter than everyone. Think you can get one over on us all." He walked up to Molnar's face and stood nose to nose with him. Molnar wasn't thrilled about it, but he didn't look down. "This is the day someone calls your bluff."

Molnar shrugged. "Then drink it."

The man looked down at the bottle. "He'd never poison me. You should have chosen a different bottle, thief. But this one did have his name on it..." He nodded at the guard. "It had to be this one so he had a story." He stared at the name on the open note, shaking his head. "I'll tell you what we're going to do. We're going to call Riffel right now."

"Great, call him."

"I will."

"OK, let's go."

The count stood there a few more beats to make it known that he was in charge. Molnar let out a short chuckle. The count turned on his heel and made his way upstairs, through the castle, with Molnar and the guards following behind him.

The count stood, ear pressed against the receiver, with Molnar held back a pace between two guards. The operator connected the call.

"Riffel!" said Riffel. He stood by his desk with a leg of lamb; he'd left his dinner to get the call. He was about to take a bite.

"This is Count Gorm." Riffel's forehead went from matte to sheen to beaded, and he fell into the chair beside him; the leg of lamb fell to his desk. "Thank you so much for the bottle of pinot noir, by the way," added Gorm.

Riffel's face writhed like a garden snake. "Count Gorm! It is my sincere pleasure. You know that I always consider my best friends as we carry on, taking back the *Reichsland*."

The count waited a moment to give Riffel the opportunity to mention anything about the wine. When he said nothing, the count prodded: "Was there anything particularly special about this wine?"

The suffocating fingers of tension tried to squeeze their way into Riffel's voice. "It's a fine pinot," said Riffel. "And 1934 was one of the best years. I got it from a particularly talented vintner. Look at that kiss mark. Isn't that attractive?"

"Riffel, I have a man here, a Mister—"

"Doctor."

Gorm's brows went up. "A Doctor"—Molnar said his name—"Molnar. A Dr. Molnar. And we caught him breaking into the cellar. And do you know what he told me? He told me this wine you sent me is poisoned and he came to get it!" Gorm started laughing, and Riffel clung to the laugh. He caught it like a cricket ball and ran with it. But Gorm's laugh suddenly stopped. "Is that true, Riffel?"

Riffel's heart halted. He went all in. "Of course not! And it is patently absurd. Dear count—and I mean this with the utmost respect—how can you believe a thief? Haven't we been friends for years? Why would I try to—" He guffawed again. "It's humorous. It's funny even."

Gorm put the bottle of wine under his arm and gave a nod to the guards on either side of Molnar. They grabbed his manacled hands behind his back and yanked them high, so Molnar's arms were bent backward. At the movement Molnar realized he'd been betrayed. The guards shoved him—bent over like a wheelbarrow—out of the room. "You're a canker, Riffel," said Molnar, before the thick-skulled guard kneed him in the mouth to prod him along.

"Is that him?" asked Riffel. "I would put nothing past him. The viper! He's trying to frame me."

"But perhaps I shouldn't drink it. Just to be safe," said the count, giving Riffel one more out, just in case he was the one who was bluffing.

"Your choice. It was a gift from a good friend, but I would hold nothing against you if you decided to be cautious." As the words rang in Riffel's ears, he knew they sounded damning. But telling him to drink it would be more damning. Then a flashbulb ignited the dark halls of Riffel's mind. It lit up a picture of two birds and one stone. "Why not feed it to the thief and find out? If he wants to go free, he must first drink the wine. Then he must admit he was lying to escape, and you'll see I have no connection to that pirate."

Riffel's flashbulb shone on the count's face and illuminated his countenance for a moment ... and then darkened. "But if he is lying, he simply gets a free bottle of wine. If he isn't lying, he'll never drink it."

"Ah, you're right, count."

"But I'll solve for that, Riffel. You have me thinking now."

"Wonderful!"

"This is the most entertaining event since *Herr* Adolf chose me for this role," said the count, gripping the receiver until his knuckles went white.

"You really must come down and see us sometime," said Riffel.

Molnar sat in a dungeon. Its thick stone walls were dark and cold. A permanent unhealthy dew beaded on the stones. Some of the drops had calcified; some were liquid. All gave off a foul, moldy odor. A thin, barred window four meters from the floor was the only light. And that night's near-full moon cast a cold white shine on the floor beside Molnar. He put his hand in and out of it to see if it gave off heat. He stood, leaning against the wall with the least mildew, and smoked a cigar.

Footsteps echoed down the stone stairwell until they brought the figure of Count Gorm into Molnar's barred vision. "I understand your psychology," said the count.

Molnar had to work too hard not to roll his eyes. So he closed them.

"It's the psychology of a thief. I have something you want. You think you're smarter than I, so you steal it. You do think you're smarter than I, don't you?"

Molnar's brows went up. "Royal lineage never did wonders for the mental faculties."

The count put the bottle of wine on a rough wooden table on the stone floor outside of Molnar's cell. There were two matching chairs at the table. Then he looked down at the bottle. "You're free to go whenever you like." He shrugged. "But first, you must drink this."

Molnar cursed and kicked at a metal bench—the only fixture in the room. He couldn't help thinking of Marilyn, safe and warm and full of champagne only ten minutes away. She'd have to run up his tab a few more days. He chuckled at that and lay himself down on the cold bench.

The count turned and walked upstairs. He was followed by the guard, who trotted at double speed to catch up with him. "Excuse me, count. With all respect, if that thief is lying, I believe he just got a free ticket out. And if he ain't, then he'll just stay put."

"I know that!" said the count without slacking his pace. "Did you think that I didn't know that?"

"Of course not, sir," said the guard. He followed in silence a moment before his finger went slowly to his brow and he added, "Then—pardon me for asking, of course—but why'd you give 'im the chance?"

"I didn't," said the count, finally reaching the top of the stairs and turning to address the guard in the voice you use toward a relatively intelligent infant. "You see, I enjoy experimenting on the human condition. If the thief relents and declares himself to be a liar by drinking the wine, my study will be satiated." The guard's brows went up. "And then you will kill him."

The guard smiled now, knowing the plan. He turned to go back down the stairs and stopped mid-step, adding, "Oh, wait, Count. What if he don't relent?"

"Well, we'll give him a day or two. And then you will kill him anyway. Can't go on feeding thieves."

The smile broadened, and the guard put a finger to the side of his nose to show they had a secret. "Ain't there a word for this?"

"A double bind," said the count. "Or we can call this"—he chuckled aloud—"the Thief's Dilemma."

By the time the guard got back to the cell, Molnar was asleep.

———

Freezing water splashed Molnar's face, shocking him awake. It had been thrown from a bucket outside his cell. "Rise and shine!" yelled the guard, laughing at Molnar's sopping figure. "Got somefin' special for ya!" He threw a stinking and molded loaf of bread through the bars at Molnar. Then he took a seat near the bars. "I want to see ya eat that thing."

Ignoring the guard, Molnar got on his feet, shook the drops off his hat and the kinks out of his muscles. He put the hat on the bench and wiped his eyes with the water. Then he sat on his bench, lit a cigar, and got into a staring match with the heavy-skulled guard, daring him to come in.

After a while, the guard lost interest and left. Molnar switched to a staring match with the bottle of poisoned wine. He walked over to it and lifted it through the bars, shaking his head at it. He was about to break it so no one got poisoned, but something made him put it back. Then he sat down and stewed.

Riffel had thrown him under the bus. That meant that Riffel had never been serious about giving him exit papers. That meant that it'd all been a waste of time. How would he get out of Denmark?

Dejected, Molnar reached into his jacket pocket for his last cigar, and his fingertips brushed the edge of Ilsa's letter. Emotion flooded over him. He removed his hand as if burnt. And then it went back in, slowly, and came back with the letter. He looked down at it and read her name several times, staring at the ink that her hand had applied. How could she have written a letter he'd never seen? Never read? It was probably like most of her lovely letters—full of encouragement and hope. That hope was dead. Why should he read it now? She was gone. He must let her go. But then again, she had words that she'd wanted him to read. That thought stuck in his mind, and he tore open the envelope and unfolded the letter.

Dear Mads,

I'm so anticipating your return that my hands shake at the movement of writing your letters: M A D S. It's as if we've been apart for years. I worry so much about you in the maw of death every day. I know you've warned me against such ruminations. But those admonitions are all mental, and I'm a woman alone in a very physical world. Mads, I have a premonition that we may not see each other for an age. Perhaps it is only because my dear sister's husband was just killed. Shot through the heart on the Kolubara River.

Oh, my love, the world in which we dwell. Will we ever see each other? I write this note to stop dangerous meditations by using a method you've prescribed. You've told me that the cure is not to focus on the consequences of the evils around us, but the solutions. So I shall. And I shall take you with me.

If anything were to happen to you, I cannot imagine life lived alone. But, Mads, if I perish, I want you to know that you were the ideal husband and would be the most doting father. I want you to know that I love you as my very soul. You've sworn to me you'd never remarry in such a case, and I know that was hubris speaking, but let me be pragmatic for us both and remove any burden that could begin to adhere itself to your perfect shoulders. If, by the evil chances of this dark world in which we live, we are to be separated by any of the myriad snares that lie between us, then know that my chiefest desire is for you to care for our child and also to discover for yourself a new mother for him or her (though I'm sure it shall be a boy) and a wife for yourself. By virtue of me writing this note, and because you love me so, my mind is now at ease. I know you shall observe my smallest desire. So my mind is at peace.

Now, that is probably all silly, Mads, but my mind works—as you have told me so often—in such circular ruminations. Consider this my therapy, and reading it as one of your husbandly duties.

Get home to me soon, Mads. May the Creator of the Heavens and Earth protect you as you fight through the awful darkness. Take courage. Remember that if good men lay down their arms, light and love will be crushed by the vicious entropy that clings to both matter and man.

Your own passionately affectionate,
Ilsa

Molnar carefully folded the letter and put it into his breast pocket. His hand came back with a cigar. He began smoking and stared at the wall for the rest of the morning.

Hours later, he heard footsteps. The same guard as before ran in. "Ooh-boy!" He moved to the cell and held up the paper against the bars. He stepped back and closed one eye, sizing Molnar up against something on the paper. "Yep. I knew it!" he said. "It is you. Ooh-boy. You're the most hated man in Germany. You better be glad you're in there."

Molnar gave the guard the raised eyebrow he was waiting for, and the guard threw the afternoon paper through the bars. It was Marilyn's photo under the headline: *Fiancée Found! Detective Thrilled! Kidnapper at Large.* Molnar's mug was busy looking mean halfway down the page. The caption beneath his photo read: "If you see this man, he is armed and dangerous. Call the local authorities and turn him in."

His eyes read the words but didn't comprehend. All his mind could hold was that Marilyn was back in the hands of the monster. And he had a new purpose. One purpose. If he ever got out of here, he'd get Marilyn and head straight for Sweden. With her, he could find a way across the boarder.

"All press is good press," said Molnar, shrugging at the newspaper—but his guts were aflame.

"Wait if I get my hands on ya, pretty boy," said the guard. "I'll teach ya to kidnap one of our girls, you sick *Scheißkerl.*" The guard worked himself into a frenzy as Molnar relit the stub of his cigar. "What'd you do to her?"

"You like to think about that, don't you?"

"I could kill you with my own hands," said the guard, grabbing the bars and shaking them as if he already were.

"Go get the count for me instead," said Molnar, taking a drag of his afternoon smoke. "I'm ready to talk. You can listen in if you like."

The guard swore up a storm of threats, but he eventually got bored and did leave to get Count Gorm.

As soon as he was gone, Molnar felt the presence of another being. He looked back at the bench to his left to see the cave-like eyes of Death staring at him.

"Worried?" asked the specter.

"No."

"Have you thought all this through? I'd hate to lose you."

"There's nothing to think," said Molnar, trying to keep the cigar aflame. "I have to get her back. If I die on the way, you and I can be better friends."

"You spend more time with me than her anyway."

"I hope this is the last time I'll see you."

"No, you don't," said Death, smiling his lipless smile.

"OK, second to last."

Death hissed his seashell whistle of a laugh.

"You sure do hang around a lot," said Molnar, giving up on the cigar stub and tossing it to the ground. "You'd think you could lend me a hand once in a while."

"In what way?"

"You know, keep an eye on Marilyn." Molnar rattled the iron bars. "Tell me how I can get out of here without drinking poison! That sort of small talk."

"Oh, that wouldn't be fair."

"To whom?"

Death sighed—it was a disturbing sound. "There are rules in place. That's why we work so well together."

Quick footsteps echoed down the stairs.

"Wish me luck," said Molnar.

Death snorted. "It doesn't exist."

The count pranced down in a light, silvery suit of chainmail, with a rapier in one hand and a fencing mask in the other. The guard looked as if he were about to watch an execution—or give one.

"Ah, Mister Molnar. You deemed it appropriate to interrupt my exercises. I suppose I did leave the timing up to you. So, are you ready?"

"It's *Doctor* Molnar. And yes. I'm a liar and a thieving wino too. Now, let me drink that thing and let me go." Death hung over Molnar's shoulder, watching the scene. Business must've been slow today.

The count looked at the guard. "That was easy," he said. "I knew from your insolent glare that you were false with me, Mister Molnar. Guard, get us a glass and an opener." The guard made a less-than-pleased exit. "I knew you would fold. What made you tell the truth?" Count Gorm took a seat and put his rapier and mask on the table.

"Some things are more important than others."

They stared at each other for a while, and then the guard was back in the room. He unlocked Molnar's cell and gestured to the open seat at the rough table. Molnar sat across from the count. The guard opened the bottle of wine and filled Molnar's glass. After that, he made apparent the MP40 slung over his shoulder.

"Cheers," said the count, holding out an empty hand.

Molnar swallowed hard and took a sip of the wine.

The count chuckled to himself. "I knew it!"

Molnar couldn't cut the frown off. He took another sip and tried not to think about burying the old man. It went down very easy for poison. So he put on a bit of a show. He looked at the reflection of the wine against the pale chain-mail mask on the table. Nice, light ruby color. He took another sip and sucked air into his mouth over the wine, oxidizing it.

"This'll be a story for the chess club," said the count. "The one about the thief who drank his way to freedom! You should be proud. At least you were creative enough to get out of there." He nodded at the cell. Molnar took another drink, sitting back and relaxing now, swirling the wine in the glass. The guard topped him off.

"Wait!" said the count to the guard, eyeing Molnar's sommelier airs. "We can't bless him with freedom and intoxication." He grabbed Molnar's glass and smelled the wine. "Smells delightful." He looked at the guard as if for affirmation. The guard shrugged. The count took a drink himself and sucked air in past the wine to get the taste, just as Molnar had done. He swished it around and swallowed. Molnar looked on, face flat as flooring.

"Hmm. It is very nice," said the count. He stuck his nose in and sniffed. Then took another drink and looked to the ceiling to begin his appraisal: "There are the red fruit flavors we would expect in a pinot. And there's something quite dry about this one. Edging toward bitter, but not quite there. Colonel Riffel did a wonderful job." The count finished Molnar's glass and nodded at the guard for a refill.

The count drank on as he berated Molnar. "This was a warning. Run far away. I'll have you jailed or shot if I ever see you near Copenhagen again."

"You won't," said Molnar, allowing a smile for the first time.

After some more of this, the count grew bored of his game, finished his glass quickly, and stood to his feet. He took up the mask. "If you'll excuse me, my partner awaits." He gave a deep bow to Molnar.

"Guard, I wash my hands of this man. As far as I'm concerned, he's free. Do with him what you will."

The guard smiled a hard smile and nodded at the count. "As you wish, count. As you wish."

The two rats stared at each other as the sound of echoing feet pranced back up the stairs. The guard held the MP40 on Molnar and put his foot up on the count's seat. He poured the rest of the wine in the count's glass and held it in his hand.

"All that talk made me thirsty," said the guard, in his all-brown Nazi outfit. He drank the whole cup and frowned. "Doesn't taste so good to me," he said, looking down at the dregs. "I prefer beer when I have the choice. Come on. Up with you."

Molnar stood, but the guard cuffed him with the automatic back into his seat. He fell back down—new blood welling up from a cut on his head.

"Now, didn't I tell you to get up? Get up!"

Molnar tried again, and again the guard belted him with the gun, opening up his old wounds from Bastick's beating. A third time, Molnar tried to stand, with the same result.

He felt the swoon of unconsciousness try to muddle his mind. But when blood trickled down into his eye, something in Molnar snapped to life. He vaulted off his seat with the explosive power of a rugby player, lifting the wooden table with him, and smashed it up into the guard's arms and face. The guard screamed and fell off balance. Molnar grabbed the heavy chair he was on and swung it in a wide arc, smashing the guard in the head so hard that he fell forward. Molnar swung again at the man's bowed head, connecting with every ounce of his strength. There was a sickening sound like splitting cantaloupe, and the guard lay still. Molnar took his MP40 off his shoulder and searched for an extra clip of bullets. As he was looking, his hand felt his own gun in the guard's jacket pocket.

Molnar fondled the beloved weapon. He pocketed it and left the MP40. Then he turned, panting, and stared behind him at Death.

"Not sure which one of us you're here for, but you can start with him."

Molnar was about to run out when he saw the bottle on the ground. Though his employer had betrayed him, an aversion to leaving a job un-done made Molnar grab the empty bottle and take it with him. He ran up the stairs and retraced his steps so he could get out the same way he'd come in. He went down the steps and through the wine cellar and some stone tunnels, found the sewer pipe, and started crawling. When he was in the middle, he left the bottle stranded on a heavy rock, where it shouldn't get washed away.

By the time he was out of the noxious sewer pipe, he was almost sick from the stench. He crawled out, bleeding, poisoned, and covered in filth, and he threw himself onto the earth. He forced himself to be sick the rest of the way, until nothing came but bile. Still, he retched and retched and lay on the ground panting. The ground felt so soft compared to the stone, and all his body wanted was to sleep. He lay his head down and closed his eyes, and the comfort of darkness covered him like a heavy blanket.

But something twinkled in his mind for a moment. He could hear his wife's words. And then her words faded away. And he remembered Marilyn. Marilyn, with that man.

Molnar mumbled to himself. His eyes flickered open. He tried to stand to his feet, but fell. He got to his knees and used a tree to stand. Then he put one foot in front of the other and lifted his hands to feel the new wounds on his head and face. But the fingers stopped just in front of his broken flesh, unwilling to discover the truth. He pulled them away and marched on.

After escaping the woods, Molnar looked half-heartedly for the cabbie, who had left. After a few minutes, he flagged down an old woman who couldn't see well enough to fully appreciate his condition. She spoke of cherry pies and grandchildren and the coming long winter nights. He just listened.

Soon, they got to Copenhagen, where Molnar genuinely thanked her and stumbled into the Palace Hotel. He wiped his forehead with a handkerchief to get rid of the last beads of blood and sweat that stood on his crinkled brow. He made eye contact with the bellboy in the suit that was still too big for him. The sleeves hung to his knuckles. The kid spotted him as well and, seeing no escape, hung his head and walked up to Molnar. The boy held out the 10 to him but didn't say a word.

"Did you see anything?"

"I didn't hear where they were going."

"Who was she with?"

"Oh!" The boy shook with anger from the encounter. "She was with a nasty kid with red hair and a face like a round of cheese."

"Anyone else?"

"Yes, there was a big man who looked like he was part horse."

"That would be Bastick," said Molnar. He looked down at the boy who still had the 10 extended in the air between them. "Keep it, kid."

"Really?"

"Yeah. It'll be more helpful to you than me."

"Thanks, mister."

Molnar patted him on the shoulder and stumped his way to the front desk. "Where did they go?" he asked the attendant, whose face betrayed that she was deathly afraid of this bleeding, dirty, foul-smelling man.

"Whom do you mean, sir?" she asked, without making eye contact. She wore a form-fitting cream dress with gold rings around the arms and a gold ribbon around the waist, but Molnar didn't notice.

"I mean the young woman from Room 31 and the trained bear that was with her."

"I'm afraid I have no idea." The woman opened a notebook to see details. "Room 31 still hasn't checked out. But that's all I can tell you. I didn't see them myself."

Molnar tried to hide his frustration. "Who was working last night?"

"I can ask Gustav," said the woman, wanting to be helpful and not cross this man, whose always-perfect hair was now knocked loose, allowing a dyed-blond apostrophe of it to crown his left eye. "He's about to go home now."

"I would be so pleased if you would," said Molnar. He took the hand-kerchief from his jacket pocket and wiped his forehead again, dabbing at the fresh cuts above his hairline.

The woman took a step back with relief. "I'll be right back," she said, and went into a little door behind the counter. In a few moments, she returned with someone.

"Hello, sir," said the praying mantis with human flesh that could only be Gustav. His gangly limbs and stretched eyes and upside-down pyramid face all worked toward this image, and when he steepled his fingers at chest height, the metamorphosis was complete. "How may I help you?"

"My friend in the room beside me, 31, left with a man the size of a city bus and a ginger kid last night. I need to know where they went. It could mean her life." He put his Gestapo disc on the counter and made sure the mantis could see the 20-mark bill beneath it.

"They must have left before I got on duty," said Gustav. His upturned, almond-shaped eyes rolled toward the ceiling as if he were trying to re-member something. His hands remained steepled, and his fingers flew like they were playing Beethoven's 9th on the world's tiniest piano. The thin slice of mouth moved, muttering things to its owner, summoning the brain. "But ..."

Gustav's digits stopped moving, and his eyes opened and leveled. He grabbed the phone beside him and lifted it to his mandibles. "City Taxi, please," he told the operator. Molnar watched the bug-being work. "Hello, City Taxi? Yes, this is Gustav Bille at the Palace Hotel. We had three guests leave last night in one of your cabs. Two men and a woman." He described them. "Well, the big man said he left his wallet. Can you please find the driver who took them and where they went? They're VIP guests, and we must know." There was a pause, and Gustav's mouth clacked some insect mating call as he listened. "Ah, thank you. Thank you. I'll wait." The clicking continued, and his eyes were as big as saucers. "Hello, there. You drove a trio from our hotel last night ..." The driver was talking fast. "No wallet?" The voice was loud and angry. "And their destination?" More yelling. "Thank you," he said, and hung up the phone. "They've gone to Kronborg Castle."

Molnar nodded at him, mumbled a thank you, handed him the 20, and headed for the bar. He got a coffee cooled by a double shot of whiskey. As he stood there, torn, filthy and bleeding, the only other client looked up at him. It was an overweight desk job with a comb-over. Molnar nodded at him.

The man was rabbit scared and kitten curious. "You in trouble?" he managed.

"Trouble is my business, buddy," said Molnar. "Trouble is my business."

The man nodded religiously. When Molnar's drink arrived, he drained it in one long draught. Then he headed for the door, the eyes of the fat man on him and the imagination of the fat man churning. Molnar leapt into a cab under the carport and told the driver to get to Kronborg Castle, offering double the fare if he could break every speed limit along the way.

———

Otto and his two criminal assistants reached the *Kriegsmarine* docks, where the last bottle had been sent to a man named Pfeiffer, *Kommodore* for the Germany Navy. Otto showed his ID at the brick entrance and descended wooden, saltwater-pocked steps toward the massive naval docks. There were several long warehouses where ships were being built. Outside the warehouses and beside the water were large metal vessels on gantry cranes. Welders worked at the hulls, throwing orange showers of sparks to the ground. Otto halted, hypnotized by the sparks. The beauty astounded him. He headed toward the shots of light, and his criminal assistants glanced at each other and tagged along.

As Otto rounded the front of a large hangar, he spotted a few workers. Moving past them, he saw a massive German destroyer in the water parallel to the hangar. Sparks flew. The deck was getting finishing touches before being sent off into the unknown, to squelch as many lives as was its lot. Otto moved toward the sparks and found a gangplank that bridged water far below. He stared at it, took a step onto it, and quickly stepped back off. He stared a bit more. Then he folded his body in two, gripped the gangplank with his fingers, and shuffled his feet behind him. The hand-and-foot shuffle continued until he was on the deck, where he breathed a gasp of relief. The assistants followed him, upright.

On the destroyer, men were yelling orders, wielding impact wrenches, and welding metal. Otto tracked the sparks. Once he reached their source, a welder, he stared at the bright light of the torch. After a while, he rubbed his eyes.

The welder noticed. He stopped welding to lift his mask. "Hey! That'll burn your eyes out if you look at it!"

Otto looked straight up in fear.

Unable to stay silent, one of the assistants asked, "Where is Commodore Pfeiffer?"

The welder looked at Otto with pity, then at his assistants. The welder took his mask off and rubbed sweat from his brow. "Commodore Pfeiffer is usually up on the bridge," said the welder, pointing to the second level of the ship, which was now a makeshift construction office.

The welder shook his head and returned to work. Otto climbed the stairs to the bridge and walked through the door. He spotted the large and portly yet impeccably neat Commodore Pfeiffer. The man had outlived his hair except for a stubbly path that spilled up his jaws and over his ears, and met above the nape of his creased neck. The Commodore pointed to a blueprint of the ship and yelled something at a worker. The worker nodded and exited. Otto stared at Pfeiffer as if he were a robin searching for worms.

"What in hell are you looking at, boy?"

"Are you Commodore Pfeiffer?" asked one assistant. "We are Gestapo agents."

"Yes, I'm Commodore Pfeiffer."

Otto stepped in front of the assistants and spilled the story to the commodore as quickly as if he'd memorized it. He told how poisoned wine was being sent to Nazi officers and how the villainous Gray Man was behind it. He asked if the man had received any pinot from Alsace.

Pfeiffer looked impressed. He nodded. Then he reached out to shake Otto's hand. The boy just stared at him. Pfeiffer took his hand by force and shook it. "Come on. I'll show you the bottle."

The four of them crossed the plank (Otto repeated his crossing routine) to Pfeiffer's office in the warehouse. The man pulled a bottle out of a locker and put it on a boring-metal table. It was still wrapped, complete with the note from Riffel. "That it?"

"*Ja.*"

"Well, I'm lucky I drink beer. And thank you. I owe you my life."

"*Ja,*" said Otto.

The commodore cleared his throat under Otto's chicken-like glare. "The only thing I can't figure out is why Colonel Karlin Riffel would be involved." The man pointed to the notecard on the bottle. "He's my friend."

"Colonel Riffel?" Otto mouthed the name as much as he spoke it. He leaned in to look at the notecard, as did the *Kriminalassistents.*

―――――

Meanwhile, Miles sat in Pest with his "big gun"—the .455 Webley revolver—in his lap, and binoculars to his eyes. There was a mug of coffee on his dashboard and a half-empty bottle of absinthe in the passenger seat. He stared at the metal door of the concrete-block building where Eva was being held. Through a few seedy connections, Miles had been able to figure out who Horváth was and where he might hide. Now, he was stalking the place, and trying to discover which liquid would most help him work up the nerve to go in.

Inside the building, Eva sat in a dark closet and stared at a chair she had propped against the doorknob, to try and keep visitors from having too easy a time getting in.

The two lean men were propped up on high stools playing cards. Empty beer bottles were strewn around the kitchen.

One lean man cleared his throat and looked over at their fat leader in disgust.

Horváth must have felt the glare, because he stood suddenly from the couch, sending bottles cascading from the cushions. "We've waited long enough!"

The two lean men released a howl and ran to the closet door that sheltered Eva. One shoved into the door, and the chair Eva had wedged under the knob threw him back. Her heart shot to 200 beats a minute. She cursed and cursed to regain composure and used some sort of feminine flexibility to step over her bound hands until they were in front of her. Then she held the chair down to give it more stopping power.

Horváth pried one of the men away. "Let's get this straight," he said to them. "I'm your superior. You all can fight out who's second-in-command." He grabbed the knob and pressed hard to get through. The two lean men tried to solve their own problem through debate. Words failed them, anger flared, and they were soon rolling around on the floor, scuffling and shouting.

Outside, Miles was staring at the bottle of absinthe. When he heard the yelling, he swallowed hard, picked up the bottle, and emptied it into his mouth. He chased that with coffee, grabbed his Webley, and kicked his car door open.

Horváth had the closet door open at the same time. He burst in on Sandor, splintering the back of the wooden chair into bits. Seeing the gleam in his eyes, she tried to kick him in the groin, but he was ready for that and blocked it, before grabbing her and pulling her toward the door. She punched him hard in the jaw, but he kept dragging her out.

"Come on!" said Horváth. "I need a hand here."

As the two men looked up, the front door smashed in and Miles came through blasting. He hit the floor a few times before turning one of the lean men's heads inside out. Then he hit the wall, and the second man ran for shelter. Horváth froze. Miles tracked the lean man with the hand cannon, which hit him in the back of the neck just before he rounded the corner. It sent him into a full spinning somersault.

Horváth reached for his gun, but Eva kicked it from his hand with one limber leg. She hit him again in the jaw, and he stepped away from her. Miles, out of ammo and full of absinthe, ran toward Horváth, bellowing, and tackled him to the ground. They landed hard. The fat man smashed a balled fist into Miles's head. He followed it with his great mass, rolling atop the thinner man and holding him down.

"Do you think I've waited this long for nothing?" He began pummeling Miles with heavy blows. Miles tried to block them, tried to writhe out from under the man, but the weight was too great. The man bellowed with every blow. "I. Am. Horváth. Commanding. Officer. In—"

Eva ran to Horváth's gun on the ground and lifted it. "All you'll be remembered as is a failed rapist," she said, and waited until he looked up at her before pulling the trigger.

By the time Eva helped Miles up, he could hardly stand. He was mostly uninjured, but the absinthe was really kicking in. Chuckling, he stared at Eva. "At least Molnar'll quit bothering me."

She didn't say anything, but pulled him close and kissed him on the mouth.

———

Molnar sat stiffly in the back seat of the cab until the salt-savaged walls and green spires of Kronborg Castle came into view. As soon as he saw these, he told the cab to pull over on the side of the road and let him out. The cabbie started to balk but looked back and noted his passenger's face and shut up. Molnar handed him a large bill and got out. "There will be double that if you can stick around for a while."

The driver nodded and did a quick U-turn, parking with his nose out. "I'll be here." After all, it was 45 minutes back to Copenhagen.

The sun was setting behind Molnar's back as he stared out at the castle and past it to the strait of Øresund. Orange hues lit up Sweden's Helsingborg across the water. Pink spilled into the tops of buildings, stratifying the view and turning the far-off city and waterway into an unreal, dream-like sherbet. But the hard metal of Molnar's gun in his hand and the biting seawater against his face reminded him of his purpose.

Long blades of wet grass soaked through his shoes as he jogged silently toward the towering silhouette of Hamlet's castle. As if on cue, the skull face of his longtime friend appeared beside him, hovering in the air.

"Ah, my Quietus," said Molnar.

"To be or not to be?" said Death.

"Kind of your job description, isn't it?" said Molnar, stooping low as he ran toward the darkening, grass-covered ramparts to keep out of view of the towers. "But for me, it's not even a question: 'Tis nobler to use even a final breath to crowd out the darkness of this world than render my mortal coil impotent by pulling the plug. And it's not from fear of the unknown. I mean, we're already pretty well acquainted."

"To be or not to be?"

"Either way, I'll be seeing you," said Molnar as he neared the ashen-stained white walls of Hamlet's castle. He moved along the north side of the peninsula on which the castle was nestled. It was protected by ramparts to the west and the Øresund to the east. The castle was the last bastion of mainland Europe, jutting out into chilling Scandinavian sea waters. And along a path of earth ran Molnar and Death—moving toward the foreboding castle, which had been turned into a tourist destination two years prior. But right now, Denmark wasn't getting much tourism. The castle was empty save for the hulking Bastick and his team.

The gates were open. Bisecting a narrow path, Molnar's shadowy figure sprinted through the first gate, over a moat, and into the bare-brick walls of the final fortifications of the castle. His soaking shoes started squeaking as he went—so, although creeping cold cut through his coat, he removed his shoes and socks and hid them behind an ancient powder keg under the fortification wall. Then he gazed across at the castle itself, only a few meters away. There was no sign of movement or light. His bare feet padded across the alley between battlement and castle wall. He tried a door and found it locked. He tried a second. It didn't budge. Then he glanced behind him and saw Death standing beside a window. Molnar ran to the window. The old glass lifted with no resistance. Molnar gave Death a quizzical look before climbing in.

The two specters moved through the castle, searching for lives to snuff. The castle itself was the shape of a hollow box. The center was a massive courtyard surrounded by long, cold rooms full of tapestries and adornments from the past. One was a life-size statue of Hamlet, complete with ruffled collar, tights, and dagger. Molnar's fingers gripped the dagger and removed it from the inanimate Hamlet. The fingers of his other hand felt the point, and he grunted in surprise that it was sharp. Then he got an idea. He squatted low beside the figure and checked the bullets in his revolver. Satisfied that no one could see him, Molnar removed the bullets from the chambers and used Hamlet's dagger to cut crosses into the soft-lead tips of the bullets so they would break apart and mushroom out on impact.

Footsteps echoed down the hall, and Molnar hid behind the wall to the other room. It was a *Kriminalassistent*. He reminded Molnar of a hyena. As soon as the darkly dressed man with shaved head and red swastika armband cleared the doorway, Molnar was silently behind him with his hand over his mouth and the dagger plunged from his Adam's apple to the tip of his skull. The man's body convulsed as Molnar lowered it to the ground. Molnar wiped his hands and Hamlet's dagger on the man's outfit and moved into the next chamber.

The whispers of a familiar and chilling voice carried on cold drafts to Molnar's ears. His bare feet padded quickly toward the sound. He squatted low and peered around the doorway and through the next room. He could see the light of a fireplace in yet another room beyond that. The fire threw long shadows on the wall. Another hyena-like man stood in the doorway. Behind him, the voice of the monster could be heard. It was speaking in calm, low notes. Piercing these was the bell-like voice of Marilyn, shaken but defiant. The voice spiked in a cry that rent Molnar's heart. The guard in the doorway turned to see what had caused the change in pitch. When he turned back with a smile on his face, Molnar's hard hand was over his mouth, and Hamlet's knife was in his throat, and his body was lifted entirely from the ground by adrenaline-filled arms and moved out of view of the doorway.

As he handed off the man's soul, Molnar listened intently. He slid his body closer to the entrance.

"You've only to tell me how Molnar is party to the poisoning," said Bastick, out of Molnar's view. "And we can move on to more pleasant activities."

"I don't know!" came her cry.

"Tsk, tsk," said Bastick.

Molnar glanced into the room to see Marilyn in a chair with her arms tied to its arms and her golden hair wild and insolent over her shoulders. Bastick stooped with a large Bowie knife in his right hand. His massive arms held the knife over the fireplace to get the blade glowing red hot. Two hyenas looked on with sadistic glee.

With the beast's back to him, Molnar was in the room beside Marilyn. Before ears rang from the gunshot, the majority of one hyena's head was

on the ceiling. He crashed to the ground as another shot exploded into
the chest of the second. Bastick spun around to see the barrel of Molnar's
gun. Molnar pulled the trigger but it hit a dud, clicking loud and hollow
through the stone room. That pause was all the time Bastick needed, and
he was upon Molnar as he pulled the trigger again. The revolver shouted
into the ceiling as Bastick's massive hand tore it from Molnar's grasp. With
a roar, Bastick threw the gun and the man to the ground. Molnar backed
up to the wall and braced himself for the attack, knowing there was no way
to beat this hulking tower. He held Hamlet's knife out as his only defense.
Bastick saw this and laughed.

"I knew you would come!" cried the girl's voice, bursting with relief.

Molnar saw the fresh red burn mark on the underside of her forearm,
and for the first time in his life, he felt the peculiar sensation of hairs raising
up, one by one, from the small of his back to the nape of his neck.

Bastick turned to glare at the girl. In the instant of inattention, Molnar
leapt to his feet and kicked the brute with all his might, knocking him
backward. Bastick toppled into the fire, burning his hand in the coals and
sending his glowing knife to the floor. Molnar was quick with Hamlet's
blade, severing Marilyn's ropes. Then he half carried, half pulled her out of
the chair. But she yanked away from him with the strength of a tiger.

"No!" she yelled. She grabbed Bastick's glowing-hot knife from the
stone floor and laid the flat of it across the giant's cheek as he was recov-
ering his feet. He fell back again with a shriek, frozen with shock, but she
followed him down, keeping the blade against the cheek.

"This is for my brother," she said through her teeth, as the blade tried
to fuse to Bastick's skin. Molnar pulled her away, and they ran off down the
hallway and past the fallen men to the room with the open window where
he'd gotten in. A deep bellow came from behind them. Bastick was close
on their heels, holding his cheek. Molnar slammed the last heavy wooden
door behind them, locking it with a wrought-iron hasp as Bastick smashed
into it. The door's frame flexed against the heavy attack. But the doors of
Hamlet's day were significantly thicker than the doors of 1940, and Bastick
was no match for this one. Molnar heard the blade thud into the door. The
man's heavy boot smashed into it next. Molnar helped Marilyn through the
window he'd come through, and the two ran across the narrow road into

the fortifications. He grabbed his shoes on the way out and ran with them in his hand.

Even through the shock and fear, Marilyn couldn't help but laugh when she saw this. "I never thought my knight in shining armor would forget his boots!" she said. But she didn't miss a beat, and they kept running side by side as they heard the grating snorts of Bastick's breathing far behind them. He must've found another way out of the building.

Molnar returned the way he'd come. He could see the cab in the distance. Thank God for the honest Danes! Then Molnar saw half a dozen criminal assistants come into view between him and the cab. He gave one last look at his escape plan and pivoted right. The pair turned and ran along the outside of the fortifications and around the bottom of the castle toward the tip of the peninsula.

"Men! Give chase! Track them down!" yelled Bastick from behind them. The pair carried on without looking back. They flew past long buildings and over a little bridge and along high brick fortifications until they reached a dock at the very edge of that Danish world.

The end of mainland Europe.

"Oh, no!" cried Marilyn, seeing that they were trapped on the dock. Molnar looked back at an encroaching Bastick and the six new hyenas catching up. Even from this distance, Molnar could see a smile sliding across the monster's face.

Molnar looked back at the water. Maybe they'd have to swim for it.

Molnar and Marilyn ran halfway down the dock and then turned back toward the group. Murder and something worse glinted in Bastick's eyes.

"Thank you anyway, Molnar," said Marilyn, gazing up into his eyes. "No one has ever—" She cut herself off and was quiet. They watched the group nearing the dock.

"Vengeance has arrived, my love!" shouted Bastick, marching toward them with the group of criminal assistants at his side.

The sunset had just passed, and Molnar glanced around for his friend. He didn't see Death anywhere, so he kept searching. And there, out of the corner of his eye, something red bobbed into his view, just beyond the edge of the high dock. He let go of Marilyn and moved down the long dock. She followed him closely.

There, tied at the end of the dock, was a little red rowboat with chipped paint and a small outboard motor. As Bastick reached the dock, Molnar threw his shoes into the boat and helped Marilyn step down into it.

Bastick saw what was happening and sprinted after them with a roar. Molnar used Hamlet's knife to cut the rope that held them to the dock. He threw the motor in the water, choked it, and yanked on the zip cord to start it up. He pulled once, a second and third time, and the engine blared.

Bastick barreled over the edge of the dock and leapt with all the power of a coiled python. He stretched his giant frame and caught the rear end of the departing boat with a claw, the rest of him landing in the water. He hung on, pulling the boat down.

Bastick's head came out of the water, his right hand getting a better grip on the back of the boat. He reached his left hand up.

Molnar revved the five-horsepower motor and turned it hard to starboard so the bare, spinning propellers cut into Bastick's clinging body. A bellow went up, and Bastick released the edge and dove into the depths for safety. Molnar hit the gas.

Bullets skipped over the water and thudded into the boat. Molnar held Marilyn's head down, pressed himself against her as a shield. They heard the gunshots lessen as they got out of range. Marilyn raised her head slowly.

"Are you all right?" he asked her over the engine, trying to survey her for wounds. She looked up at him with eyes that sparkled in the light of the full moon. It was the kind of look that only some women could give, and it could heal a man's very soul. She grabbed his shoulders and buried her face in his neck.

The little red boat puttered closer to the middle of the strait. Off in the distance, back on the Danish side of the water, the sound of other, larger engines roared out like air-raid sirens.

Molnar turned back to see a large boat skipping over the surface of the water toward them. It was a 10-meter-long, shrunken version of a *Schnellboot*, capable of running sprints at 48 knots. Molnar turned back to Sweden, and his mind flew through possible outcomes. None ended well. He imagined Bastick bearing down on their boat and running it over or cutting it in half. The speedboat grew quickly in the distance.

Molnar turned to Marilyn. "I have an idea," he said, putting his hand on her shoulder.

"You'd better," she said, staring at the approaching boat.

"You can hold your breath much longer than you think," he said, his eyes searching her face as if he wanted to say more. "When we go under, know that. Whatever you do, don't breathe out. Just hold it in. We'll make it."

"I don't like your idea."

Molnar turned back toward the approaching boat. "Come on!" he said, locking the throttle and the motor into position so their boat wouldn't spin in circles when they jumped. He grabbed her hand, and they leapt into the chilling Scandinavian strait. The little red boat held its course and kept skipping off toward Sweden, if a bit cockeyed. Marilyn swam beside Molnar.

Bastick and six assistants barreled toward the red boat. Bastick's arm hung strangely at his side, the black sleeve soaked dark red and torn in a dozen places at the shoulder, just above the gunshot wound Molnar had inflicted earlier. He ran out to the nose of the vessel and watched the red rowboat. Two 20-mm cannons pulled the boat into focus. "Now!" shouted Bastick. The cannons roared, and the red boat exploded into fragments.

A moon-white circle from a spotlight onboard Bastick's boat moved across the face of the disrupted waters—searching, seeking. It halted on some bits of broken wood and, satisfied, moved on. Then it paused on one of Molnar's shoes, floating upside down in the water. Bastick's shotgun laugh reported. "Keep searching," he said.

Two dark silhouettes bobbed out of range of the circle, but it moved toward them like a ghost—noiselessly, effortlessly, gliding across the choppy waves. The circle's reflection danced in Marilyn's pupils as she stared at Molnar for answers.

"OK, remember what I told you."

She nodded.

"Take a deep breath with me." As the moon of light approached, the two silhouettes disappeared beneath the water. The circle kept moving. A hyena with a shaved head and red goggles wore an uncomfortably heavy backpack and held a pipe from which flames poured like the mouth of a breathless dragon. Fire filled the surface of the water all around Bastick's boat, hanging on its face or riding on the shattered red wood like mice on a raft. Two pairs of eyes gazed at the fireworks from below.

How long can humans hold their breath? How long until panic sets in? Can a kiss and a breath fill another with oxygen? How soon do the contractions in an empty chest force the body to breathe?

Two silhouettes bobbed to the surface of oily water. A beautiful figure breathed in deeply. The other did not. Flames rode around the silhouettes. The one figure panted. The other did not. One figure's heart swelled with sadness and longing and regret. The other's did not. One figure said, "Wake up, you bastard, Mads, you bastard, Mads, you bastard!" and slapped the face of the other over and over again. The other figure floated, hanging in the water like a dark star, only visible at a slant.

Marilyn put fat lips to his mouth and started to blow—and then screamed. He laughed. She slapped him and shoved him away.

"You!"

"What?"

"You! You!" She smiled at him now, but she was shaking. "You."

"I love you," he said.

"I hate you!"

"I love you."

"I hate you!" she laughed, shoving him again. "I hate you."

"I love you." His hands brushed her wet hair into rows that lost form when they entered the water and splayed around them both.

"I love you," she said. And he pulled her against him so he could feel her heartbeat, and he pressed his lips against hers. It lasted until it didn't, and neither of them said anything more.

The boat with seven hateful souls aboard it went on through the water, burning everything it found. The biggest, most hateful soul touched his newly disfigured cheek and hated even more. He yelled at his bald helper and took the flaming gun and burnt and burnt and burnt as the boat floated on, in the middle of the strait, halfway between a raging, battle-worn world and one untouched by war. And as this man went on burning and swearing and fighting for revenge—for a cleansed and pure strain of mankind to enjoy the Earth—two silhouettes parted the water and tried not to giggle as they moved closer and closer to another shore and to another life, one in which they could go forth and multiply.

THE END

EPILOGUE

It was one of those rare, warm, and sunny autumnal days in Berlin. Colonel Riffel was sunbathing in his backyard—in the nude, as many an aging German was wont to do. His eyes were closed, and he had an angle of mirrors around his neck, shining light on his mustachioed face. Beneath the mustache, the corners of his little mouth were fixed in a permanent upward bent. Molnar was gone, the bottles were gone, and the sun was shining on all his glory.

Charles was meant to hold another mirror on the man, and was doing so to the best of his ability while averting his eyes from the scene. His face was grim, disgusted.

The doorbell rang, and Charles's face underwent a shocking change. It was as if an internal light started shining in the pit of his stomach and its rays bloomed slowly into his every feature.

"Well? Aren't you going for the door? You're doing a shoddy job mirroring anyway," said Riffel without opening his eyes. "Tell them I'm not at home. I'm celebrating."

Charles lowered the mirror without a sound and moved toward the door.

As he waited, Riffel readjusted the mirror on his face. A door opened and closed, and then another. Riffel blindly reached to a round glass table at his elbow to attain a sweating gin and tonic. His lips stretched forward to meet the drink. They stretched and stretched, his mustache prickling his nose as the lips extended. But the drink didn't come. His hand encountered resistance. Blinding sunlight shone into Riffel's eyes when he opened them. He squinted up to see a hand like a flank steak crimped around the rim of his glass, holding the drink at bay. The hand took the glass and brought it to its owner's slick black mustache. Above that mustache was a flexible, flaring nose, like two rounds of rubber hose. The nose rippled, breathing in. Riffel squeaked.

"No dulling of the senses, my dear colonel," said the bellows-like voice of Detective Wolfram Bastick. "You smell of sweat and putrescence." He sniffed again. "And now: fear." Bastick returned the glass to the table and sat in a chair beside Riffel's flabby supine shape. He stared at the figure; he sniffed. "No matter. Now! There is someone I must thank for this chance at vengeance."

Riffel's eyes nearly bugged out as he waited for Bastick to continue.

"Me!" said Charles, from behind Riffel. "It was me!" The young man was shaking as he shouted. "Bastick got your name. I led him here." Charles ran up to Riffel, who sat halfway forward. The boy had the start of tears in his eyes, and he lifted the glass of gin and threw its contents in Riffel's face. Riffel sputtered.

"But—!" he started to say.

"That's the last drink you get from me," interrupted Charles. And turning on his heel, he trotted through the back door and out the front door and was gone.

"Charles!" squeaked Riffel, trying to get out of his chair. But Bastick's half-kilo hand helped him lie back down and get comfortable.

"What a pity," said Bastick. "Your drink is gone. But it's so hot out. We can't let you get parched." His hand went up, summoning his own loyal helper.

Otto presented the 12th bottle of wine. He uncorked it and placed it on the table before beginning to intensely ponder the clouds.

Riffel stared at the bottle in pure horror. His mouth opened and shut like a goldfish.

"You really are a cad, Riffel. Your foolery killed my father—a much greater man than yourself—and lost me a very ... *advanced* bride." Bastick turned his hands heavenward and shrugged as if the situation were beyond his control. "Otto!"

The young man pulled his eyes from the clouds and gripped Riffel's wrists, pinning them above him in the chair.

"Normally, I'd beat you to death," continued Bastick. "But instead, I have a greeting from my father."